DRY HEAT

A NOVEL

LEN JOY

North Carolina

Published in the United States by BQB Publishing
(an imprint of Boutique of Quality Books Publishing, Inc.)
www.bqbpublishing.com

Printed in the United States of America

978-1-952782-52-7 (p)
978-1-952782-53-4 (e)

Library of Congress Control Number: 2021953353

Book design by Robin Krauss, www.bookformatters.com
Cover design by Rebecca Lown, www.rebeccalowndesign.com
First editor: Caleb Guard
Second editor: Allison Itterly

PRAISE FOR DRY HEAT AND LEN JOY

"*Dry Heat* is a page-turner with heart. A tale of star-crossed lovers and best-laid plans run amok, this smoothly written novel is full of friendship, family, and redemption."

– Nickolas Butler,
author of *Shotgun Lovesongs* and *Godspeed*

"Through misunderstanding and bad luck, a young man of real integrity gets on the wrong side of the law. But the real test of Joey Blade's integrity will involve the people he loves—his girlfriend Mallory and his locally influential father. *Dry Heat* exposes in picturesque Phoenix a corrupt level of society, which a young man must navigate using only his own moral compass."

– Louis P. Jones,
author of *Innocence and Prodigal in the City*

"Len Joy delivers in this page-turning coming of age story. Joy's signature style brings the story of an innocent teen forced to navigate the criminal justice system to life. Engrossing and heartbreaking. *Dry Heat* is unputdowable."

– Jen Collins Moore,
author of the *Maggie White Mysteries*

"Award winning author Len Joy is back with another action and character driven thriller. Joey Blade is a high school sports superstar with a free ride to a major university's football program. Everything changes when he makes bad decisions about the company he keeps, and he is charged with a serious crime. Adding more bad choices to the first, he finds himself negotiating a world filled with hardened criminals. Two decades later, difficult choices still bedevil him. In the end, he faces a choice that could end his life or his freedom but which promises to save his family from ruin. Memorable characters, some deeply flawed but also worthy, given the world in which they must live, populate the story. Fans of courtroom drama will especially enjoy the book."

– Drew Bridges, author of
A New Haunt for Mr. Bierce and *Billion Dollar Bracket*

". . . The novel is straightforward but effective, employing direct prose to show how incompetence and innocent mistakes snowball into life-changing personal catastrophes. . . "

– Eileen Gonzalez, *Foreword Reviews*

"The novel reads like a play, with the characters' own words, particularly in court scenes, conveying most of the action. Joey's tenderness and candidness toward Mallory convincingly set him apart from his mates' brash talk and lack of sportsmanship. Visually captivating attention to people's appearance and references to 1990s pop culture enhances the stark Arizona scenery depicted. . . Celebrating the hard work of maintaining human dignity, this is a fiery story of just rewards."

– Mari Carlson, *The US Review of Books*

"Len Joy's *Dry Heat* takes the reader through Joey Blade's tumultuous journey of lost love, lost dreams, and betrayal. Joey is not a character you will soon forget. Len Joy is a master storyteller whose skillful use of gripping action scenes and captivating dialogue result in relentless pacing that keeps the reader glued to the page. Tension mounts throughout the story as the reader aches for Joey to find his way, ending in a riveting climax. Well done, Len Joy."

- Gregory Lee Renz, author of *Beneath the Flames*.

OTHER BOOKS

BY LEN JOY

American Past Time
Better Days
Everyone Dies Famous

PART I

Joey

CHAPTER 1

The gangs were always stealing the nylon basketball nets, so the park director had replaced them with galvanized steel chain, which rattled obnoxiously on every bad shot. Joey frowned as his jump shot clanked off the front rim.

"Your shot sucks today, Joey Blade," Mallory said as she bounced the ball back to him.

"Your boobs are distracting me. Maybe it's time you started wearing a bra." Blonde, with a pixie cut that framed her cute little-girl face, Mallory could have passed for a twelve-year-old if it hadn't been for her huge breasts. She was fifteen, two years younger than Joey, and they had been playground buddies for ten years. She lived with her creepy father in a rundown brick house a block away and escaped to the park most afternoons.

"Come on, concentrate, Mr. All American." She lifted up her sweatshirt, flashing him as he took his next shot. An airball.

"Aargh." Joey chased after the errant shot, hip-checking Mallory as he grabbed the ball. He dribbled out to the corner and swished a turnaround jumper. "Yes! No distractions that time." He pumped his fist.

Mallory smirked. "Better get used to it. You'll have plenty of distractions when you're in Lala Land next week."

Lala Land.

Joey was out of time. He had to make a decision about his trip to USC and he had to make it now. He clanked another free throw off the rim.

"What's wrong, Joey?"

"Dutch."

Mallory scowled as she bounced the ball to him. She knew what Joey's dad was like. Dutch Blade was an unfiltered, heart-on-his-sleeve guy. He could chew someone out one moment and be hugging them the next.

"He doesn't want you following in the immortal footsteps of O.J.?"

Joey gave her a look. Mallory was always a smartass. Three weeks ago, in his last high school football game, the Shadow Mountain Matadors had defeated Apache Junction, last year's state champion, 28 to 24. Joey rushed for 264 yards and scored all four touchdowns for Shadow Mountain. After the game, he was contacted by every school in the PAC 10, all promising that he would have a bright future playing football for their university.

He thought it would be cool to have all that attention, but it was really like trying to date five girls at once. Everyone insisted their school was the best choice for Joey. He didn't like disappointing people and he didn't want to string anyone along, so he quickly narrowed the search to USC in Los Angeles and the University of Arizona in Tucson.

He dribbled out to the foul line and took another turnaround jumper. The shot was a foot short and wide left.

Mallory scampered over and picked it up. "You can't blame that one on me."

Joey tried spinning the ball on his index finger, but he couldn't keep his focus. "Dutch grew up in Tucson. He loves the Wildcats. He's always said that if his folks had had the money, he would have gone to U of A instead of Vietnam." He glided out to the corner again. "Ball!" he shouted. Mallory fired a chest high pass to him and he swished a fifteen-footer.

"Maybe he just wants to keep you close so you can help with the family business," Mallory said with a faux expression of innocence.

Dutch had started Blade Engine and Crankshaft when he returned from Vietnam. With the help of Joey's mom, Callie, it had become the largest engine rebuilder in the southwest.

"My dad thinks anyone who goes to California just wants to be a movie star."

Mallory tilted her head and squinted at him. "You're pretty cute with that curly hair and those girly eyelashes. I could definitely see you in the movies."

"Shut up, Mallory. This is serious."

"What do you want to be when you grow up? A football player? Or are you planning to take over the business?"

Joey gave her the finger. They'd had that discussion before. "I want to be a writer. USC would be better for that, but to my dad, a writer is even worse than a movie star. He doesn't think it's a real job unless you're sweating."

"So, your big problem is deciding between a free education in California or Arizona?" Mallory arched her eyebrows, suggesting that was the kind of problem most people would love to have. Then she grinned and said, "You want to come over to my place for a glass of ice tea?"

"Uh . . ." Joey stared down at his feet. Mallory was cool, but he couldn't stand her father. Donny Stewart worked at Blade Engine as a mechanic doing engine installs. He thought he was some kind of comedian. He was always telling stupid, dirty jokes and his delivery sucked. He acted like Joey was disrespecting him for not laughing his ass off. Joey knew Stewart resented him because he was the boss's kid. Donny Stewart was an all-around creepy guy.

"My dad's running the install center today." Mallory said. "He won't be home for two hours."

"Ice tea sounds great," Joey said.

o o o

Joey sat down on the yoga mat on Mallory's screened porch. She brought out two glasses of ice tea and handed one to him. "This is my workout studio," she said. "You okay with the floor? I can get you a chair."

"No, this is good." He took a gulp. "Thanks. I really sucked today."

"You were definitely not Joey Blade, All-American."

Joey shook his head. "It's Solita's fault. She came home today from ASU with her latest boyfriend. I'm pretty sure he's gay. We all sit down for a special family lunch and she tells me how cool it is that I'm visiting USC next weekend. She wasn't supposed to blab that because I haven't told Dutch yet. She did it just to get a rise out of him. She's been fighting with him all her life."

"Solita's cool. I wish I had a sister who could tell my old man to go fuck himself."

Joey shifted his position, trying to get comfortable. "I love Solita, but she makes it so difficult. When Dutch heard about USC he blew a gasket. Told Solita that no kid of his is attending some granola-munching fag school. I thought her boyfriend was going to faint. So then Mom got angry and told Dutch to watch his language. Callie Blade's the only person on earth who can stop Dutch in his tracks. He got all contrite and told the boyfriend that there was nothing wrong with granola."

Mallory laughed so hard she snorted tea through her nose. "Your family meals sound like so much fun."

"After dinner, Dutch drags me into his office and starts giving me the hard sell. Telling me all the reasons I should go to U of A. 'Closer to home,' he says." Joey shuddered. "That's not a good reason. He tries to tell me it has a better football program, but he knows that's not even close to true. So then he tries the career angle. Tells me I'll make better connections. But that's only true if my career is working for Blade Engine, and that's never going to happen. So then—get this—he says the weather is better. The weather! Can you believe that?" Joey took another gulp of ice tea. "I say, 'The weather, Dad, come on.' And he says 'It's a dry heat. Very comfortable.'"

Mallory laughed again. "Dry heat. Your dad's a trip."

"He even tries reason. Says the Wildcats need me. Says I'll get lost in the shuffle cause USC drafts ten tailbacks a year. But the USC recruiter compared me to Marcus Allen. Probably because we're both six two and neither of us are speedsters. Not like O.J. Hah! They never talk about O.J. That's what happens when you fuck up as badly as he did. Anyway, Dutch wants me to go down to Tucson for a meet and greet next Saturday and I want to go to that USC game." Joey paused to catch his breath.

Mallory giggled.

"What's so funny?" Joey asked.

She set her ice tea on the floor and cupped his face in her hands. "You talk too much." Then she tongue-kissed him. Joey's heart raced. He had ignored most of the stories, but he knew Mallory had a reputation.

He slipped his hands under her T-shirt as she tugged down his cargo shorts. He unsnapped her shorts and she wiggled out of them. They lay together on the mat, their naked bodies pressed together. It was really going to happen.

Joey tried not to show how nervous he was. He rolled on

top. He wasn't sure how to proceed, but Mallory helped him. Joey came in ten seconds.

"Sorry," he said, embarrassed.

Mallory was cool. "That's okay. Have another ice tea and I'll bet you'll be ready for another round."

He was, and it was much better the second time. Afterward, they spooned on the yoga mat. Joey cupped her breasts and tried to think of something to say, but he'd already talked too much and he couldn't think of anything that wasn't lame so he kept his mouth shut.

Mallory scrunched around and rolled on top of him, pinning him to the mat. "You don't have to say anything, Joey. That was nice."

"Nice?" Joey said. He was hoping for more than nice.

"Nice is good."

As he was heading out the door, Mallory wrapped her arms around him again. "I think your father is right."

"About what?"

"Arizona. That's where you should go."

"Why?"

"Because then we could do this again. Have more nice times." She giggled and Joey had to admit it sounded appealing.

CHAPTER 2

Six Weeks Later

8 P.M. – FRIDAY – DECEMBER 31, 1999
SHADOW MOUNTAIN HIGH SCHOOL –
PHOENIX, ARIZONA

Joey parked Dutch's pickup in the teacher's parking lot at the far corner of the school property. The millennium celebration bonfire wasn't an official school event so there would be no teachers using the lot tonight. All the other high school kids were parking in the visitor's lot next to the football field, but Joey didn't want to park there with this ugly truck and its stupid BLADE ENGINE & CRANKSHAFT logo plastered on the doors.

The little S-10 was a '93 with over six hundred thousand miles on it. The engine was tired—a Corolla passed him on the way over—and the cabin stunk. Even after Joey hung three New Car Scent tree deodorizers on the rearview and under the visors it still carried the smell of dried sweat, cigarette smoke, and fast food from the three dozen drivers who had used it to deliver parts over the last seven years. Blade Engine was only using it now for emergency deliveries, so his dad let him drive it on the weekends. It was most definitely not a cool ride, but better than walking.

Wendy Chang, Joey's new girlfriend, refused to ride in it. "It's disgusting, Joey. We'll take my car to the party." Wendy's father was some big-time lawyer. For her seventeenth birthday, he had given her a '99 Infiniti J—a lady car for sure—but a nice ride. He had met Wendy at a party at Lookout Mountain the weekend after Thanksgiving—the week after he had been with Mallory. He hadn't seen Mallory since that day, and he never saw her in school. He felt like he should say something to her about Wendy, but he wasn't sure what.

Joey walked past the tennis courts and entered the football field at the north end. He hadn't been on the field since the big game with Apache Junction. This morning he had called Coach Meyer at the University of Arizona and told him he was signing the letter of intent and would be heading to Tucson in the fall. He couldn't go against his father's wishes. Tomorrow he would let USC know of his decision.

Today was his eighteenth birthday. He was officially an adult. A man with a full-ride scholarship. Even Wendy would be impressed. A sex breakthrough was definitely a possibility tonight. Thanks to Mallory, he wasn't totally inexperienced. He felt a little guilty that he was grateful for that.

The bonfire was being built just beyond the south end zone near the pole vault pit. Lua Tupola pulled up towing a hay wagon loaded with wood and scrub brush. Lua was a giant. Six foot four, two hundred forty pounds. As nose tackle, he anchored the Shadow Mountain Matadors' defensive line. Lua had corralled a bunch of younger kids to unload the wagon. A swarm of them were streaming from the wagon carrying armloads of wood and brush for the fire.

Wendy, with her legs tucked, was perched on a hay bale. She was wearing white jeans and a powder-blue cashmere sweater. Her long black hair was gathered into a silky ponytail and designer sunglasses wrapped the top of her head like a tiara. She reminded Joey of one of those Disney princesses, except for the joint she was smoking. She spotted Joey and gave a little finger wave with a coy smile he hadn't figured out how to read yet. TJ Grimes, her pot supplier, sat next to her on the bale holding a pint of Southern Comfort.

TJ was a scrawny, freckle-faced redhead with greasy long hair. He moved to Phoenix a year ago and lived with his older brother, who everyone said was a serious drug dealer. He was a year behind them in school and had the hots for Wendy.

"Joey!" TJ jumped up from the bale. "Just keeping it warm for you, buddy. Have a seat."

Joey ignored TJ and sat down next to Wendy. "Sorry I'm late. You know how my mom is."

Wendy draped her arms around Joey's neck and ran her fingers through his hair. "I would die for those caramel curls." She feathered a kiss on his neck and whispered in his ear,

"I was worried that you'd stood me up on your birthday."

"Dude, it's your birthday?" A trickle of a Southern Comfort slipped down TJ's chin. "You're eighteen? Congratulations." He held out his pint. "Take a hit. Get your birthday buzz started."

"No thanks," Joey said. He glared at TJ, hoping he would get the message to disappear, but the kid was too drunk to notice.

Lua was walking toward them. The giant Samoan moved with the grace of a big cat. "Happy Birthday, Joey Blade. Come here, brother." Lua's voice, like his walk, was smooth and light and soft. He held his arms opened wide. Joey couldn't help but smile when Lua was around.

Joey stood up and braced himself. "Don't hurt me, man."

Lua wrapped his meaty arms around Joey and lifted him off the ground. "Don't be a pussy, Blade." He gently set Joey back on his feet and turned to TJ. "Hey, Grimes, I hear you got good weed."

"Absolutely. Primo Mexican Red."

Lua scowled. "Don't shine me, shitbird."

TJ rubbed his hands together. "It's true. I got a connection in Rocky Point. I'll give you a dime bag for five bucks. New customer special."

Wendy handed her joint to Lua. "Try it, Lulu. It's good stuff."

Lua took a deep hit. The joint disappeared between Lua's huge thumb and forefinger. "That's tight," he said, his eyes watering. "You got a bag in your little purse there?"

TJ clutched his fanny pack protectively. "No, I don't carry. It's in my car."

"Okay. I'll take two of those discount dime bags."

TJ screwed up his face to complain, but then thought better of it. "Okay, ten bucks. Special favor. Don't tell no one. Come with me. It's in my car."

Lua had turned to look at the crew building the fire. He shouted at the group, "Hey, dipshits, start with the small stuff." The fire was more smoke than flame.

"Come on. I got lighter fluid," TJ said.

Lua scowled. "Bring it to me. I gotta go help those numbnuts before they smoke us all out."

TJ shrugged and started to settle down next to Wendy on the hay bale. "You better get Lua his grass before he throws you on the fire," Joey said.

"You don't want to disappoint a new customer," Wendy said.

TJ was all attention when Wendy acknowledged his existence. "Yeah. You're right, Wendy. I'll be right back."

He did a quick about-face and stumbled into a face plant. The pint of Southern Comfort bounced out of his hand. "Goddammit." He jumped up and grabbed the bottle. It was unbroken, but most of the whiskey was gone. He took one last pull from the bottle and tossed it aside. "Fucking Lua. Screw's me on the price and now he wants free delivery." When he saw Joey staring at him, he blanched. "Just kidding, man. Me and Lua—we're cool."

Joey stared at him walking away. "Grimes is too stupid to be a drug dealer."

"I know," Wendy said. "But he does have good weed." She kissed him with feeling. "Happy birthday, babe."

Her lips tasted faintly of strawberries and Joey's heart raced as her tongue probed teasingly. He tried to prolong the kiss, but she pulled back. "Hold that thought. I have to talk to Lawrence about something. It won't take long." Lawrence Darville was Wendy's old boyfriend. She pushed herself up from the bale and kissed him again. "Keep an eye on the fire." She grinned as if running off to talk to her ex-boyfriend was a big joke.

Darville had pulled into the student lot in his new midnight-blue Toyota Tacoma. A super cool ride. A model year 2000. Fresh from the factory. He stood in the bed of his pickup wearing a leather bomber jacket looking disinterestedly at the kids building the bonfire. With his mop of white-blond hair and his pretty face, he looked like a young David Bowie. When Wendy approached, he jumped down and climbed into the cab. Wendy got in the truck.

Damn thing probably still had a real new car smell. Joey thought about his piece-of-shit S-10 with its sweat and taco smells and its duct-taped upholstery. He didn't blame Wendy for not wanting to ride in it.

Wendy and Darville had been on and off all throughout high school. Even after she dumped Darville and started dating Joey, there were more than a few times when she had run off to talk to him about something. Joey didn't really care. He never expected to date someone like Wendy. He wasn't in her league. She was a snob, but she was beautiful. Exotic. She had a right to be stuck up. She was a preppy, like Darville, but smart like all the Asians. She applied to Harvard and didn't even bother with a backup school. Her bigshot old man told her there was no need to. Harvard was his school. End of story.

Joey Blade wasn't part of her long-term plan, but that was okay with Joey. Wendy would be a perfect end-of-the-school-year girlfriend. In the fall she'd go east and Joey would head down to Tucson. He didn't need to hassle her if she wanted to gossip with Mr. Too Cool. After the bonfire, some of Wendy's preppy friends were having a party at Darville's home. His parents were in Cabo for the New Year. Joey would have preferred making out over at Squaw Peak.

It was a typical Phoenix winter night. Once the sun went down the temperature dropped quickly. Lua had managed to organize the fire-builders and the dark clear sky was now dotted with sparks. Joey shivered. He should have worn something more than his flannel shirt, but all he had was his varsity letter jacket. He was so proud of that jacket when he earned it as a freshman, but now he felt silly wearing it. Maybe that was Wendy's influence. She wasn't into sports. The wind was whipping up and he was getting cold. He was about to get up and move closer to the fire when he spotted Mallory walking toward him.

Damn.

When he started dating Wendy, Joey forgot about everything else. He should have at least called Mallory. Now as she headed toward him, he felt like a shit.

Mallory looked different. Serious. She sat down on the bale next to him. Close. The heat of her body took the edge off the chill Joey was feeling.

"I saw your girlfriend leave you to go talk to her old boy-friend." She was staring at the fire, not looking at him.

"Yeah. They're still friends."

Like you and me. We're still friends, right?

She was still staring at the fire. Not looking at him. "I'm pregnant."

A simple declaration, delivered as information, not an accusation.

Joey's throat tightened, like some invisible specter was choking him. Even if he had known what he wanted to say, he wouldn't have been able to get the words out. He hesitantly lifted his hand and covered Mallory's hand that was resting on her thigh. "Uh . . . what . . ."

Mallory flipped her hand over and squeezed his hand. "I'm keeping the baby. I don't want anything from you. I'm not telling anyone that you're the father. I just wanted to let you know. You have a right."

A father. A baby. "You . . . you have to tell someone," he said. "I can help."

Mallory jumped up from the bale. "If you tell your parents, my father will find out and he will make trouble."

"Are you sure?"

Mallory looked fierce, not angry. "He's an evil man," she said. Her voice level, but determined. "I will never tell him. Now go enjoy your bonfire. And your beautiful girlfriend. Everything will be fine." She turned and walked quickly away toward the parking lot without giving Joey a chance to say anything more.

CHAPTER 3

J oey watched Mallory walk away. He tried to gather his thoughts. Everything wasn't going to be fine, that much he could figure out. It was hard to breathe, like the wind had been knocked out of him by a blindside tackle.

His father would go ballistic.

Dutch had been giving Joey sex lectures since he was twelve years old. "Don't be thinking with your little head, Joey. Get a girl pregnant and you can kiss your fancy dreams good-bye."

No one knew he had been with Mallory, but there was no way that this would stay a secret.

A baby? He shouldn't be thinking about himself or worrying about what his father would say. He knew he was being selfish. Mallory was having a baby, *his* baby. How could that be possible? Who would take care of the kid? It couldn't just be Mallory. He would have to help her. With what? Money? Changing diapers? What would happen when he went off to college? Would this fuck up his chances to get a scholarship?

Joey kicked himself again for making this about him. The wind picked up and now he was shivering for real. Mallory's news drained all the warmth from his body.

The burst of wind stoked the bonfire's flames, and something in the pile of burning logs and brush exploded. There was a chorus of screams as the kids circling the fire retreated. Then, an ungodly howl, as TJ burst out of the crowd running madly toward the parking lot, his jeans and hoodie on fire. Lua chased after him, but TJ was pulling away.

Joey leaped off the bale and raced toward TJ.

"He spilled lighter fluid on his pants!" Lua shouted as Joey raced passed him.

Joey unbuttoned his shirt and peeled it off as he ran down the sidewalk that flanked the parking lot. TJ was careening through the lot, running around cars, changing directions like a broken-field runner. He was faster than Joey expected. They were halfway across the parking lot before Joey pulled even with him. Joey wrapped his shirt around his hands and was about to grab TJ when he turned sharply to avoid a parked car and ran smack into Joey. TJ went down like a cornerback leveled by a pulling guard.

Joey quickly patted out the flames with his shirt. TJ's baggy ghetto jeans and his black hoodie were trashed, but they had protected him. He wasn't burned, just scared shitless. He lay on the ground whimpering, his face pressed into the asphalt.

"You're okay, Grimes. The fire's out."

TJ stopped crying and covered his head with his hands. "How bad is it, Joey? I can't look."

A ghostlike cloud of smoke hovered over TJ as if his soul had left his body. There were scorch marks on his jeans and hoodie. "Good thing you were wearing those baggy ass pants," Joey said. "With Wranglers your skinny butt would have burned for sure."

Lua ran up to them, gasping. "Nice tackle, Joey. You might make it on the kickoff team next year."

Joey gave him a look. "Kickoff team is for crazy fuckers like you." He slipped his shirt back on and brushed off his jeans.

TJ sat on the ground with his arms around his knees as he inspected his smoldering jeans and rearranged his fanny pack so it was in front instead of on his ass. "Damn. You saved my life, Joey. You should get a medal."

Lua scoffed. "This is Sheriff Joe Arpaio country. That ol' man gives medals for killing skanky drug dealers. Not saving them."

TJ's face screwed up like he was about to cry. "I ain't a—"

Another explosion from the fire. This time a fireball of debris enveloped the athletic shed next to the field. The kids who had been watching Joey run down TJ now started racing in full-bore panic mode back to their cars in the parking lot.

"Jesus Christ," Lua said. "That fire's out of control. I gotta get my fucking truck out of there. You guys better book; the law will be here soon."

Thick black smoke billowed from the shed as the tarpaper roof ignited.

TJ moaned as he got to his feet. "My hands are shaking. I can't drive like this. Can you give me a ride, Joey?"

Darville's truck was rumbling down the center of the parking lot headed for them. He stopped and Wendy jumped out. "Babe, are you okay? That was crazy brave." She hugged Joey and combed her fingers through his hair, rearranging it. "There. That's better."

"Hey, I was the one on goddamn fire," TJ whined.

Wendy stared at him with disgust. "You're a fucking idiot."

The piercing wail of a siren could be heard coming from Shea Boulevard. A firetruck rumbled into the school parking lot, bounded over the curb, and headed down the track that ran adjacent to the football field. The bonfire engulfed the shed and was closing in on the bus garage.

"Wendy! We need to get out of here!" Darville said, his cool façade cracking.

"He's right," TJ said as he dragged his smoky ass into the pickup bed. "Let's get out of here before the cops show up."

Wendy looked at Lawrence and then Joey. "Can you get in the back with TJ to make sure he doesn't do something even more stupid?" She nuzzled his neck and ran her hands under his shirt. "Okay?" She gazed up at him. Her dark eyes mysterious and inviting. Her hands warm on his chest.

Joey felt himself grinning like a fool. He gave her ass a quick squeeze. "No problem," he said. He put his hands on the side of the pickup and vaulted cleanly into the truck bed. It was a showoff move.

Darville revved the truck engine. Two metro cop cars pulled in behind the fire truck and blocked the exit to the parking lot so Darville turned his truck around and headed across the baseball field that was just north of the football field. The powerful Tacoma rumbled across the infield, and Joey clung desperately to the sidewall to keep from being bounced out of the truck. As Darville slowed down to turn onto Thirtieth Street, Joey scrambled to the front of the truck bed and leaned back against the cab wall. He was directly behind Darville and could see Wendy in the passenger seat. Joey braced himself as the big truck fishtailed into the northbound lanes. "Fuck!" TJ yelled. He lost his grip on the sidewall and rolled across the truck bed. A handgun clattered out of his fanny pack. Joey reached over and picked it up. He looked over at TJ. "What the fuck, Grimes?"

TJ crawled over and sat next to Joey. "Protection," he said. He reached for the gun. "Fuckers are always trying to rip me off."

Joey handed him the gun. "Keep it out of sight."

"Sure thing, boss. I ain't stupid."

Darville turned on to Cholla Street. He took the ramp for Highway 51, the new Squaw Peak Parkway, heading north. The truck rode smooth as glass on the new road. He pulled into the HOV lane. The cars in the other two lanes were a blur of lights and chrome as the Tacoma rocketed past them.

"Fucking rich boy drives like a maniac," TJ said, his teeth clenched. The wind was whipping his scraggly long hair into his face.

Joey didn't respond. Darville was racing to his home in north Scottsdale. His New Year's Eve party was still on. Joey had been all hot for a sex breakthrough with Wendy, figuring that party would be a great opportunity, but now he just wanted to go home and figure out what to do about Mallory.

TJ scrunched low in the truck bed and shook his hair out of his face. "Sort of sucks, you sitting back here while that prissy, rich boy gets to sit up there with your girl."

Joey ignored him, hoping TJ would shut up, but he knew that wasn't likely.

"Of course, you being a big football hero, I guess you get pussy anytime you want. You fuck Wendy yet? I hear she's a screamer."

"Grimes?"

"What?"

"Shut the fuck up."

TJ nodded. like Joey had told him he had something in his teeth. "Sure thing. I hear ya." He raked his hands through his singed hair again. "Holy shit!" he shouted, pointing at a black Silverado that was closing fast on them.

The Silverado was inches from the Tacoma rear bumper when it swerved out of the HOV lane. The driver was wearing a straw cowboy hat and had a beefy tattooed arm. As he passed them, he shouted, "Hey faggots! Piss in your pants?"

Darville punched the truck into overdrive and closed fast on the Silverado. Joey glanced at Wendy. She was leaning forward, engaged, her face animated. This was her kind of sport. They came up fast on the Silverado, inches from their bumper, and then Darville gunned it past them on the right side.

TJ flipped off the two men in the Silverado as the Tacoma sped past. "Piss on this, you chickenshit motherfuckers!"

Joey stared down at the truck floor, holding his head between his hands. This was stupid and dangerous. As soon as they got to Darville's house, he would call his dad and get a ride home. He didn't care what Wendy or Darville or any of their rich friends thought.

The Silverado wasn't done. As they sped past, the tattooed dude hurled his beer can at the truck. It hit the top of the cab splattering TJ and Joey. It wasn't beer, it was piss.

"Motherfucker!" TJ unzipped his fanny pack and pulled out the handgun as he slithered over to the driver's side of the truck.

"TJ! Put that gun away!" Joey screamed.

TJ pulled himself up behind the cab like he was driving a chariot. With a madman grin, he peered over the top of the cab and, holding the gun with both hands, aimed at the Silverado.

Joey grabbed TJ by his hoodie and whipped him to the truck bed. TJ lost his grip on the gun and it bounced toward the tailgate.

"You stupid fuck!" Joey slammed TJ's head into the truck bed.

The gun rattled against the tailgate, and as Joey stretched to grab it, Darville swerved the truck into the passing lane, rolling Joey into the wall of the truck bed.

The gun bounced back into the middle, and TJ grabbed it just as Darville pulled even with the Silverado. "Fuck you!" He fired wildly at the Silverado as Darville rocketed past them. The first two shots missed, but the third shot blew out the windshield.

The Silverado fishtailed, skidding into the HOV lane and then back across the highway. The driver slammed on the brakes as the truck skidded off the road, with a plume of black smoke trailing from the rear tires. The truck flattened a highway sign and did a 180, coming to a stop facing the wrong direction on the shoulder of Highway 51.

Joey wrestled TJ to the floor of the truck. He didn't resist as Joey ripped the gun from his hand. "Oh my God! What did you do?" Joey screamed as he kneeled over TJ, holding his gun. He stared down the road. A police car was closing fast, lights flashing and siren blaring.

"Throw the gun away!" Wendy had slid open the truck cab window. Her eyes were wide, frightened.

Darville slipped in behind a U-Haul van that was driving well below the speed limit.

"Jesus Christ, Joey!" Wendy screamed. "Throw it away. Now!"

Joey looked from Wendy to TJ, who remained curled up in a fetal position, and then to the police car in hot pursuit. As they crossed over the Arizona Canal, Joey flung the handgun toward the canal as if he was lobbing a grenade. He couldn't see where it landed.

Wendy slammed shut the cab window and leaned forward, her head practically resting on the dashboard as she pulled out her cell phone. Over the sound of the traffic rushing by and the growing din of the police siren Joey could hear the desperation in her voice.

"—on the Squaw Peak. Just past the canal," she said. She took a quick peek back at Joey and then continued in sort of a shout whisper. "Yes, he's here." She paused. "Okay, Daddy. I won't. I promise. Tell Tommy to hurry."

Darville brought the truck to a stop on the shoulder of the highway. The high beams on the car were blinding and the whoop-whoop-whoop of the siren deafening. Joey knelt down in the truck next to TJ, who was face down hugging the floor of the truck. He gave himself a pep talk. *Stay calm. No sudden movements. Keep your mouth shut*

The siren stopped and the loudspeaker on top of the squad car squawked. "Turn off the engine." The driver, a tall Hispanic with a weightlifter build, stepped out of the car holding a handset in one hand and a .38 police special in the other. As he ducked his head to talk to his partner who was still in the vehicle, TJ slipped over the passenger side of the truck bed, and, with surprising athleticism, scaled the chain-link fence that lined the highway and disappeared into the night.

The DPS trooper appeared not to have noticed TJ's escape. "Keep your hands on the wheel where I can see them!" he said.

Joey's heart pounded. The trooper was focused on Darville and hadn't even noticed him. Joey didn't want to raise his hands suddenly and startle him.

"Hey, you in the back," the big trooper said with a Mexican accent. "Put your hands on your head!"

His partner stepped out of the car. He was young. Blonde. Even with his Mountie hat he appeared short and unthreatening. He was tugging on his gun but it was stuck in the holster. His partner, annoyed, was about to say something when the younger trooper figured out that he needed to unsnap the flap holding the gun in place. He braced his arm on the top of the open car door and aimed his gun at Joey. His face was screwed up with concentration, lips pressed tight, as he struggled to keep the gun steady. "Facedown!" the trooper yelled, his voice breaking.

His nervousness scared Joey more than the gun. There was nothing about Joey Blade that should make a cop nervous. Joey laid facedown in the truck and interlaced his fingers behind his head, like he'd seen it done on a dozen cop shows.

"Secure him," the lead trooper said as he marched up to the driver's window.

Joey kept his face buried in the floor of the truck bed. He tried not to move a muscle. He heard the crunch of gravel as the rookie trooper approached the truck.

"Uh, Luis, how do I . . .?" The kid's voice cracked again. He wasn't tall enough to reach Joey in the middle of the truck bed. Joey thought about scootching closer so he could reach over, but decided he better not move.

"Make him sit on the edge of the truck wall. Then cuff him and take his ID."

The rookie pounded the wall of the pickup. "Sit here!" he said. He had a fake deep voice and sounded like a kid imitating an adult. "Hands behind your back."

Joey crawled on his knees and sat down. He put his hands behind his back and the trooper slipped a nylon cord over one wrist and then the other and pulled them tight.

"Anything sharp in your pants pocket?" the rookie asked.

"No sir."

He tugged Joey's wallet from his jeans pocket and removed Joey's license. He put the wallet back in Joey's shirt pocket.

"Leave him there and give me his ID. Get the girl out and curb her," the trooper named Luis said.

The boy trooper opened the passenger door. "Step down, ma'am."

"Of course," Wendy said. She jumped down from the truck, smiling. No sign of the desperation she had shown moments ago. Joey had seen that smile before. "I'm so sorry. This is all a misunderstanding. Hitchhikers, you know?"

Hitchhikers? "I'm not a hitch—"

"Keep your mouth shut." The rookie flashed Joey his I'm-in-charge look. "You talk when I tell you to." He led Wendy ten yards in front of the truck and told her to sit on the ground. Joey couldn't hear what she was saying, but she continued to talk to the boy, who was nodding his head like he understood her.

Trooper Luis asked Darville for his license and registration. He took them and the car keys and Joey's license and headed back to his squad car. Wendy was smiling and then she laughed at something the boy trooper said. It reminded Joey of how she acted when they first met.

As Joey sat on the wall of the pickup with his hands cuffed behind him, he noticed cars slowing as they passed to check out who was getting busted. Hitchhiker? Wendy must have panicked. She had to be explaining to that cop that Joey wasn't shooting at anyone.

Joey's shoulders throbbed and his back ached. He wanted to shift his position, but he didn't want to upset Wendy's new friend. The young trooper had been talking to her for at least ten minutes. She just kept smiling and giggling like she was on a date.

What was taking that cop so long? Does Darville have outstanding tickets?

Another DPS patrol car pulled up behind the first and then a black Lexus rolled slowly past and parked in front of the Silverado. A stubby, middle-aged white man in a polo shirt and dark pants got out and walked over to Wendy. He shook hands with the rookie and then he pointed to his car. Wendy, who hadn't been cuffed, strolled nonchalantly over to the Lexus and slid into the back seat.

That was a good sign. Joey got a knot in his stomach as he thought about having to call his dad to come pick him up. But at least this clusterfuck of a day would be over. This was the worst birthday of all time.

Luis was talking with the other two troopers and now they were all marching over toward Joey.

"Get him down from there," Luis said.

They each grabbed him by the arm and lifted him out of the truck.

Luis's walkie-talkie squawked. "Adam Twelve, do you copy?"

"Twelve. Copy. Go ahead."

"Adam Eight found the gun. Break . . ."

"Go ahead."

"Kick the juvies. Bring in your party. Break . . ."

"Copy that. On our way. Ten-four."

Luis addressed the other two cops. "Tell Sidney he can take off now. I'll transport Blade."

Joey wondered how they knew his name and then he remembered the license.

Luis waved to his partner. "Come on, Randy. We gotta roll." He tightened his grip on Joey's arm.

"Wait a minute. I didn't—"

"Save your breath. Big mistake shooting at a cop. They found the gun so you are fucked."

He marched Joey to the squad car and pushed him, not roughly, but not gently either, into the backseat. With his hands behind his back, it was difficult to sit.

Joey had a sinking feeling. *Those cowboys were cops?*

"I didn't shoot anyone," he said. "Ask Wendy. Or Darville. They'll tell you."

"Shut up, kid. I've heard it all before."

They pulled onto the highway with the lights flashing. Joey would not be home for his birthday.

CHAPTER 4

If you're arrested in Maricopa County for anything from public drunkenness to murder, the police—or in Joey's case the Arizona DPS—take you to the Durango jail on Fourth Avenue for intake processing. If the system is running smoothly, intake can be completed in less than two hours. On December 31, 1999, intake was not running smoothly.

Chaos reigned. It's always crazy on New Year's Eve, but on the millennium, it was a thousand times crazier. The parking lot was full, and cop cars were double-parked up and down the driveway to the station.

The DPS officer stared at Joey in the backseat like it was his fault everyone had gone crazy. "You get him processed, Randy," he said to his partner. "I'll get us coffee. Maybe it will clear up by the time I get back."

Randy escorted Joey into the station. "Won't see him for an hour," he said.

Joey felt like he'd been knocked out and was still trying to figure out what hit him. Wendy and Darville should have been able to straighten everything out. "Didn't my girlfriend tell you I didn't shoot at anybody?"

"Girlfriend? You were in the back of the truck. She said you hitched a ride." He grinned like he had made some kind of special connection to her.

Hitched a ride? Why would she say that? Joey wouldn't even have been in the truck bed if Wendy hadn't asked him. If Joey hadn't stopped TJ, the fool might have actually shot those cops. And what were those cops doing, street-racing on the Squaw Peak?

They stepped through the door and it was like waiting in the crowd for the doors to open for the Smash Mouth concert last month. Only here, half the crowd didn't really want to go in.

"Oh geez," Randy said. "Is there a line? There should be an intake officer somewhere." He craned his neck to see around the crowd.

"I think that's the end of the line," Joey said, nodding toward a big biker dude and his escort. What appeared to be a random crowd was actually a line that snaked from one end of the reception area to the other and back at least four times. It ended at a counter where a beleaguered officer was logging in a drunk who could barely stand.

"Golly, this will take forever," Randy said. He shrugged. "My shift ends in a couple hours. Guess I'll make some overtime."

"Don't I get a phone call?" Joey said. His shoulder sockets throbbed. Being handcuffed was a lot more uncomfortable than it looked on television.

Randy shook his head. "You don't get anything until you get put in the system."

An hour later they were still at least an hour away from the intake desk. Finally, another cop came out from behind the counter with a box of plastic bags and a roll of masking tape. He went down the line and handed each escort cop a plastic bag and a six-inch strip of masking tape.

"Put his personal effects in the bag, rip the tape in two pieces and put one tape on the bag and one on his wrist and write his name on the tape. Then take him over to G40."

Joey handed Randy his wallet, watch, truck keys, and high school ring. Randy wrapped the tape on Joey's wrist and then with schoolboy perfect penmanship wrote out his name: **JOSEPH BLADE.** He marched Joey across the room to the staircase. "G40's on the second floor," he said.

"What about my phone call?" Joey asked.

Randy's face twisted into a frown and he straightened up like he was trying to make himself taller, more in charge. "You still aren't officially processed."

A portly correctional officer who resembled the fat Elvis, but with rust-red hair was sitting on a tall stool at the door to G40 with a clipboard. "Name?" he said, barely looking up from his clipboard.

"Blade, Joseph," Randy said.

The guard wrote the name on his sheet. "Forty-three dot five nine eight. Write it on his wrist tape," he said to Randy, his voice weary. "Put that number on your O-43 so we know who we're holding."

He cut the nylon cuffs off Joey and pointed into the room. "Find a place to sit. It'll be awhile."

Joey glanced over his shoulder at Randy, but the rookie was already walking away. G40 was a rectangular room about the size of the Shadow Mountain girls' gym. When the new century arrived, Joey Blade was sitting cross-legged in the center of the room. The side walls of the room were lined with benches, but those were all occupied by Mexican and Chicano gang members. The far wall was lined with garbage cans that reeked of vomit and piss. In the front of the room, four guards leaned against the wall. They were all sloppy big—not muscle big like Luis the DPS trooper. None of them were happy to be working in G40 on New Year's Eve. Most of the room, other than the gangbangers, was occupied by drunks. Dirt-tanned, rail-thin, scraggly-haired men, like the dozens Joey saw every day panhandling on the street corners with cardboard signs asking for work.

Joey parked himself in the center of the room, equal distance from the gangs, the stink of the garbage cans, and the disinterested guards.

All of sudden, some of the gang members stood up and started shouting. "*Diez, nueve, ocho, siete, seis, cinco, cuatro, tres, dos, uno! ¡Feliz año nuevo, hijo de puta! ¡El mundo no terminó,* bitch!"

New Year's! Joey instinctively glanced at his wrist, but all that was there was his masking tape bracelet. He scanned the room. Over the door where he entered, there was an old-fashioned clock like in grade school with a white face and large black numerals. It was one minute past twelve. The world hadn't ended like some of the wack jobs had been predicting, but the new century was definitely not starting out the way he planned.

The traffic into the room slowed to a trickle. At ten minutes past the hour, a thirty-something white man in a blue blazer and a white dress shirt stumbled into the room, wide-eyed and looking like he was afraid to breathe. His head swiveled around until he saw one of the guards. He walked toward him, but the guard brandished his Billy club and pointed to the room. "Sit the fuck down, turkey. Over there!" He pointed in Joey's direction.

Joey stared down at his Nikes. *Don't come over here. Don't come over here.* This was like being a new kid in school and sitting all by yourself in the cafeteria. The last thing you want is for the school dork to come and sit down with you. *Don't come over here.*

"Mind if I sit down?" Two shiny black loafers appeared in Joey's field of vision.

Joey looked up and shrugged, which the man took as an invitation to sit down.

He extended his hand. "Name's Gordon Smith. Friends call me Smitty."

Joey didn't want to shake his hand, but his father had ingrained that habit in him. "Grip the man's hand like you mean it and look him in the eye. Tell him your name. Repeat his. That way you won't forget it."

"Joey Blade. Nice to meet you, Gordon."

"Smitty. Call me Smitty."

Smitty was nervous as a kitten and he was making Joey nervous. Joey had tried to be as invisible as possible in this room of gangbangers, drunks, and hot rodders. Gordon's arrival was like someone flashed a spotlight on him.

"They didn't let me make a phone call," said Smitty. "Aren't they supposed to do that? Did you get to make a call? I got caught in one of them damn speed traps. Wasn't even drinking. Cop said I had outstanding tickets. Hell, that ain't no reason to run me in. What'd they get you for, Jimmy?"

"Joey. Speeding." Joey turned away and retied his shoe, hoping Smitty would get the message he didn't want to talk.

"Sorry. I'm terrible with names. Amanda—she's my wife—says it's 'cause I don't listen." He sighed, and his nervous face got even more wrinkly. "She's going to be worried about me." He started fidgeting with his gold cufflinks. Joey wanted to tell him to hide the cufflinks but he was too late.

"Hey, boss, those are pretty. Can I take a look?" One of the gang members was standing over Smitty. He was bony and missing two front teeth, and with his shaved head and jack-o-lantern grin, he could have been mistaken for a goofy kid except that the gang name "Vatos Locos" was tattooed on each arm. The Vatos Locos were a Mexican national gang with a vicious reputation.

Smitty tugged his sports jacket sleeves down to cover the

links and he wrapped his arms around himself. His face screwed up tight, like his arm was being twisted.

"I just want to look at them, *jefe*. You think Fernando's a thief?"

Smitty smiled nervously. He popped the cufflink through the buttonhole and handed it to Fernando.

"Sweet. That looks like real gold. Let me see the other one."

Smitty handed him the other cufflink. "My wife gave them to me," he said, like that might make a difference.

"Tell ya what, holmes. I'll hold them for you. Keep 'em safe."

Smitty scrambled to his feet. "No thank you, Jose." He held out his hand.

"Jose? What the fuck, holmes. You think every *mojado* is named Jose?" He closed his hand into a fist, palming the cufflinks.

Every instinct in Joey's body told him to not get involved. But he had a bad habit of ignoring his instincts. He stood up next to Smitty. "Give them back," he said.

Fernando grinned. "Ooooh, Pretty Boy wants to be a hero. Bad place for a hero, holmes."

He started to slip the cufflinks into his jeans pocket, but Joey grabbed his arm and easily pried open his fist and grabbed the cufflinks.

"Big fucking mistake, *nino bonito*," Fernando said, huffing like a cartoon bull getting ready to charge. "That face won't look so pretty when I get done with it."

"I don't want any trouble," Joey said, his voice almost a whisper. He hoped Fernando wouldn't notice that his legs were shaking.

"Let him have them, Jimmy" Smitty said, his voice quavering.

Fernando smiled. "Listen to your friend, Pretty Boy."

Gang members silently surrounded Joey and Smitty.

Joey stared at Fernando, who had his hand out. "Give it up."

Joey clenched his fist and he could feel the gold jewelry pressing into the flesh of his hand. Joey knew he should just give them up—he was in enough trouble—but he was Dutch Blade's son, and the one thing he knew for certain was that he wasn't giving up those goddam cufflinks.

"Joey Blade?" A gangster with a trim goatee and an eye patch was staring at Joey like he knew him. He was lean and muscular and dressed all in black.

"Y-yeah . . . I'm Joey Blade."

"Dutch's kid, right? You're the big football hero." He turned to his gang members and said something in Spanish. And then in a harsh tone he said something to Fernando.

Fernando bowed slightly. "Sorry, man. I didn't know you were familia."

Joey stared at Fernando and then at Eyepatch, trying to figure out what was happening.

"You got balls, Joey Blade. Just like your old man. When you get out, you tell Dutch that Chico Torres had your back." He scowled at Fernando and headed back to the gang bench. Fernando and the other gang members followed him.

Smitty was staring at Joey, his mouth agape.

"Put these away," Joey said. He pressed the cufflinks into Smitty's sweaty hand.

Joey watched Fernando sitting on the bench, apart from the others. "I will tell him," Joey said softly.

CHAPTER 5

An hour after the encounter with Chico and the Vatos Locos gang, Joey was taken to Central Intake for official processing. It wasn't like television. It took four hours for Joey to be fingerprinted, medically examined (the actual exam took less than a minute) and finally escorted by a skinny Black deputy, whose bald head gleamed with sweat, into a stuffy, windowless room in the basement of the jail.

"Sit there," he said. "Someone will be in soon to take your statement."

Joey had given up asking when he could make a phone call. He was tired, hungry and desperately thirsty. "Can I have some water?" he asked.

"Do I look like a fucking waiter? Wait for your interview." The deputy made a note on the clipboard he was carrying and then hung it on the post outside the room. "Don't mess with the furniture," he said as he pulled the door shut.

Joey tried not to think about how thirsty he was. The more he tried to ignore his thirst the more he craved water. He put his head down on the desk and took a deep breath. The desk, the whole room, had a farty smell. He made a list in his head, but he couldn't keep it straight. His mouth was dry. He couldn't spit if he wanted to. He sucked on his forearm, but it didn't help. He was dying of thirst. Finally the doorknob turned, and the door opened slowly. A middle-aged balding guy with a bad comb-over shuffled into the office studying a clipboard.

"Joseph Blade?"

Joey lifted his head off the table. He nodded. "Water." He didn't recognize his own voice. It was a guttural croak. A death rattle.

The man frowned. "Shit. They didn't get you any water?" He quick-stepped out of the room and was back in two minutes with two dixie cups. "Here. It's Phoenix tap water so it sucks, but better than nothing."

Joey gulped down both cups. "Thank you," he said.

The man settled into the chair across the table from Joey. "I'm Lieutenant Carnes. Sorry about them not giving you water. Okay. First I got to read this." He pulled out a bookmark shaped card from his shirt pocket. It was feathered like it had gone through the wash once or twice. "You have the right to remain silent. Anything you say can and will be used against you in a court of law. You have the right to an attorney. If you cannot afford an attorney, one will be provided for you. Do you understand the rights I have just read to you?"

Carnes sounded like Sipowicz on *NYPD Blue*. But he wasn't intimidating like one of those TV cops. He reminded Joey of his guidance counselor, Mr. Coots. Joey nodded his head.

"You have to answer audibly, Joseph."

"Yes. I understand."

"Good. With these rights in mind, do you wish to speak to me?"

"I want to go home," Joey said. His voice almost broke. He took another deep breath.

"Understood. If you want a lawyer, it's going to take some time. Most lawyers are not too available on New Year's Day. And the legal aid guys are buried. It might be days before you can get one of them. Talk to me now and we might be able to get this all cleared up."

"Okay," he said.

"Joseph, do you go by Joseph?"

"Joey."

Carnes made a note on his clipboard. "Okay, Joey. You are waiving your right to counsel. Is that correct? Sorry for the legal jargon, but we have to do this by the book. You know how the bosses are."

"Yes. I am."

"Good. Just give me a minute." Carnes flipped through the pages that were tacked to the clipboard.

"Okay. What is your birthdate?"

Joey remembered how he thought his birthday had turned to shit when TJ caught fire. That was just the beginning. He should have let that shithead burn. "December 31, 1981."

Carnes made another note and then smiled ruefully. "Wait a minute. Yesterday was your birthday? You just turned eighteen?"

"Yes sir."

"So, you were out celebrating? Joyriding on the Squaw Peak?"

"Uh, no. See, there was a fire and—"

"A fire?"

"It was a bonfire at the school. Uh, Shadow Mountain . . . for the millennium."

Carnes frowned. "Where did you get your gun?"

Joey shook his head. "I don't have a gun."

Carnes scowled as he flipped through the pages of the file. "According to the statement of two undercover police officers, they were fired upon by someone riding in the back of a dark blue Toyota Tacoma. Were you riding in the back of a dark blue Toyota Tacoma on New Year's Eve on the Squaw Peak Parkway?"

"Yes, but I didn't shoot the gun."

Carnes studied the report again. "The officers are certain that the shots came from someone in the back of the truck."

Joey didn't want to be a rat, but he didn't owe TJ anything. "It was TJ who shot at the truck. It was his gun."

"Who is TJ?"

"TJ Grimes. He goes to Shadow Mountain."

Carnes frowned. "He wasn't in the truck when you were stopped. Just the two minors and you."

"He jumped out when Darville stopped the truck."

"There is no report of another person in that truck. Just the two juvies and you. The arresting officer said he saw you try to toss the gun into the canal. Unluckily for you it didn't make it to the canal. The lab will check it for fingerprints on Monday. Will they find your fingerprints on that gun?"

"Yes, but—"

Carnes held up his hand. "Okay. I've got enough." He stood and pulled a set of handcuffs from his jacket pocket. "Joseph Blade, you are under arrest for the attempted murder of a police officer. This is a class A felony, and you will be arraigned later today where you will have an opportunity to enter a plea." He cuffed Joey's hands behind his back and led him out of the cell.

Attempted murder of a police officer. Just when Joey thought things couldn't get any worse, they did.

CHAPTER 6

Carnes handed Joey over to the same Black officer who had brought him to the interrogation room. He escorted Joey to a new holding cell with bolted-down metal benches along both walls. He was told to sit down and then the officer handcuffed him to a ring in the wall. There were three other guys in the room, two sleeping drunks and to Joey's dismay, Gordon Smith, who was handcuffed to the opposite wall across from Joey.

He beamed like Joey was an old friend. "Hey Jimmy. We meet again. Didn't get a chance to thank you before. I appreciate what you did. That was a scary proposition. Good thing your old man is connected."

Joey slumped on the bench. He didn't have the energy to respond. He was so tired he couldn't even keep his eyes open. Something awful had just happened. He was being charged with a serious crime. He should be trying to make a plan, figure out what to do, but weariness permeated his body. If he hadn't been chained to the wall, he would have melted into a puddle on the floor. He just wanted to sleep, but Smitty wouldn't shut up.

"Hell of a way to start the new century, isn't it, Jimmy? Did they charge you? They're taking us all to court soon. Judge will kick us. That's what I hear. Got too many to deal with. Man, I could use a good meal."

The new century. Yesterday, before he left for the bonfire, Joey told his father about signing the letter of intent accepting U of A's football scholarship. He had never seen Dutch so happy. In less than twelve hours, Joey had gone from not having a care in the world to so many problems he didn't even know what to do next. He knew this screw up with the shooting would be cleared up soon. Wendy and Darville knew what happened. They must have seen Joey trying to stop TJ from shooting. TJ would be found one way or another. But even if it got cleared up today, the word would get out and it wouldn't be a good way to start his relationship with the Wildcats. He needed to stop fretting about that.

Think about Mallory. She can't take care of a baby all by herself. *Come up with a plan, Joey.* But every time he tried to make his brain focus on Mallory, Chico's words kept coming back to torment him. "Tell Dutch that Chico Torres had your back." What did his father have to do with the Vatos Locos gang?

Smitty, undeterred by Joey's silence, continued talking. He didn't stop until the guard returned. He rousted the drunks and the four of them were led down the corridor to a courtroom where they joined a dozen other scruffy men on two long benches along the wall. In the front of the courtroom, there was an elevated podium for the judge, tables for the prosecutors and defense attorneys, and a desk for the court stenographer. The bailiff, a large Black man, announced that the court was in session with the Honorable Morris Crenshaw presiding.

Judge Crenshaw was a slight, owlish-looking man with wire-rimmed glasses and a horseshoe of hair on his otherwise bald head. The gallery was half-filled. Joey's chest tightened when he spotted his parents in the back row with the company attorney, Everett Blainey.

His mom, Callie, was wearing her ASU sweatshirt. She had

probably been getting ready for her daily hike when they got the call. Callie was lithe and fair-skinned, and with her red hair pulled back into a tight ponytail she could have been mistaken for a college girl. She had been Miss Tucson of 1969. She had met Dutch Blade at the NAPA Auto Show where she was working a booth. Dutch had offered her a job as a customer service rep for Blade Engine, the engine rebuilding company he'd just started. Six months later, they were married. She nodded as she caught Joey's eye, her jaw set with determination.

Blainey was whispering to Dutch, who looked fierce and ready to take on the whole court. Dutch was built like a fire hydrant, and his curly black hair, even at age fifty, showed no traces of gray.

Joey swallowed hard and wiped away a tear that leaked from his right eye. It felt so good to see his folks. They would get him out of this situation and if he could convince Mallory to let him tell his parents, he was confident they would be able to help.

The bailiff called out Smitty's name. He got up from the bench and stepped over to the lectern. The clerk read the charges against him. The judge exhaled wearily and said, "I'm dismissing the charges, Mr. Smith. Pay your outstanding tickets. I don't want to see you in my courtroom again."

"Yes, Your Honor. Thank you, Your Honor." Smitty looked around and the bailiff pointed to the door. A minute later he was out of the courtroom, a free man again.

"State versus Joseph Blade. Charge is attempted murder of a police officer."

The feeling that everything would be okay was erased in an instant. *Attempted murder.* Even knowing he was totally innocent, Joey felt dirty having his name linked to that charge.

The murmuring in the defendant box ceased and the men all

turned to look at Joey as he rose uncertainly. A deputy took Joey by the arm and walked him to the lectern.

Judge Crenshaw leaned forward. He was focused. The serious charge grabbed his attention. "Do you have counsel, Mr. Blade?"

Joey felt a hand on his back. "Everett Blainey, representing the defendant. I request a few moments to confer with my client."

Judge Crenshaw smiled. "Don't usually find you in my courtroom, Everett. By all means, confer. Briefly." He waved his hand and then motioned for the bailiff.

Everett Blainey would come to Blade Engine a few times a year to advise Dutch on legal matters, mostly employee disputes and the occasional customer lawsuit. Dressed in jeans and a polo shirt, Blainey was easygoing and friendly and never let Dutch's temper ruffle him. He once told Joey that his most important job was to protect Dutch from Dutch. But today he was dressed in a black suit, and with his wavy white hair combed, he looked like Hollywood's version of a corporate attorney.

He put his arm around Joey and whispered, "We'll talk later. For now, say nothing unless I tell you to speak. Do you understand? I mean nothing." Blainey showed none of the good, old boy affability he exhibited with his father.

"Okay, Your Honor. We're ready."

"How do you plead, Mr. Blade?"

Blainey whispered to Joey, "Tell them you plead not guilty."

Joey cleared his throat. "Not guilty." He sounded croaky, but his voice didn't break.

"Bail?" The judge addressed his inquiry to the prosecutors' table.

A young man with a military crewcut—he didn't look much older than Joey—stood up as he thumbed through a manila file folder. He was trim, but his suit was too big for him, which made him look even younger than he was. "Your Honor, this is a serious offense. Attacking—"

"Excuse me, son." Judge Crenshaw peered at the prosecutor over his glasses. "Would you please identify yourself for the court?"

The attorney reddened. "Sorry, Your Honor. Lonnie Clark, Assistant District Attorney. Your Honor, attempted murder of an officer of the law is a serious offense. We request the defendant be held without bail."

Joey locked his knees to try to keep his legs from trembling.

Blainey squeezed Joey's neck. "Your Honor, my client has no record. He has strong ties to the community and is a well-known and respected scholar-athlete. He lives with his parents, who are here with him today—his father is a reputable small businessman—and it will become apparent very soon that Mr. Blade is innocent of these charges. We request he be released on his own recognizance."

"Can't try the case today, Mr. Blainey," the judge said. He looked over at the young prosecutor. "While I respect and want to protect our law enforcement officers, I think the defendant is entitled to bail. One hundred thousand dollars. Cash or bond."

Joey groaned. *A hundred thousand dollars?*

"Thank you, Your Honor," Blainey said, as though the judge had extended him a huge favor. He patted Joey on the back.

Joey looked at him, perplexed.

A deputy took Joey by the arm and Blainey lifted his arm off Joey's shoulder.

"Trust me, Joey. Your dad has the resources. We'll have you out of here in an hour. Remember what I said. Don't talk to anyone. About anything. You got that?"

"Got it," Joey said, still trying to process Blainey's words. How would Dutch come up with a hundred-thousand-dollar bail?

CHAPTER 7

Everett Blainey was right about Dutch Blade. He did have the resources. Three hours after they took Joey back to his cell, Dutch and Blainey returned with a one hundred-thousand-dollar cashier's check. It took longer than Blainey promised because Dutch's resources were in a safe deposit box at Thunderbird Bank. Krugerrands. Hundreds of them apparently. Dutch had persuaded his banker to drive in from Scottsdale, open the branch, and then purchase 350 of Dutch's gold coins. Blainey advised Dutch to use a bail bondsman, but Dutch didn't trust those men who had billboards up and down the highway.

They were waiting in the reception area when Joey emerged. Dutch's face lit up when he spotted him, and he gave him the royal Dutch treatment—a crushing bear hug. "Joey. Joey. Joey. Joey." He pressed Joey's head to his chest, and Joey could smell the Aqua Velva. His father must have had a lifetime supply. It brought back memories of when he was a little boy and his dad would hug him when he came home from work. Even after a day working in the sweaty engine factory, Dutch always smelled like Aqua Velva.

"I'm sorry, Dad."

"Wait till you get to the car," Blainey said.

"Where's the truck?" Dutch asked.

The truck. Joey was numb from lack of sleep and food. "Darville's truck?"

"The S-10, Joey. You took it last night, right?"

Finally, his brain slipped back into gear. "It's at Shadow Mountain. I got a ride from—"

Blainey put his hand on Joey's arm. "Later."

Blainey's Fleetwood was parked in front of the jail. He and Dutch sat in the front, and Joey slipped into the back seat. It was a '97 with soft gray leather upholstery. It felt great to sit on something that was cushioned and didn't stink. On the twenty-minute drive to Shadow Mountain, Joey told them everything that happened except for the encounter with Mallory and the altercation with Fernando or Chico's cryptic comment about Dutch. He would ask his father about that in private.

As they pulled into the Shadow Mountain parking lot, the S-10 was the only car left in the lot. TJ's car was gone, so he must have retrieved it after his escape. Joey winced as he remembered the bonfire. The equipment shed was still intact but badly scorched.

"Jesus Christ," Blainey said. "That was some bonfire." A snow fence had been installed around the structure with yellow caution tape at the opening and a Keep Out sign planted in front. He tapped Dutch on the forearm. "I'll call Terry Quinn and get you an appointment. Top-notch criminal lawyer. A Brophy man. You're going to need him."

Dutch grunted. "Okay. Thanks. Come on, Joey, let's get you home. Your mom's got breakfast ready."

They rode in silence until Dutch steered the truck into their driveway. As he turned off the ignition, he looked at Joey, who was struggling to keep his eyes open. "So that Wendy girl? Will she back your story?"

"It's not a story. I'm telling the truth."

"I don't doubt you. You ain't a storyteller like your sister. But that girlfriend of yours didn't do you any favors with the cops."

Why hadn't Wendy cleared it all up when that cop asked her? What had her father made her promise? She knew it was TJ's gun and she had to know TJ was the shooter. And why did she make that stupid comment about hitchhikers?

"I'm sure she'll tell the truth. Why wouldn't she?"

Dutch shook his head, smiling sadly. "I hope you're right," he said. And then softly like he was praying, "Goddamn, I hope you're right."

Joey just slumped in the seat, almost too tired to open the door.

Dutch gave him a friendly punch in the shoulder. "Come on. I can smell that bacon sizzling."

His mother had prepared a feast for Joey's return. Scrambled eggs, bacon, sausage, biscuits and gravy and her famous hash browns. Joey sat at their kitchen table and inhaled a full plate of eggs, six strips of bacon, and two helpings of hash browns. His mom sat across the table, studying him, her brow furrowed.

As he reached for the orange juice pitcher to refill his glass, she finally spoke.

"Tell me what happened, Joey."

Joey tried to give his mom the condensed version of his story, eliminating Wendy's pot smoking, Lua's weed transaction with TJ, and any mention of Mallory. It was what his coach would have called a tactical mistake. Callie's face flushed and her freckles seemed to glow. She had competed in beauty pageants for ten years, handled all personnel matters for the company for over two decades, and had lived with Dutch since she was nineteen. She had a very well-developed bullshit detector.

"How did the bonfire get out of control?"

"Who is this Grimes character and why did he have a gun?"

"Why were you riding in the back of the truck?"

Her interrogation was ten times tougher than Lieutenant Carnes's. In the end, Joey told her everything, except he again left Mallory out of the picture and didn't mention Chico's comments about Dutch.

"I just need some sleep and then I'll go out and find TJ and this whole thing will be cleared up," Joey said as he pushed back from the table.

Callie shook her head. "That boy's gone with the wind. You need to get your rich, Japanese friend to tell the truth."

"Wendy's Chinese, Mom."

His mother waved him off. "Chinese, Japanese. It's all the same. Her family's got money, and her daddy has a fancy reputation. Mark my words, they're going to be trouble."

CHAPTER 8

Joey slept for fifteen hours. He awoke to the smell of fresh-brewed coffee. He didn't like coffee, but the aroma triggered the memory of lazy Sundays when he was a kid playing Crazy Eights with Solita on the patio while his parents relaxed inside with their giant mugs of coffee. Sunday was the one day Dutch didn't work. When Joey stepped into the kitchen, he knew in an instant that this was not going to be one of those idyllic Sundays.

Callie was sitting at the kitchen table with the newspaper spread out in front of her. Dutch was on the phone, grunting, his face flushed.

"Putting it on hold? What the fuck is that supposed to mean?" He was gripping the handset so tightly his knuckles turned white. "Fuck you." He slammed the phone into the wall cradle, shattering the bracket. That triggered another torrent of swearing. He glared at Joey. "Motherfuckers put your scholarship on hold." He bit off the words as if they were poison. "Fuck them." He stormed out of the kitchen, slamming the kitchen door behind him.

"On hold? What does that mean, Mom?"

Callie bit down on her lower lip. "It's just their chickenshit way of saying they don't want you."

Joey sunk back into his chair. "But how . . . why?"

"They read the papers, Joseph." She pushed the front page of the *Arizona Republic* across the table. The banner headline screamed, "World Embraces New Millennium." Below the fold was a smaller headline: "Mayhem Mars Start of the New Century." And the column recap read, "Shadow Mountain superstar shoots at police officer." Halfway down the column was Joey's grainy mugshot photo.

Joey slumped over the table, holding his head in his hands. Every time he thought it couldn't get any worse, it did. For the first time since this nightmare began, he truly felt like crying.

His mother reached across the table and took hold of his hands. "Look at me, Joey." He knew from the way her mouth was set that there was more bad news. "I called your girlfriend's house. Talked to her mother."

Joey had never met Wendy's mother, but Wendy made her sound like a barracuda. Joey's mom was not known for her diplomacy. There was no chance the conversation could have gone well.

"A very unpleasant woman," Callie said.

"What did she say?" Joey asked.

"She said you've been stalking her daughter, and that if you tried talking to her she would call the police."

"What?" Joey jumped up from the table, knocking his chair over. "That's bullshit! I'm going to go see her. I haven't been stalking her!"

Callie stepped in front of Joey and grabbed his arms. "No, Joey," she said, using her calm mother voice. "That will just make things worse. Those kinds of people play by different rules. We have to be very careful. We need to talk to Blainey's lawyer before we do anything."

CHAPTER 9

After Callie convinced Joey that trying to get to Wendy right now might make things worse, Joey called Lua and told him everything that happened. "I need TJ to come clean. He can't let me take the rap for this," Joey said.

Lua scoffed. "Grimes is a lowlife. He might need some persuading."

Joey winced. Lua smacking TJ around would just add to his troubles. "No, no, no. Don't touch him, but let him know I'm getting screwed because of what he did. Already lost my scholarship." Joey had tried not to think about that, but saying the words made it more real, and for an instant, he wished Lua would rough up TJ.

"That sucks," Lua said. "I'll make sure the little shit understands he needs to step up or else."

o o o

Everett Blainey had arranged for Joey and his parents to meet with Terry Quinn at Quinn's offices at eleven a.m. As Joey was getting dressed for the meeting, Lua called Joey on his cellphone. "TJ's not in school. And he wasn't selling out in the parking lot this morning either. His buddies haven't seen him. They said Monday is usually a big sales day for him. Dude's run off."

TJ was hiding out and Wendy's parents were calling Joey a stalker. Clearing his name would not be as easy as he had hoped.

Terry Quinn might have been Joey's first lucky break since TJ caught fire. Quinn was in his mid-thirties, sandy-haired, and flat-bellied with piercing blue eyes. He had been a wide receiver for Brophy Prep, the premier Jesuit high school in Phoenix. His office was in a high-rise with a great view of the city, but the furniture was functional not fancy. It seemed like he wanted his client to be comfortable, not impressed.

The four of them sat around an oval table in the center of his office. Dutch on one side of the lawyer and Callie on the other, with Joey sitting across from him.

After the introductions, Quinn said, "Joey, I'm glad your parents are here. This will be an ordeal and family support is critical." He nodded at Callie and then Dutch. "But make no mistake. The law of the land has deemed that you are an adult. And I'm not your parents' attorney. I know they are paying my bill, but that makes no difference. I'm your attorney, and I will advise and defend you. I think it is important that we are all here for this initial meeting, but going forward I don't need to meet with anyone but you. Unless they offer us a deal. Then, of course, I'll brief everyone together. Understood?"

Joey could tell immediately that his parents liked the lawyer. They both respected honesty and detested bullshit.

"Do you think they'll offer a deal?" Callie asked.

"Can't say. I don't know the facts. Most criminal cases don't go to trial, but let's not get ahead of ourselves." He clasped his hands together and stared at Joey. "Now it's your turn to talk." His icy blue eyes drilled Joey. "Take me through all the events that led to your being arrested. Be as specific as possible."

Joey told the story with the same level of detail he provided to his parents. Once again, he omitted any mention of Mallory or the incident with Chico Torres. Quinn was focused and silent while Joey talked, only taking his eyes off Joey to make notes on his legal pad.

It took about twenty minutes to run through the story. When he finished, Quinn scanned his notes, stone-faced. Joey had no idea whether he believed him or not.

After what seemed like an eternity, but was probably less than a minute of silence, Quinn looked up from his notepad and asked, "How well do you know Wendy Chang?"

"Uh, you mean—"

Quinn waved him off. "No, I don't care about your sex life. At least not right now. When did you start dating?"

"We met in November at a party at Lookout Mountain."

"So, five or six weeks?"

"Yes."

"Ever meet her parents? Her father?"

Joey could see Callie's mouth tighten, like she was trying to prevent herself from sharing her opinion of Mrs. Chang.

"No. We would usually meet someplace. Wendy always drives her car. She doesn't like my truck."

Dutch snorted. "That should have told you something."

Quinn sat back and his expression softened. "Cary Chang is a real estate attorney. But he's a lot more than that. The man's very well-connected. Good friends with the mayor and the governor and lots of judges. Works both sides of the aisle. A smooth operator."

Wendy told Joey her father was a powerbroker, but she made it sound like a joke. Whatever her father was, Joey didn't see how it made any difference.

"Wendy saw that TJ had the gun. She'll have to testify, right?" Joey asked.

Quinn sighed, and Joey knew immediately that more bad news was coming. "Wendy Chang flew to Switzerland yesterday. Finishing school. To get her ready for Harvard."

Callie gasped, and Dutch pounded the table. "That son of a bitch."

Joey felt like he'd been gut punched. "She's run away? Why?" he yelled. He stood up and leaned over the table. "All she has to do is tell the goddamn truth. I didn't do anything wrong. Grimes is the shithead who shot at the truck. And those assholes in that truck didn't act like cops."

Quinn was unfazed by the family outburst. He gestured calmly with his hand for Joey to sit down. "The whole thing stinks," he said. "Starting with those hot-rodding cops. They were cowboys in the worst sense of the word and they should be fired, but instead they go after you. Cary Chang doesn't care if you're guilty or innocent. He doesn't want any part of this mess to touch him or his daughter. Cary cares about Cary. So we have our work cut out for us. But we'll get there. The cops need to bring in that kid who was driving—what's his name?" Quinn flipped through his folder.

"Lawrence Darville," Joey said. "He lives in north Scottsdale."

"Yeah, here it is. Nice neighborhood. I'll make sure they bring him in for a formal interview. We don't need the girl if Darville backs your story. And I'll make sure they're looking for TJ." He stood up and extended his hand. "Go back to school, Joey. We'll get this figured out."

CHAPTER 10

Joey didn't go back to school on Tuesday. His parents left for work at six every morning so he didn't even have to make an excuse. He had a good one. All the bullshit of the last three days had worn him out. He stayed in bed until ten.

Lua called him in the afternoon and told him that he was the talk of the school. "You wouldn't believe the bullshit stories. They make you sound like Wyatt Earp at the O.K. Corral. Like you are totally badass. I tell them they're full of shit, that it didn't go down like that, but nobody's listening. It's fucked up, man."

Joey felt a cold tightness in his gut. He didn't want to be the talk of the school. Not for that. He wished he could go to some fancy finishing school just so he didn't have to face everyone. "I gotta find Grimes," he said.

"Rumor is that he's in Rocky Point," Lua said. "Staying with his dealer friends."

Rocky Point—or Puerto Peñasco—was just over the border. TJ had bragged that was where he had his connection for weed.

After Lua hung up, Joey wanted to go back to bed. He wanted to sleep and not wake up until everything was back to normal again. The insanity of that idea scared him enough that he grabbed his basketball and headed out to Roadrunner Park. He jogged down the road. At first it was like he was running through water, his legs heavy, almost lifeless. But after a few blocks his rhythm returned, and by the time he got to the park he was running easy and feeling better.

As he approached the basketball court, he spied Mallory on the swing set lackadaisically swinging back and forth, her feet dragging in the dust.

Joey was surprised at how good it made him feel to see her. He didn't want to admit it to himself, but he had been hoping she was at the park. She waved to him—not that little finger wave like Wendy. Everything about Mallory seemed more real. More honest.

He walked over to the swings. "Mind if I join you?" he asked.

"Are you okay?" She studied his face like she would be able to read how he was feeling.

Joey tried to smile. He wasn't okay and he really wanted to talk to Mallory about how he was feeling, but it seemed wrong with everything she had to deal with. "Not my best birthday. How are you doing?"

She was wearing a Dixie Chicks T-shirt with the three singers entwined in an oval. She pressed the tee shirt against her chest. "I read in a book that my boobs will get bigger. Just what I need." She grinned. "But I don't feel any different. No one will notice for at least another month."

"What are we going to do, Mallory? I don't know anything about babies."

"*We* are not going to do anything. I know you want to help." She stared at her feet, dragging her toe in the dust. "This will sound bad, like I'm the town slut, but I'm glad this is your baby. Not one of those other guys. You're a good person, Joey. I hope the baby will be good. Like you. But there is nothing you can do now except to keep quiet. I don't want my dad to find out."

"But—"

"I'm not ready to talk about it right now. Be patient." She

looked down at her shirt front and smoothed out the Chicks. "They'll be here in June."

"Your boobs?"

Ha ha. Very funny." The Dixie Chicks. They're playing at the stadium. I love their music. They have such passion." She started singing "You Were Mine." It was a song of lost love and heartbreak and her voice was light and clear, like a whispered prayer. A tear slipped down her cheek. She wiped it away. "Sorry. It's hormones. I'm blaming it on the baby."

He must have appeared stricken. Mallory shook her head. "It's not about us. My mom disappeared when I was four. My father said she ran off because she didn't want to be a mother. He said it was my fault. I believed him, but I couldn't understand what I had done to make her run."

Joey settled into the swing next to her and took her hand.

Mallory gave his hand a squeeze. "When I was eleven, I found out my mother had a sister in Seattle. I wrote her a letter. I asked if she could help me find my mom. She drove down from Seattle and met me at school so my father wouldn't know about the visit." She closed her eyes. "My mother never ran off. She died of an overdose. Maybe accidental. Probably not."

"I'm sorry, Mallory." Joey wanted to say something more. How could Donny Stewart do that?

She took her hand back and dried her eyes. "So that's why we're not telling him anything, okay?"

"Of course."

Mallory frowned. "You weren't in school. Everybody was talking about you."

"I just wasn't ready to face all that bullshit." He tried to find a comfortable position. "I hate these strap seats. The wood seats were way better."

"I remember how you and your friends used to swing standing up and then jump off."

"We pretended we were parachuting." He grinned, remembering something.

"What?" she asked.

"All the guys used to love watching you play tetherball. You had great form."

"Very funny." She stopped swinging and grabbed hold of his swing so he had to look at her. "Are you going to be okay?"

"I'll be fine. Don't worry about me," Joey said. "We just need to find TJ and the whole thing will go away. TJ is the one who shot at those guys. I tried to stop him."

He tried to give her his "everything's cool" smile, but she wasn't buying it. Her face had darkened and her eyebrows were peaked. "His asshole friends say he's in Mexico. In Rocky Point."

"Yeah, that's what Lua told me." He didn't bother trying to tell her that that wasn't a problem. Everyone knew that finding someone who didn't want to be found in a place like Rocky Point was near to impossible.

"He's not."

Joey stared at her, not sure he heard her correctly. "He's not what?"

"TJ's up at Lake Pleasant. That's his hideout."

Joey almost slipped out of his swing. "You're sure? How do you know?" Then he waved his hand as if to erase that question. He didn't care how she knew. "Do you know where? An address?"

She glanced at her watch. "I have to get home. But I can show you. Do you still get your stinky truck on the weekends?"

"I can get it Saturday, but I don't want to wait that long. We should tell the cops. They can pick him up right now."

Mallory gave a slight tilt to her head. "Even if they were willing to go up there, which I doubt, they'd never find him."

She jumped out of her swing and started to walk toward the park entrance, but Joey grabbed her hand and drew her close to him. She placed her hands on his chest and gently separated their bodies. "You have enough trouble, Joey. I'll meet you here on Saturday afternoon. Two o'clock."

CHAPTER 11

Joey returned to school the next day and by Friday he had almost gotten used to everyone going out of their way to act like nothing had happened. But not quite. The forced nonchalance and the way conversations stopped when he walked by was almost worse than if they had just come out and asked him why he shot at those cops.

None of his teachers said anything to him. After school, he stopped at Coach Klein's office to tell him the situation with U of A.

Coach Klein had been a linebacker for the Citadel back in the eighties. He prided himself on being "lean and mean" and with his military crewcut he looked ready for active duty. Joey was one of the few players on the team who could keep up with him on his insane conditioning drills. He was in his office, feet propped on the desk, reading the *Arizona Republic,* when Joey walked in. He forced a smile and quickly stood up. A week ago, he would have kept reading just to bust balls. More proof that everything was different now.

"Joey. Sit down. Take a load off." He folded up his paper and gestured for Joey to take a seat.

"Gotta a minute?" Joey asked.

Coach Klein leaned forward. His right hand drummed nervously on the table. "What's on your mind, son?"

Joey eased into the straight-back chair. "I wanted you to know I didn't shoot at those cops."

"Hell, I know that. Tupola gave me the details. Lousy deal. How you holding up?"

Joey shrugged. "Arizona decided they don't want me. I wondered if you thought there was a chance with USC?"

The coach stared down at his hands. He was considering whether to give Joey a bullshit answer or tell him the truth. He went with the truth. "Probably not," he said. "They don't know ya, Joey. So, they're not willing to stick their neck out. And after that OJ shitstorm, USC is probably the last place you'd have a shot."

Joey wasn't surprised. That was a change for him. He used to always expect things to fall his way. Now he expected things to go wrong. "I appreciate your being straight with me." He pushed back his chair.

Coach Klein stood up again. "Get this deal behind ya and I'll make some calls. Some smaller schools, Division 2 or even 3. There are some good programs out there. It's not over yet."

His whole life had been put on hold because of TJ Grimes. But he would have never been in the back of that truck with that asshole if it hadn't been for Wendy. He had been a fool. "Thinking with your little head," as Dutch would say. He wouldn't make that mistake again. With Mallory's help, he'd find TJ and get his life back on track. Maybe none of those schools would want him to play football for them, but at least people would know Joey Blade was innocent. He would get his good name back.

○ ○ ○

When Joey got home, he retrieved his copy of *A Separate Piece* from his nightstand and went down to the kitchen where he usually did his homework. He sat at the kitchen table to work on his long overdue book report. He had read the book a half dozen times—it was his all-time favorite. It was the only story he had ever read where the athlete wasn't a dumb jock or a self-centered asshole. Phineas was noble and pure—too pure to be believed—and that was his downfall. It was a great story, heartbreaking and true, and Joey hated trying to reduce it to three pages. Hated trying to explain what the "theme" was. He had made several lame attempts at an opening paragraph when Dutch and Callie walked in the door.

They were *so* not talking to each other that it was obvious they'd been fighting. Or discussing, as his mom would always correct him. It had to be about him. They used to have Solita discussions all the time, which often created those rare but always short-term silences.

Callie opened the refrigerator. "Finally finishing that book report?" she asked.

"I'm trying," Joey said.

"Where's the beer . . . never mind." His mother pulled out a Dos Equis from the back of the fridge where she always hid it to avoid tempting herself. The after-work beer, another sign they'd been fighting.

"Hey, Dad. Can I borrow the S-10 tomorrow?"

"Joey. You can't go out carousing," Callie said, her voice rising. "You have to be extra careful right—"

"I just want to drive up to Lake Pleasant and hike the trails." It was not exactly a lie.

"Who are you hiking with?" Callie asked.

"Nobody. I want to be alone." Joey looked at Dutch. "Okay on the S-10, Dad?"

"Yeah, but I need you to come to work in the morning. We're shorthanded in the install center. Need someone to handle the phones. Just until noon."

Mallory's father, Donny Stewart, was working Saturdays. Joey wanted nothing to do with that creep, but he would have to suck it up. "Cool. I'll drive it home. Thanks, Dad."

CHAPTER 12

T he plan was for Joey to ride to Blade Engine with Dutch when he went in to work and then Joey would take the S-10 home at noon when his replacement in the installation center showed up. The ride into work would give Joey the opportunity to finally ask Dutch about Chico Torres. After Coach Klein had given him the straight scoop on his scholarship prospects, Joey decided it was time to regain control of his life. The Chico comment had been festering in the back of his mind, distracting him. He didn't want to ignore it any longer.

Dutch was driving a '93 Lincoln Continental. Powder blue. It was a godawful ugly car—the owner brought it in for an engine install and never returned. When no one claimed the car, Dutch took it in payment for the engine installation. That was over a year ago.

"I thought you were selling this boat," Joey said as they headed east on Northern. Blade Engine was on the southwest side of Phoenix, Twenty-Seventh Avenue and Cypress.

"I was. Had a deal to sell it to Donny Stewart, but he backed out at the last minute. Drank up his down payment. Too bad. I was giving him a smoking deal."

"Donny Stewart's an asshole." Joey never bad-mouthed any employee to his father, but he didn't mind making an exception for Stewart.

"Lots of assholes in the world," Dutch said. "Donny's a good mechanic. You're working with him today. He's the lead."

"I know."

As Dutch turned on to Twenty-Seventh Avenue, traffic was light. They would be at the plant in another ten minutes. If he wanted to ask his father about Chico Torres, now was the time.

"Hey, Dad . . . when I was in jail, I met a guy named Chico Torres. He said he knew you."

Dutch glanced at Joey, and maybe just for a moment, his face betrayed something that looked a lot like fear. But that couldn't be. His father was afraid of nothing.

"Chico?" Dutch returned his eyes to the road. "Yeah, I know Chico. We do some business."

"Business? Isn't he like a gang leader?"

"I buy turbos and four barrels from him. He has good prices on late-model stuff. Fucking dealerships rip us off on those late-model parts. Especially Ford. Those sons-of-bitches . . ."

Dutch had a hard-on for Ford. They had their own engine-rebuilding operation, so he considered them competitors, but dishonest competitors because they made their dealers buy engines from them. If Chico Torres was selling late-model turbos and carburetors, they had to be coming from stolen cars. Chop shops. Joey was silent, not certain what to say.

"We don't buy that much. Just when we're in a bind," Dutch said. When Joey still didn't say anything, he added, "Hector Torres—Chico's father—saved my life in Nam. Hector was killed at Khe Sanh. Chico was only two years old. He never knew his dad. I want to help his kid in anyway I can. I owe it to Hector."

"They're stolen goods, Dad." Joey knew he should keep his mouth shut. Especially when Dutch was driving, but he couldn't help himself.

Dutch swerved around a pickup and barreled down Northern, twenty miles over the speed limit. "Sixteen hundred fucking dollars!" Spit showered the steering wheel and dash. "For a goddamn Ford turbo. Chico sells them for three hundred. Sixteen hundred fucking dollars!"

"Dad! The light!"

Dutch slammed on the brakes and the car skidded to a stop at the intersection. Dutch seemed oblivious to the near-death event. "When you run the fucking company, you can buy your fucking parts from those cunts!"

Joey wanted to say that he would never run the company, but this time he knew enough to change the subject. "Chico helped me out that night. Some of his gang buddies were giving me a hard time."

"Chico's stand up," Dutch said.

Stand up was Dutch's highest form of praise. It trumped everything but family. If Hector Torres had saved his life, Dutch's loyalty would have no bounds. When Dutch Blade was in your corner, it was for life. Even if your son was head of the most vicious gang in the southwest.

"Think it'll be busy today?" Joey asked.

Dutch shook his head. "Nah. Folks still recovering from the New Year. But once they realize the fucking world hasn't ended, I expect it to pick up again."

o o o

Blade Engine had twenty install bays with thirty mechanics installing two hundred rebuilt engines a week. Joey liked working the install center. It was his job to sell the potential customer on the value of a Blade Engine installation. The only problem was that Donny Stewart was the lead mechanic on Saturdays. The lead mechanic had to play the straight man when Joey needed someone to help him close the deal. So, like it or not, he would have to work with the man.

Around ten o'clock, a burgundy 1990 Buick Park Avenue with a gleaming new-car shine rolled into the parking lot. The body was in great shape, no dings or rust. The owner had clearly taken good care of this vehicle, but there was telltale blue smoke trailing from the exhaust, suggesting serious oil leaks around the piston rings.

The driver, pudgy with wispy blond hair, was in his mid-forties. He wore shorts with the T-shirt tucked in and high-top Converse basketball sneakers. Dutch said a good salesperson was a like a detective and he needed to look for clues to figure out who he was dealing with. This car was well maintained. That told Joey that the customer was careful with his possessions. The guy's clothes were dorky-casual and seemed like he didn't know how to kick back and relax. The Park Avenue was a semi-luxury car, but it was ten years old. Everything shouted practical. Conservative. Maybe a college professor.

"Welcome to Blade Engine, sir. I'm Joey Blade."

The man took notice immediately. "Chuck Estes. You the owner?" He grinned like he didn't actually believe Joey was the owner.

"My dad. Nice car. What is it, a '96?" Joey knew it was a '90, but Dutch warned him that those kinds of questions were like guessing a woman's weight. "Pick a number that's ten pounds less than you really think."

"This is a 1990 Park Avenue," Estes said, beaming.

"You looking to replace the engine?" Joey asked.

Estes rubbed his chin. "Maybe a ring job?"

"How many miles you got?" Joey asked. Estes suggested a ring job just to show Joey he knew something about engines. Enough to be dangerous.

"Five hundred thousand miles," Estes said, thrusting his chest out. His pride at that accomplishment was clear. It was something Joey could use.

"That's fantastic," Joey said. You know how few customers we see who get that kind of mileage out of their engines? Nice work."

"Thank you," Estes said. He smiled broadly. Joey's praise actually made him blush.

Estes, like Dutch, was used to being the boss and making all the decisions. Joey figured he probably wouldn't want to be sold by some kid. Better for Joey to play the humble role.

"Mr. Estes, I'm just learning this business. Maybe all you need is a ring job. Would it be okay if our head mechanic checked it out? Give you his opinion?"

Estes agreed and Joey waved to Donny Stewart, who was acting busy at one of the bays but was really waiting for Joey's signal. He walked into the service center wiping his hands off on an orange engine rag.

Joey had to admit that Stewart was a good mechanic. He didn't act like he had an ounce of salesmanship in him, which worked to their advantage. "What you got, Joey?" he asked, acting almost surly.

"This is Mr. Estes. He's thinking maybe just a ring job. What do you think?"

Stewart frowned. "Pop the hood. Crank the engine."

Joey raised the hood as Estes slid behind the wheel and started the Buick.

"Give it some gas," Stewart said. Estes revved the engine. "Okay. That's good. Turn it off." He shook his head. "Engine's shot. You need a replacement, sir."

Estes nodded as if he expected that answer. Donny Stewart's

certainty was persuasive. "Do you have the engine in stock?" Estes asked.

"Hell yes. We can have that swapped out in three days." Stewart patted the car hood like it was a horse. "Sweet ride. They don't make them like this anymore."

That was all it took. Joey wrote up the quote and by the time the paperwork was signed, Mrs. Estes had arrived to pick up her husband.

After they had driven away, Stewart came into the office, looking self-satisfied.

"Nice work, Donny," Joey said.

Stewart plopped into the customer chair and started knocking his pack of Lucky's on the counter. He pulled one out and lit up. It was joke time.

"Listen to this one, Joey. A husband comes home from work. The wife's got her suitcases all packed. 'Where the hell you going?' he asks. 'I'm off to Vegas,' she says. 'I hear blowjobs go for four hundred bucks there. I figure I might as well earn money for what I do to you free.' Man thinks about it for a minute and then runs upstairs and packs his bag. 'What are you doing?' she asks. He says, 'I'm heading to Vegas too. I want to see how you can live on eight hundred dollars a year.'" Stewart slapped his knee and took a deep drag on his cigarette.

"That's one of your better ones," Joey said, trying to smile sincerely but failing. He stared at the phone, willing it to ring. No luck.

"What's the difference between your wife and your job?"

Joey shrugged.

"After five years the job still sucks." He laughed even harder. "I'm on a blowjob kick today."

"Yeah, I can tell. Don't quit your day job."

Stewart frowned like Joey had insulted him. "Heard you had

a pretty wild New Year's." His jokey manner was gone. There was an edge to his voice.

"Don't believe everything you hear." Joey started shuffling through the pile of sales tickets on the counter, like he was looking for something.

"Easy, kid. I know what you're dealing with, I've been there." Joey stared at Stewart. "Been where?"

"I heard about your little legal problem. That rich Chink bitch was your alibi and she took a powder. Fucking women. They're all alike. Love you till things get tough and then they leave you holding the bag. They're all cunts."

Mercifully, the phone rang and Stewart stopped ranting and strolled back into the install center. Joey ignored the phone. The invoices he had been playing with were crumpled in his fists. He set them on the counter and tried to smooth them out.

CHAPTER 13

Mallory, bundled up in a purple Arizona Diamondbacks hoodie, was on the park bench next to the swing set. A mother and father took turns pushing their little boy on the swing. Mallory was watching the young family and didn't see Joey as he approached. "Higher, Mommy! Higher! Come on Daddy! Higher!"

When he was within ten feet, Joey stopped. Watching Mallory study the young family made him feel happy and sad at the same time. "Hey, Mallory," he said, his voice just above a whisper.

She looked up at the sound of his greeting and smiled. Everything about Mallory seemed so real. So genuine. She would make a great mother. Someday.

She skipped over to him. "I like your sweatshirt. Go Wildcats!"

Joey was wearing a new Arizona Wildcats sweatshirt. "It was a freebie from the recruiter. Thought I better wear it before they ask for it back."

"They made a big mistake." She frowned at his shoes. "You sure you want to wear those Nikes? We might have to do some hiking. It will be muddy."

"I don't care. How much hiking? Where is he?"

"TJ hangs out at a cabin off Pipeline Canyon Trail. It's his brother's. It's about a mile from the trailhead. We need to get there before dark."

Five minutes later, they were on the Squaw Peak headed north. "This is where TJ blew out the windshield of the undercover cops' truck," Joey said. There were black streaks on the highway where the truck had careened off the road and flattened the Highway 51 sign. The sign was gone, but the skid marks remained. A moment later, they crossed the canal, and Joey laughed bitterly as he thought about that night.

"What's so not funny?" Mallory asked.

"That's where I tossed TJ's gun," he said, nodding toward the canal.

"Why did you do that?" Mallory asked. She put her hand on his shoulder and she was staring at him.

"I don't know," he said. He twisted his shoulder away and she let her hand drop. He really didn't know. "That's where they stopped us and TJ escaped." There was a ten-foot-high chain-link fence along the highway and TJ had scrambled over it like a guy used to being chased. Beyond the fence was the frontage road. Joey hadn't noticed it that night, but opposite the highway there was a small shopping mall anchored by a Fuddruckers and an Office Depot.

They drove in silence until Joey exited the Squaw Peak and headed west on the Carefree Highway. "I was scared. Wendy was screaming to toss the gun, the sirens were blaring, and I was afraid those guys were really hurt. I didn't know what to do and I panicked. Hurled that sucker. Didn't even make it to the canal. Stupid."

Mallory rested her hand on his forearm. "You took the gun away from him. That's what counts. You might have saved those cops' lives."

"Too bad Wendy didn't tell the cops that."

Mallory turned and gazed out the window. Most girls would have bad-mouthed Wendy—she deserved it—but Mallory wasn't like most girls. Maybe she'd heard enough people saying shit about her that she wasn't ready to pile on. She changed the subject instead. "I love the desert in the winter. Everything is so green."

Joey hadn't driven out into the desert since last summer. In July and August, the temperature seldom dropped below a hundred degrees during the day, and the blistering sun baked the land hard and brown. But now the desert teemed with life. Birds circled above the saguaro cacti that dotted the landscape. There were splotches of green everywhere. The land appeared almost habitable.

"It is pretty," Joey said, "but I like summer. Can't beat that dry heat."

"You're the only one I know who runs in the heat of the summer."

Joey laughed. It was true. He would run the desert mountain preserve trails behind his house, sometimes at two or three in the afternoon. "Perfect time to run. No crowds. When the temp gets to 110, not even the birds come out. I love it. Can't explain. It's like I'm the only one left in the world. No sound but my feet hitting the trail stones."

"You are crazy." Her brow furrowed as she studied Joey.

"What?"

"When we find TJ, what are you planning to do with him?"

Joey chewed on his lower lip. "I don't know. Tell him to do the right thing?" He hadn't really thought about how he would convince TJ to cooperate.

From the look on Mallory's face, it was clear she thought that was naïve. "You know what guys who have guns do on New Year's Eve? They shoot them up in the air to celebrate. That can be TJ's story. He was just celebrating early and he lost his balance. Total accident. He's a juvie, and they can't do anything to him. He doesn't have a record here. That is as close to the right thing as you'll get from TJ."

This girl had a plan for everything. "How do you come up with this stuff?"

Mallory frowned. "Survival."

It only took fifty minutes to cover the forty miles to Lake Pleasant. The lake had been a large irrigation reservoir until the state built the Central Arizona Aqueduct in the seventies. The aqueduct diverted waters from the Colorado River into Lake Pleasant, tripling its size and turning it into a major recreation spot for Arizonans. It was a great spot for scuba diving, water and jet skiing, and even windsurfing.

"That's where Lua launches his boat," Joey said as they passed a sign for Scorpion Bay Marina. Almost every weekend last summer Lua drove Joey to the lake. Lua owned a nineteen-foot Four Winns powerboat with 280 horsepower. Enough power to even get Lua up on skis.

"You had a lot of fun up here," Mallory said.

"What do you mean?" Joey asked.

"All the girls wanted to ride on Lua's boat. A chance to ski with that tall, dark, and handsome football hero, Joey Blade." She giggled.

"Fuck you, Mallory."

"It's true. I was up here one weekend, but you didn't pay me any attention. Too many cute girls from ASU in their string bikinis for you to notice the little girl next door."

Joey stared at Mallory's chest. "You're not so little. And you don't live next door." It was true that there were always girls from ASU looking to hitch a ride if you had a cool boat and a cooler of beers. And most folks thought Lua was at least twenty-one so his boat was a popular option. "I think Lua was the main attraction," Joey said.

Mallory sat back in the seat, arms folded. "No. He wasn't. Turn left here. The trailhead's just a mile beyond the ridge."

"Do you think he'll be there?"

"He's probably sleeping. TJ's a night owl."

A few minutes later, a sign indicated the Pipeline Canyon Trailhead was less than a mile away.

"Take that road." Mallory pointed to a rock-strewn dirt path with ten-foot high banks. It was a dry riverbed, barely wide enough for one vehicle.

Joey drove cautiously, winding from one bank to the other, trying to avoid the larger rocks. It took ten minutes to go a few hundred yards. Ahead of them was a muddy stream at least twenty feet wide. Joey stopped the truck. "I can't drive through that."

Mallory frowned and bit her lower lip. "This was all dry in the summer. I guess we'll have to hike. It's not far. We can cross here." She jumped on to a tree that had fallen across the stream and tight-roped across.

"What are you? A goddamn Billy goat?" Joey said. He frowned and searched for an easier option. There wasn't one. He crawled onto the log and carefully slid one foot forward and then the other. A slow shuffle.

"Come on, Mr. All American. We don't have all day. Don't be a sissy."

Joey was afraid to look up at Mallory. He took a deep breath and lifted his left foot off the log. He pushed off hard with his right foot, yelling like he was running the gauntlet in football practice, and he surged forward. Right. Left. Right. Left. Four steps and he was over. He jumped down and sprinted toward Mallory, who was cheering and laughing. He grabbed her at the waist and lifted her up, her breasts brushing his face as he held her high in the air.

"I knew you could do it," she said. "You just needed a little coaching."

"Thanks for your help." Joey copped a feel as he set her down. She still wasn't wearing a bra.

Mallory shoved him with both hands, laughing. "Stay focused, Blade. Follow me."

They hiked up the road for another mile and then turned onto a trail that led up a steep hill. At the top of the hill was an old jeep and beyond the jeep a small hunting cabin. TJ was seated on the porch in a ratty armchair reading a book.

"He looks comfortable," Joey said. "Didn't know he could read."

Mallory put her finger to her lips. "Shhh." She scampered up the path to the cabin and jumped on the porch. "What you reading, TJ?"

TJ screamed and dropped the book. "Goddammit, Mallory. What the hell you doing sneaking up on me like that?"

Joey picked up TJ's book. He was reading *Kiss the Girls* by James Patterson. "Any good?" he asked as he handed it back to TJ. He stood right in front of the armchair so TJ couldn't get up.

"Joey! Great to see you." He took the book and set it aside. "It's all right. Lots of hot babes getting captured and kept in this big underground prison."

"Prison, huh?" Joey said, leaning in closer to TJ. "That's where I'm headed if you don't come back from your little reading retreat and tell the authorities it was you who shot at those cops."

"Prison? What are you talking about?" TJ pressed back in the chair, trying to get farther away from Joey, who was leaning in menacingly.

Mallory stepped up next to Joey. "Don't act stupid, TJ. You know what's gone down. That's why you're up here."

TJ glared at her and then turned to Joey, smiling nervously. "Joey, I swear I didn't know they were putting the rap on you. What can I do?"

Mallory poked TJ in the shoulder. "You tell the cops it was an accident. You were just celebrating the new century and you lost your balance. You didn't mean to shoot anyone. It'll just be a juvie charge for you. A slap on the wrist."

TJ snorted. "Slap on the wrist? Only underage whores like you get that kind of treatment."

Joey yanked TJ out of the chair by his throat and slammed him up against the wall of the cabin. "Watch your mouth, Grimes."

Mallory grabbed Joey's arm. "Stop, Joey. You can't bring him to the cops all busted up. It won't look good."

TJ held up his hands in surrender. "I'm sorry. I'm sorry. I'll give them a story that will take it off you. Let me put away my stash and grab some of my gear."

Joey released his grip and stepped back so TJ could enter the cabin. Mallory and Joey followed him in. It was just one room, surprisingly neat. TJ pulled up a floorboard, then hid his gym bag filled with pot and pills under the floor. He stuffed some clothes into his backpack.

"Okay, let's get this over with," TJ said.

He was subdued, not acting like an asshole for once. When he stepped off the porch, he stopped. "I gotta take a dump." He pointed toward the outhouse that was near the cabin.

Joey looked at the outhouse and then at TJ, who was shifting from one foot to the other with a pained expression. "Okay."

"No funny stuff, TJ," Mallory said.

"You wanna come in with me? Be my guest." TJ hustled

over to the outhouse and opened the door. Even from the porch where Mallory and Joey were standing the stench was impressive.

"I think I'd have my shithouse a little farther from my cabin," Mallory said.

"Probably didn't want to make that long walk on a cold winter night," Joey said. He peered into the window of the cabin. "He's got a nice place here. I thought this was all park land."

"I don't think it's legal. His brother probably bribes the rangers—"

Behind them, at the base of the hill, an engine started.

"Fuck!" Joey jumped off the porch.

TJ was driving down the trail in his jeep. He peeked over his shoulder and flipped them off. "Eat shit, football hero!"

Joey ran after him, but the four-wheel-drive jeep climbed over the rocks with ease. When TJ reached the S-10, he jumped out and stabbed two of the tires.

By the time Joey and Mallory reached the truck, the jeep had vanished down the highway. Two tires were flat.

"Fuck me," Joey said. "That son of a bitch."

"What do we do now?" Mallory asked.

Joey stared glumly at the tires. "I'll call my dad. He can bring me an extra spare."

"He's going to be pissed, isn't he?" Mallory said.

Joey hunched his shoulders. "He won't be happy, but this kind of thing doesn't get him as upset as other stuff." He kicked at the slashed tire. "Goddamn TJ." He sighed. "Let's go back to the cabin."

Mallory checked out the outhouse while Joey called his father. As he suspected, Dutch didn't go ballistic. He took down the location and told Joey he'd send one of the mechanics from the install center.

Mallory was walking back from the outhouse, shaking her head. "There's a hole in the back. Just big enough for a skinny guy like TJ to slip through."

"Must be a special precaution for drug dealers. Dutch is sending out a tow truck from the plant. They should be here in about ninety minutes."

They stepped into the cabin and Joey sat down on TJ's bed. He held his head in his hands and stared at the floor. He had been confident his problem would be solved as soon as they found that little weasel. He had underestimated TJ.

"Now we'll never find that son of a bitch," Joey said.

Mallory sat down next to him and leaned her head on his shoulder. She didn't say anything. Didn't try to offer some cheery bullshit. She knew the score. She tilted her face and looked up at him. "You can kiss me," she said.

They kissed and then Mallory fell back onto the bed and dragged Joey on top of her. As they kissed, Joey slipped his hands under her shirt and stroked her breasts.

She whispered in his ear, "I'll bet I can get naked quicker than you."

They both jumped off the bed. Clothes went flying. Mallory won easily.

"It's not fair," Joey said as they tumbled onto the bed. "You didn't have any underwear."

"Come here, sore loser." She pulled him down on top of her.

Joey ran his hands over her body. He could feel his heart racing out of control as he slipped inside her.

"Breathe, Joey."

Joey exhaled and his heartbeat slowed. They found a rhythm. It was an exquisite feeling and Joey wanted it to last forever. He kissed her eyelids and cheeks and lips and ran his hands through her short hair. Mallory giggled.

"What?" Joey asked.

"Have you been practicing?"

"Fuck you, Mallory."

"Well, yeah," she said, and they both started laughing.

Afterwards, they spooned and Joey nuzzled the soft blonde hairs on the back of her neck. "Was that nice?"

"Super nice," Mallory said. "Five-star nice. Do you think we should wash TJ's sheets?" She giggled.

Joey pulled her closer. Her body was warm and sticky and her short pixie hair was matted with sweat. It was oddly sexy. Joey's vision was blurry. A tear trickled down his cheek, and he pressed his face into her back to wipe it away. He took a deep breath and tried very hard not to cry. With everything else falling apart, it seemed like Mallory was the one good thing in his life. She was special. He could see that now.

"I love you, Mallory."

"Don't say that. You don't have to." She pulled her knees up and curled into a fetal position.

"I'm not just saying it. I do. I love you."

Mallory grabbed him and kissed him hard. "I'll bet you say that to all the girls you fuck."

Joey pushed her down on the bed and straddled her. His eyes were still moist and he swiped at them with the back of his arm.

"Joey . . . ?"

"Let's get married, Mallory."

"You are crazy, Joey Blade. We can't get married."

"Why not?"

"Because you aren't thinking straight. Getting married will just fuck up your life. Don't worry about me, Joey. I'm honored you asked, but I can't marry you. I won't marry you."

"Do you love me?"

"It doesn't matter if I do or I don't."

Joey swung his feet on to the floor and reached for his briefs. Then he remembered another of Dutch's lessons. "Don't say no, Mallory. Not right now. Just say you'll think about it."

Mallory gave him a look like "What I am going to do with this guy?" but she sort of smiled, which was a good sign. "How long until that tow truck arrives?" she asked.

Joey looked at his watch. "About forty-five minutes."

Mallory leaned back on the bed. "Well, we can fight about this until they get here, or we can go another round."

Joey let go of his briefs and rolled back on top of her. "So, you'll think about it?"

She elbowed him in the ribs. "Don't push your luck, cowboy."

CHAPTER 14

It was bad enough that they allowed TJ to elude them. The collateral damage from the failed mission was epic. Dutch had sent out Frank Ross, one of the mechanics and a drinking buddy of Donny Stewart. Ross was three hundred pounds and he didn't do tire changes. He insisted on towing the truck back to Blade Engine instead of just replacing the tires, so Joey and Mallory squeezed into the truck cab. And it was a squeeze because Ross took up more than half of the bench seat. Joey scooched over as far as he could, but Ross's gut still oozed all over Mallory.

Joey wasn't interested in sharing the TJ escapade with him, so their story was that they were out hiking the trails and vandals slashed the truck tires. Ross nodded like that kind of vandalism was to be expected. "Probably one of them Mexican gangs. Fuckin' Beaners takin' over the Valley."

Mallory sat in the cab while Joey helped him hook up the S-10. "Didn't know you were dating Donny's kid."

"I'm not," Joey said. But he knew Donny Stewart would learn about this Lake Pleasant adventure before the end of the day. Mallory's fantasy of keeping everything a secret was not going to happen. People would start connecting the dots.

If Frank Ross and Donny Stewart knew he was out at Lake Pleasant with Mallory, it would only be a matter of time before

Dutch learned about it too. When Ross dropped Joey off at his house, he thought about asking him not to say anything. But that would just make things worse—make him look guilty—and Ross would have just lied to him. So he thanked him for the ride and went into the house and told Dutch and Callie what happened. Not about the sex or the baby, but the TJ part of the story. Dutch didn't yell, but he came close to the same color as when Joey told him he wanted to go to USC.

"Jesus Christ, Joey. You grab a punk like that, you don't let him out of your sight. Let him shit in his pants. What do you care?"

Callie was more interested in Mallory. "I thought you said you were hiking on your own."

"I didn't want to worry you. Mallory knew where he was staying. I needed her help." He could tell by Callie's freckle-flush that she didn't believe him.

"Have you called the police yet?" she asked.

"No!" Dutch said, banging his fist on the table. "Call Quinn. Cops ain't gonna do shit."

Dutch almost never argued with Callie. At home she was the big boss and the last time Dutch raised his voice to her was back when Solita was a teenage brat making everyone's life miserable. Joey didn't want a repeat of that hell. "I'll call Mr. Quinn right now. He has a good relationship with the police so he might want to be the one who lets them know."

Callie pursed her lips but said nothing more. Joey escaped the kitchen hoping the parental truce would hold. He picked up the hallway phone—Dutch still hadn't replaced the busted kitchen phone—but decided it would be better to call from his cell phone in his bedroom so he wouldn't have to talk to Quinn with his parents listening. He climbed the stairs to his room and was about to dial the number again when he noticed he had a voicemail message. It was a strange number he didn't recognize.

"This is Wendy. Wendy Chang. My parents said you've been trying to reach me. My mother was quite upset. I think your mother said some nasty things to her. She acted like we'd been dating. I'm sorry you're in trouble, but that has nothing to do with me. Please leave my family alone. Stop harassing us. My father can be very difficult."

Joey dropped the phone on his bed and sat down. He wasn't even angry. Not at Wendy, anyway. Not even at himself. He dated Wendy knowing he was just a short-term thing. A diversion for her until she went off to college. He'd been okay with that. He thought he might get lucky. Fucking Wendy Chang would have been a cheap thrill. But the only luck he had with her was bad. Big time. This was another of Dutch's lessons. "Don't mess with women who aren't stand up."

Wendy Chang was definitely not stand up.

CHAPTER 15

Joey's cellphone call to Quinn went to voicemail. Joey left him a short version of what happened with TJ, but not about Wendy's voice message. Quinn called him back ten minutes later. He was in the middle of a doubles tennis match and couldn't talk. He told Joey to call the office in the morning and make an appointment. He didn't sound pissed, which Joey thought he might be, but he didn't sound happy either. A tough dude to read.

The receptionist led Joey back to Quinn's office. He was on the phone but gestured for Joey to sit at one of the comfortable padded chairs in front of his desk. The top of the desk was bare except for a yellow legal pad, a box of pencils, and a small figurine of the Notre Dame leprechaun.

Quinn frowned as he listened to whoever he was on the phone with. Finally, his mouth twisted downward and he said, "Okay. Thanks." He gave a slight shake of his head as he hung up the phone and picked up a yellow legal pad.

"All right. Let's hear the details of the almost apprehension of TJ Grimes."

Joey took him through all of his Saturday adventure but left out the sex with Mallory part.

When he finished, Quinn studied his notes for a minute then said, "This Mallory . . . what's her last name?"

"Stewart. Her dad's a mechanic at Blade."

"New girlfriend?"

Joey felt his face warming. "Uh . . . uh, no. Well, uh, yeah. I guess. Maybe."

Quinn laughed. "Well, it sounds like she's an improvement over the last one." He frowned as he reread his notes. "Grimes admitted he was the shooter?"

"Yes."

"And Mallory heard him say that?"

"Yeah. Is that good?"

Quinn frowned. "It's hearsay, but . . ." He tapped his pencil. "It's an excited utterance. And against penal interest. Yeah, it is good. Mallory will testify to that, right?"

"Yeah, but if the police pick up TJ, she won't have to, will she?"

"It's not clear. First the police would have to find TJ, and they aren't looking, so that's not very promising. But even if he walked in the door right now, we can't make him testify against himself. Maybe we can convince the police to drop the charges against you and pursue him, but no guarantees."

Joey hung his head. "It seems like I'm screwed."

"No. I'm just being a lawyer. Looking at the cloud, not the silver lining. If we get TJ to come in, the situation becomes a whole lot easier. But I can't plan your defense on that hope. That's why we need Mallory."

"What about Darville? He was there. He saw the whole thing."

Quinn sighed in a way Joey had come to recognize when someone was about to deliver bad news. "Darville claims he was focused on his driving, eyes straight ahead. No idea he was being chased. Didn't hear any gunshots or see anyone shooting a gun. It's like he was in a totally different vehicle."

"He's a fucking liar," Joey said.

"Yeah, I know. He also said you were harassing his girl. Said she left the country just to get away from you."

A week ago, that would have knocked the wind out of Joey, but now he almost expected it. Whatever could go wrong would go wrong. Darville acted so cool, but he couldn't stand losing his girl to some jock like Joey. Darville and Wendy deserved each other.

"I got a voicemail from Wendy. She said the same thing."

"When?"

"Saturday. Just before I called you. Want to hear it?"

"Hell yes. You got to tell me these things, Joey. You have to tell me everything. No matter how embarrassing or painful. I can't do my job if I don't have all the facts."

Joey's throat tightened. "I didn't harass her. They're lying. She went after me."

"I believe you. Let me hear what she said."

Quinn tapped his pencil on the pad as he listened to Wendy's message. He scoffed. "Chang's covering all his bases. He complained to Reynolds—he's the one handling the case— and said you were harassing the family. That's who I was talking to just now. Chang has a lot of juice."

"What are we going to do?" Joey tried not to sound desperate.

"I know it's tough. You gotta keep cool. We haven't even begun to fight. If we go to trial, I'll put Darville on the stand. The threat of perjury can often improve a reluctant witness's memory. Or in his case, his vision."

"My buddy Lua could help jog his memory," Joey said, deadpan serious.

"You're joking, right?"

"Sort of."

"I don't want you even making eye contact with him in the

hallway. These guys twist everything. I want to talk to your girl-friend. The new one."

Joey frowned. He didn't want Mallory mixed up in this mess. He realized he should tell Quinn about the whole Mallory pregnancy situation, but he couldn't. Not yet. "Her dad's an asshole. He won't let her. He doesn't want her hanging out with me."

Quinn peered at Joey with his usual poker face. He could never tell whether his lawyer believed him or not. "Okay, but if we end up going to trial, we might have to persuade him. I need some aces up my sleeve. Mallory might be an ace."

"Yeah," Joey said. Mallory was definitely an ace.

CHAPTER 16

For most of the first week, Joey followed his attorney's instructions and went out of his way to avoid Lawrence Darville. Wendy's ex-boyfriend traveled with a pack of preppies, all of them way too cool for Shadow Mountain High School. With their annoying snob accents, Joey had fair warning when Darville was headed his way and would duck into a classroom or study the student council bulletin board while the entourage passed. But on Saturday, Joey took the SAT exams. Now that his football scholarship was gone, if he wanted to go to college he would have to do it the old-fashioned way. The exam was no big deal. Some of the math questions were actually fun to try to solve, and he enjoyed the essay test question: "Explain how Martin Luther King Jr. builds an argument to persuade his audience that American involvement in the Vietnam War is unjust."

The exam was held in the girls' gym. There were only about twenty students, mostly those who didn't like their score on the fall exam. Darville was one of them. He was sitting in the back row with some of his friends. Joey took a seat in the front row as far from him as possible.

After the exams were collected, Joey quickly gathered his things and left the gymnasium. He rounded a corner in the empty hallway, and there was Darville opening his locker.

Joey tried to ignore him, but Darville spotted him and smirked. And that was all it took.

"Why are you fucking lying, Darville?" Joey asked.

"I don't know what you're talking about," Darville said, still staring into his locker. His voice sounded like he had a mouthful of marbles. There was a photo of Wendy in a pink bikini hanging on the locker door. He turned to face Joey, acting as though having to deal with Joey Blade was clearly a waste of his cool time.

"You know it was TJ who shot at those cops." Joey was close enough to smell Darville's girly cologne and see the flicker of fear in his eyes.

"I didn't see anything. And I don't know anything about your creepy little friend."

"You mean Wendy's dealer, don't you?"

Darville scoffed. "Did you think Wendy dug you? You were just her plaything. A boy toy distraction."

Joey grabbed Darville and slammed him into the lockers. He didn't resist; he just went limp. "You fucking little pussy. Tell the truth."

Darville swept his hair out of his eyes and tried to regain his cool. "Big mistake, macho man. Better get yourself a good lawyer. You're going to need one."

Quinn wouldn't be happy that he locker-slammed Darville. Joey loosened his grip. "I've got a good lawyer and he'd love to talk to you. Bring it on, asshole." He poked his finger in Darville's chest and then turned and walked away.

o o o

With everything that had happened in the last month, Joey had stopped believing he was living a charmed life. The New Year's

Eve fiasco had knocked him off his feet. He was going to be on trial for attempted murder, he'd lost his scholarship, his reputation had been trashed, he learned Dutch was buying hot parts from gangsters, and, of course, there was the situation with Mallory. But despite all that, Joey continued to believe it would all work out somehow. He couldn't be found guilty of something he didn't do. Something he'd tried to prevent. He had taken a standing eight count, but he wasn't knocked out. Things would eventually get fixed.

But each day, he was a little less confident. If TJ didn't turn up, and if Quinn couldn't get Darville to tell the truth, and if Wendy continued to hide out in Switzerland, it was finally occurring to Joey that he might be convicted. He could actually go to prison.

Quinn said it would probably take a few weeks before the prosecutors started paying attention to the case. Joey couldn't just wait for something to happen. He needed to find TJ.

Mallory had instructions for Joey too. She told him he needed to act like she didn't exist, but she needed him to give her a ride to the clinic in Ahwatukee.

The clinic in Ahwatukee was twenty miles south. Beyond the airport. There must be closer clinics, but at least that meant spending more time with her.

On Saturday morning, he got to the park just before nine. Mallory was waiting at the curb. "Okay. Why Ahwatukee?" he asked as she slipped into the pickup.

"I don't want someone to recognize me. And it has a good reputation. And I like to say Ahwatukee. Thank you for driving me. I usually take the bus, but I have to babysit my neighbor's kids tonight so I need to get back by three."

"The bus? Where do you get a bus?"

"It's actually three buses. It takes a little over two hours."

"You're crazy. I'll drive you next time. I don't mind at all. You don't need to spend five hours on the bus."

She patted his knee. "No. You have enough to deal with. I like the ride. It gives me time to think."

Joey huffed. "I don't have anything to do. My damn life's on hold. Let me help. I want to help."

"You don't know my father. If he finds out he'll make big trouble."

"He's going to find out sooner or later."

Her lips were pressed tight. "I know. I have to come up with a plan before that happens." She clasped his hand. "You need a plan too. Not for me. For your, uh, situation." Mallory was a master at changing the subject.

"As a matter of fact, I do have a plan," Joey said.

"Really?"

She didn't believe him. Joey didn't really have a plan, but he did have an idea. He figured he might as well share it with Mallory.

"When I was in jail, I met this dude, Chico. He's head of the Vatos Locos gang. He sells auto parts to my dad, but he's also a major drug dealer so I figure he'll have an idea where TJ is holed up since, you know, they're sort of in the same business."

Mallory nodded like what he'd said made sense to her. "When are you asking him?"

Joey frowned. It was a good question. "I haven't figured that out. I don't know how to reach him."

Mallory sat back in her seat. "The clinic's off the next exit," she said. "There's a gap-tooth dealer who hangs out at Shady's on Van Buren and Central. Creepy little guy. He has Vatos Locos tats on his arms."

"That sounds like Fernando."

Mallory shrugged. "Don't know his name. I was just a passenger. He was ugly."

"What's Shady's?"

"It's a coffee shop. Don't order a latte."

"Huh?"

"Look. I always have to wait at least an hour at the clinic. Drop me off and go check out the place. Gap Tooth's probably there. Lots of demand on Saturday."

Joey wanted to know how she knew so much, but he didn't want to ask. Maybe he didn't really want to know. "Let's wait and see. Maybe it won't be so crowded and you'll get in right away."

She gave him a look like he was clueless. Which was true.

It was standing room only at the clinic. The room was packed with pregnant women, babies, toddlers, and runny-nosed pre-teens. An elderly Black man, dressed like he was on his way to church, stood up when they entered the waiting room and offered Mallory his seat.

Joey could tell she was about to decline the offer. "Thank you, sir," he said. He guided Mallory by the elbow and sheep-dogged her into the chair. "Okay, I'll go to Shady's and see what I can find. Don't give up your seat."

o o o

Shady's was not at all like Joey imagined. He'd heard Van Buren Street was hooker territory and he visualized a sleazy, smoky joint with scantily clad women hanging out looking for johns. It was actually a tidy coffee shop, with an impressive selection of quiches and deli sandwiches as well as the usual array of coffee and tea beverages. Joey was tempted to order a latte just so he could bring it back to Mallory, but he didn't want to make the wrong impression. He ordered a coffee from the girl behind the counter. "Uh . . . is uh Fernando around?" he asked when she brought him his coffee.

She wrinkled her forehead and stared at him as though she was trying to decide if she had ever seen him before. Without answering she turned around and slipped through the swinging doors into the kitchen.

A moment later Fernando emerged. He stared blankly at Joey and then his eyes lit up and he offered his jack-o-lantern smile. "Pretty Boy! You here for the coffee?"

"Uh . . . I was hoping to talk to Chico."

Fernando stopped smiling. "Chico's a busy man. What you need?"

Joey didn't want to piss off Fernando, but he wasn't about to discuss TJ's whereabouts with him. "Dutch said I should only talk to Chico. Sorry, man. No disrespect."

When Joey played his Dutch card, he didn't really know if it would have any impact. He was half hoping it wouldn't, but the instant he said, "Dutch," Fernando's attitude changed.

He leaned over the counter and offered a fist bump. "Disrespect? No sir. That's cool. I'll page Chico."

A moment later, the waitress returned from the kitchen and handed Fernando another phone. It was one of those new flip phones, a Motorola StarTAC. It looked super cool.

"Yo, *jefe!*" Fernando said, turning away from Joey. "Dutch's boy wants a sit-down."

Joey wanted to protest. That made it sound like he was here for some kind of drug deal.

Fernando took the phone away from his ear and peered over his shoulder at Joey. "Tonight. Graham's Central Station. Nine o'clock. That cool?" It sounded like a question, but it was really a command.

Graham's was a raucous party bar. A country bar no less. It

didn't sound like a place where a notorious Mexican gang leader would meet someone. Maybe that was why he chose it.

"I can't get in there. I'm not old enough."

Fernando doubled over laughing and almost dropped the phone. "No problemo, holmes. Tell the bouncer you're Chico Torres's guest."

When Joey drove back to the clinic, Mallory was sitting on a park bench, her eyes closed, soaking up the cool winter sunshine. She looked so innocent. But obviously she wasn't. Every time they went somewhere, she revealed another aspect of her life Joey knew nothing about. The girl had secrets. Lots of secrets.

She climbed into the cab, then leaned over and kissed Joey on the cheek, just like they were an old married couple. It gave Joey a tingly feeling and took his mind off the anxiety he was feeling over the meeting with Chico Torres.

"Did you find him?" she asked.

"Yep," he said, unable to keep himself from grinning with pride at his accomplishment. "I'm meeting Chico Torres tonight at Graham's." He half-expected Mallory to have some story about Graham's too.

"Isn't that a cowboy bar?" she asked.

"Yeah. I'm his special guest. They're waiving the age limit for me."

"Cool. Do you know how to line dance?"

He put the truck in gear and headed out of the parking lot. "I don't think Chico dances."

CHAPTER 17

Graham's Central Station on the west side of Phoenix was a twenty-minute drive from Joey's home. He'd heard it was the second largest bar in the country, only Gilly's near Houston, Texas—the bar that was in that *Urban Cowboy* movie with John Travolta—had been larger. Graham's took over an indoor mall that closed in the early '80s. The mall parking lot was already more than half filled when Joey arrived at 8:30. He was a half hour early, figuring Chico Torres wasn't someone he should keep waiting.

That was a good plan because even with four tough-looking bouncers checking IDs, the lines were long. Joey picked the line with the blonde woman bouncer as she appeared slightly less scary than the three dudes. He cowboyed up for the meet so he wouldn't look so out of place or so much like a high school kid. Last Christmas, Solita had given him a black Stetson and a black denim shirt with mother-of-pearl snap buttons. It was his sister's idea of a joke. He passed on the hat—he didn't like to mess up his hair—but he wore the shirt with his boot-cut Wranglers and Frye harness boots. The boots were scuffed and comfortable. He usually wore them instead of the clunky steel-toed boots whenever he worked at the install center. He definitely looked more like a real cowboy than those guys in line wearing felt cowboy hats and fancy snake-skin boots.

When he got to the front of the line, the all-business bouncer held out her hand for his ID.

"I'm supposed to meet Chico Torres," Joey said.

A sly smile creased her face. "I guess that makes you a VIP cowboy. But I still have to search you."

She ran her hands up and down his sleeves, squeezing his biceps, and then patted his chest and reached around and cupped his butt. She hadn't done that to anyone else.

"Dottie! Knock it off," said the musclebound bouncer next to her. "Just check the IDs, girl."

She faux pouted at her partner. "You're no fun." She stepped aside to let Joey pass. "Okay, sweetie, you can go in. Those senoritas give you any trouble, just ask for Dottie. Chico's in the big room. He's got a table back behind the bar."

Joey had never been in a bar before, but Graham's was different from anything he'd ever seen on television. It was more like an amusement park. Shops selling all manner of cowboy gear lined the interior of the huge lobby. He walked through the swinging double doors of the lobby into a cavernous space as large as a football field. In one corner there was a whooping throng surrounding a wannabe cowboy trying to ride a mechanical bull. In the other corner there was a cluster of arcade games: a shooting range, Skee-Ball, a free throw machine, and a strength tester where guys used a sledgehammer to try to ring a bell.

In the center of the room was a horseshoe-shaped bar with at least two dozen bartenders handing out bottles of beer as fast as they could. The sign above the bar read, "Twenty-nine-cent longnecks." It didn't appear the bartenders were making any change. Dollar bills were piled six inches high on the counter behind them.

Dwight Yoakam's cover of "Crazy Little Thing Called Love" was blaring from huge speakers positioned around the room. It was chilly in the lobby, but it was warm and stuffy in the arena, like a packed gymnasium. Joey unbuttoned the top two buttons of his shirt. He was glad the shirt was black because his armpits were already damp and sweat was trickling down his back.

The horseshoe bar was opened in the back and Joey figured that must be where Chico was hanging out. He started to slip around behind the crowd that was five and six deep at the bar. Yoakum's twangy song finished and suddenly the room was filled with the heartbreaking plaint of the Dixie Chicks singing "You Were Mine." Joey remembered when Mallory sang that song. She said it reminded her of when her mother left her when she was young. *Mallory deserves better. She's a good person. You can't abandon her. Or the baby.*

Maddy.

That was the baby name he came up with. Mallory and Maddy. He liked the way that sounded.

"Hey, hey, Joey Blade! You're looking lost."

Two buxom blonde cowgirls with cut-off jeans shorts and halter tops that were barely legal stepped in front of him.

"Chico's busy right now. He told us to show you a good time while you wait. I'm Krissy."

"And I'm Darlene," said the other girl. "That's a nice shirt." She ran her hand up and down the sleeve. "I love those buttons."

Joey could tell he was blushing. "Uh . . . are you twins?" It was a lame question. His mouth was disengaged from his brain.

The girls giggled. "No darlin'. Do all blondes look alike to you?" Krissy said, primping her hair and jutting out her breasts.

"Do you want to ride the bull?" Darlene asked him. She wrapped her arm through his.

Joey shook his head. "I think the free-throw shooting would be safer."

"Cool," Krissy said, taking hold of his other arm. "Free drinks for the winner!"

They strolled back around the bar to the arcade. At the basket-shooting cage, three contestants stood behind a counter and tried to make as many baskets as they could in thirty seconds. Each shooter had a bin of undersized, overinflated basketballs that bounced like crazy when they hit the rim.

It cost a buck to play and the winner won two shots of booze and the right to play again for free. They watched for about five minutes. A pint-sized dude in shorts and an ASU T-shirt was handily beating everyone.

"You can beat him, Joey," Krissy said. "Darlene and I will help."

"How?" Joey asked.

Darlene giggled. "You'll see."

When it was their turn, Joey took the left basket and the girls crowded together at the center station. They introduced themselves to the shooter whose name was Todd.

"That's my brother's name," Darlene squealed.

As soon the bell rang, the girls started bouncing up and down, screaming and throwing wildly.

Joey figured out that the secret was to get into a rhythm and shoot fast. Don't wait for the shot to land before you fired up the next one. After he missed the first two, he found the sweet spot and made ten in a row in less than ten seconds. Meanwhile, Darlene and Krissy were upsetting Todd's rhythm with their bouncing boobs, non-stop screams, and crazy shots.

Joey outscored him 22-19.

"You win, Joey! You wanna play again?" Krissy asked.

"Let's quit while we're ahead," Joey said. He figured the next guy might not be as good a sport as Todd.

A waitress came over with a tray and handed him two shots filled with a green-colored liquid. "Kamikazes," she said.

"We love Kamikazes," Darlene said.

He handed the shots to the girls. "I don't drink."

"Such a gentleman," the waitress said. She held out another shot. "On the house."

"Bottoms up, Joey," Krissy said and drained her shot.

Joey swallowed it quickly. It tasted like limeade. "That's good," he said.

Darlene hooked his arm again. "Come on, let's watch the bell ringer thing. I love to watch boys showing off."

They strolled over to the High Striker booth. A big guy, sloppy fat, not muscular, in a sweatshirt with cut-off sleeves, was getting ready to try his luck. There was a bunch of sledge-hammers to choose from. He picked the largest one—a twenty-pounder with a thirty-six-inch handle. He raised it over his head, but the hammerhead wobbled and he hit the pad with a glancing blow. The ball only made it about halfway to the bell.

Joey had played the bell ringer game at the county fair last summer. Acceleration was more important than weight. He whispered to Krissy, "He'll never do it with that big hammer."

At least he thought he whispered. The guy who was about to make his third attempt, looked back over his shoulder and shouted, "You think you can do better? Put your money where your mouth is, kid."

Joey raised his hands. "No offense. Just try the smaller hammer. You'll get more torque."

"Fuck torque. Ten bucks. You can use the pussy hammer."

The guy's friends started taunting. "The kid's too pretty to swing that hammer. He don't want to mess up his hair."

Darlene gave the guy the finger. "Y'all are ignorant rednecks. Let's go, Joey, Chico is ready for us now."

The man raised the hammer over his head. He was gripping it so tightly his knuckles turned white. With a loud bellow, he brought it down on the pad. It was a much more direct hit than his first two attempts and the ball came within a foot of ringing the bell. "Goddammit!" He tossed the hammer at Joey's feet. "Beat that, you little shit."

Joey picked up the big hammer and pulled a ten-dollar bill from his wallet. He handed the hammer and the bill to the barker. "Okay to play?" he asked.

"Absolutely. Pick your poison."

He passed over the twenty- and twelve-pound sledges and selected the six-pound hammer with a sixteen-inch handle. He raised it over his head, cocked his wrist, and slammed it down hard on the pad, snapping his wrist as he made contact. The ball shot up the pole and rang the bell with a resounding clang. He did it two more times just to show it wasn't a fluke and to show off.

"Here you go, pardner," the barker said, handing him his and Daryl's ten-dollar bills.

He walked away arm in arm with Krissy and Darlene, feeling ridiculously good about himself and enjoying the catcalls the crowd rained down on poor Daryl.

Krissy squeezed his bicep. "You got some nice muscle hiding under that shirt, Joey Blade. Time to go see Chico."

They guided him around the horseshoe to the back of the bar where Chico and several of his associates were sitting. They might have been the same group he encountered at the jail, but he only recognized Fernando, who was wearing a girly, flaming red tank top and about ten pounds of gold chains. Chico was dressed in a black T-shirt and black jeans. He was lean and ripped, and looked handsome with his trim goatee and eyepatch.

As the girls brought Joey to the table, Chico stood up. "Thank you, ladies." With a nod of his head, the other men and women at the table picked up their drinks and moved to the surrounding tables. All except Fernando, who was grinning at Joey like they were pals.

"Hey, holmes, you made it," Fernando said. There was a pail of Coronas on the table and he pulled one out. "How about a nice cold cerveza?"

"No thanks," Joey said. He was already feeling a little tipsy from the Kamikaze shot.

Chico extended his hand. "Hello, Joey." He turned and glared at Fernando like Joey's football coach would when someone didn't know their assignment.

Fernando's grin got tighter. He nodded at Joey and took the beer with him to another table.

Chico beckoned for Joey to sit down in the chair next to him. Their backs were to the wall and they faced the open end of the horseshoe bar. "How's my friend, Dutch?" he asked. He was staring straight ahead and if they hadn't been the only ones at the table, Joey wouldn't have been certain he was talking to him. Except, of course, he asked about Dutch.

And called him his friend.

Joey decided he shouldn't look at Chico either, so he studied the counter folks serving beers. It was an impressive effort. Grab a bottle, twist off the top, hand out the beer—only one to a customer—take a dollar bill, and throw it on a pile behind them. Over and over and over again.

Joey was so mesmerized by the process he almost forgot Chico had asked him a question. "Uh, Dutch is fine. He's pissed off."

Chico laughed. "He's always pissed off. Man needs a hobby."

"Not happening." Joey didn't know what the protocol was for asking a gang leader for help. Were they supposed to indulge in small talk like the supplicants did in *The Godfather*?

They were silent for a moment, both just staring out at the bar and the dance floor. A Lonestar tune finished and Willie Nelson's "Mamas Don't Let Your Babies Grow Up to Be Cowboys" came on.

"I like Willie Nelson," Chico said. "Serious pothead. Good for business."

Joey twirled his thumbs, not sure what to do with his hands.

"You can have one of those beers if you want. They're good with a lime."

"No, that's okay. Uh . . ."

Come on Joey, you're acting like a kid afraid to ask for a first date.

"What do you want, Joey?"

Joey took a deep breath and started talking. He told Chico that TJ shot at the cops who they didn't know were cops, and how he found TJ at Lake Pleasant but that he escaped and now Joey had a problem. If he didn't find TJ he could go to jail for a long time. "I was wondering if you might know where he is."

Chico sat back in his chair. "Those undercover cops are dirtbags," he said, more to himself than Joey. His face was impassive. He was harder to read than Quinn. He waved to one of the men at the tables in front of him. A light-skinned Mexican with a scar from the corner of his eye to his chin walked over, and Chico whispered in his ear. The man nodded and said something to Chico. Joey stared straight ahead, not wanting to look like he was eavesdropping. He was, but he couldn't hear anything. Scarface returned to his table.

"We'll take care of it," Chico said.

"Uh . . . I need him to testify," Joey didn't know how to put it diplomatically. Taking care of it didn't sound good. It sounded final.

"We'll persuade him, Joey. We do some business with his brother. We're not gonna hurt him." Chico had the hint of a smile, like someone holding an ace.

CHAPTER 18

Mr. Coots, Joey's guidance counselor, asked to see him after seventh period on Friday afternoon. Mr. Coots ran the booster club for the school and never missed a Shadow Mountain football, basketball, or baseball game. He was a good guy. Before each period, he would stand in the hallway jingling the coins in his pocket and offering an "I'm cool" grin to anyone who walked by. He reminded Joey of one of those oldie's singers like Frankie Avalon or Paul Anka. When he learned that Joey had lost his scholarship, he reached out to him and made sure he took the SATs. He encouraged him to apply to other colleges. Joey figured that was probably what he wanted to talk about today.

Mr. Coots was in the bullpen of the administration office sitting on the corner of Miss Helfer's desk. Rail thin and severe, like the woman in the *American Gothic* painting, Miss Helfer was the principal's secretary. She intimidated everyone, including the principal.

Mr. Coots' voice rose as he delivered the punchline to his latest joke. ". . . and she says, 'Whatever you do, don't sell that cow.'"

Miss Helfer laughed out loud and some color actually showed in her cheeks. Joey had never seen her smile, but that was classic Mr. Coots. He got along with everyone. Mr. Coots spotted Joey and slipped off the desk. "Joey, my man! How ya doin', buddy? Come on in." He wrapped an arm around Joey and led him back to his office. Mr. Coots's office was a mess. College brochures were stacked everywhere, including the seat where he beckoned Joey to sit. "Just put those on the floor. One of these days, I'll get organized." It didn't sound like he believed it.

"You stole that joke from *Bonnie and Clyde*," Joey said. His sister, Solita, had a crush on Warren Beatty and used to watch that film every week for a year when she was in high school.

Mr. Coots chuckled. "I didn't figure Edie saw that flick. And I think I tell it better than Gene Hackman." He shuffled through a stack of papers on his desk and pulled out a corporate blue folder. "Here's what I'm looking for." He flipped through the pages, shaking his head, his eyes hooded with concern. Joey thought he'd done okay on the SATs but that was probably just another thing he fucked up.

"You've been sandbagging, Blade."

"Excuse me?"

"Playing the part of a dumb jock. You knocked it out of the park—seven hundred on your math, and seven sixty-six on your verbal." He grinned so hard his eyes disappeared. He was sincerely excited about Joey's test scores.

"Really?" Joey said.

"Have you submitted your applications like we talked about?" he asked. "I mean with these scores you can get in a bunch of schools. Top schools." He pushed the report across the desk to Joey.

"Not yet," Joey said. He studied the graph. There was a bell curve and a star printed on the curve at the far-right tail of the curve. His verbal score was in the top 1 percent of all applicants. "Cool."

Mr. Coots scowled. "Very cool, but worthless if you don't get your applications in before the deadline."

"I've been, you know, sort of waiting for my legal problem to get . . . figured out." Thinking about the New Year's Eve fiasco killed the good buzz of the SAT scores. Mr. Coots was right; they would be worthless numbers if things didn't work out for him.

Mr. Coots nodded sympathetically. "I know. I feel for you, buddy. But it's going to work out. And you have to plan for that. Where's that Joey Blade confidence?"

"It's hard to think about college right now." He actually did have a plan, but he wasn't ready to share it with Mr. Coots. Not until he talked to Mallory.

"Get the applications in, Joey. Just do it. Please."

Joey looked at the report again. "Can I keep this?"

"Absolutely. Show your folks. It's an excellent result. The scores will open doors. Now get out of here. And don't tell Edie about that joke."

Joey stood up. The bell for eight period rang. If he hurried, he could catch Mallory before she got to her class. "Your secret's safe with me, Mr. Coots."

CHAPTER 19

The only time Joey had ever given someone a Valentine was when he was in grade school and all the students were required to give a Valentine to everyone in the class. Joey had wanted to get Mallory something special. Not one of those sappy Hallmark type valentines—that was definitely not Mallory. And it couldn't be something typical like flowers or candy.

He was reading Mr. Lynch's comments on his *A Separate Peace* book report when he got an inspiration. Mr. Lynch gave him an A on the report and wrote that his writing was poetic. He could write Mallory a poem. It took him all Saturday afternoon, and he nearly filled his spiral notepad with failed attempts. He came up with something, but he wasn't sure it was a poem.

Someday You'll Be Mine

I remember the first time I saw you
Waiting in line for your turn at tetherball.
Tommy Jackson said, "Girls can't play";
You gave him that look
And then you beat him.
Someday You'll Be Mine

I remember all those hot summer days
Shooting free throws.
I said you were a pest.
And you gave me that look.
But you didn't run away.
Someday You'll Be Mine

I remember the day you invited me for ice tea.
I wish I'd known then that I was going
To fall in love with you.
Don't give me that look when you read this.
I love you, Mallory.
Someday You'll Be Mine.

That's a promise.

He was rewriting the poem with his best handwriting, list-ening to KNIX when they played a new song by the Dixie Chicks—"Goodbye Earl." A song of friendship and sweet, justified revenge. The Dixie Chicks were take-charge, just like Mallory. When the song finished the DJ duo, Tim and Willy, started talking about how the Chicks were coming to Phoenix for a concert at America West Arena in June. Yesterday, Joey had driven over to the Ticketmaster office at the Biltmore Plaza and bought two tickets. On the floor. It cost him fifty dollars but he didn't care. It was the perfect gift, so even if his poem sucked Mallory would be thrilled.

Joey caught up to Mallory just before 8th period. Without looking at her, he said, "Walk you home from school?"

"Meet me at Bosa Donuts at 3:30," she said, as though she had been expecting him to ask her. She slipped into her classroom without another word. The whole exchange took less than five seconds.

Joey got to the donut shop at 3:20. They were offering large, heart-shaped sugar cookies with pink frosting for a dollar. "I'll take one," Joey told the plump Italian lady at the counter.

She held up a big frosting tube she was using to decorate the cookies. "No charge, I'll put you and your sweetheart's name on the cookie."

Joey was tempted. It would be cool to give Mallory a cookie heart with their names inscribed, but he knew it would upset her. "No thanks. Just a plain one."

"Ohh. No one? A handsome young man like you must have a special girl."

Joey could feel his face flushing. "Not right now."

The lady clucked her tongue and slipped the cookie into a paper bag. "Happy Valentine's Day," she said.

Joey took the bag and left the shop. Mallory had just crossed the street and was heading up 32nd Street. She looked around and then bobbed her head as she continued up the street. Joey caught up to her as they reached Cholla. They crossed together, not saying anything, just two kids walking home from school.

As they headed north on Thirty-Fourth Street, a driver in a red Corvair honked his horn and pulled over to the curb just ahead of them. "Hey, *jefe*! Didn't know Blondie was your girl. How's it going, man?"

The Hispanic who jumped out of the car was dressed like one of those kids from the AV club—Diamondbacks baseball hat, dorky green Dockers, and a long-sleeved plaid flannel.

"Fernando?" Joey asked. He could hear Mallory mutter "shit" under her breath.

"Hah. You didn't recognize me." Fernando grinned, showing his missing teeth.

"What are you doing here?" Joey asked.

"Chico wanted me to do some recon at the school where

your boy was dealing." He lowered his voice. "I'm undercover. Come on, I'll give you a ride."

"No way, Joey," Mallory whispered. She started walking on ahead.

"Hey, Blondie, I thought we were friends."

Mallory gave him the finger and kept on walking.

"Sorry," Joey said. He wanted to find out what was happening with the TJ hunt, but he didn't want to let Mallory walk away.

"No problem, *jefe*. I dig it." He winked at Joey. As he was getting back into his car, he said, "Chico's going to be surprised."

Joey stopped walking. "About what?"

"That TJ dude was moving a lot of product." His grin was tight, like this wasn't the kind of news he wanted to deliver to Chico.

Joey caught up to Mallory as she headed east on Cortez Avenue. "You okay?"

"That guy gives me the creeps."

Cortez was a quiet side street and Joey took Mallory's hand. "At least he doesn't know your name."

Mallory giggled. "You're not doing a good job of ignoring me," she said.

"I'm trying." He handed her the cookie. "Happy Valentine's Day."

"Thank you," she said.

He patted his windbreaker to make sure the envelope with the poem and tickets was still in his chest pocket.

Mallory broke the cookie in two and handed him half. "It's good. Thanks. I didn't get you anything. I'm sorry. My dad's getting suspicious."

"Of me or—"

Mallory laughed bitterly. "I could be twelve months pregnant and he wouldn't notice. But he asked what I was doing with you up at Lake Pleasant."

"I figured Ross would tell him we were together."

"You can't walk me all the way home. I don't want any of the neighbors to see us."

Cortez Avenue ran into Thirty-Sixth Street. There was a bench for the bus stop at the corner. "Let's sit down," Joey said. "Enjoy this beautiful sunny day."

"More dry heat?" Mallory asked.

The days were getting warmer but it was still only mid-seventies. They sat together hip to hip. Joey closed his eyes and let the sun warm his face. Mallory leaned into him and rested her head on his shoulder. It was quiet and peaceful and Joey felt ridiculously happy sitting on that bench with Mallory. He reached into his pocket and handed her the envelope with the poem.

"Happy Valentine's Day, Mallory."

"A valentine?" She ripped opened the envelope.

As she read the poem to herself, Joey stared down at his sneakers, afraid to even breathe.

Mallory put the poem down and stared hard at him.

"I know. It's not really a poem. I'm sorry—"

Mallory giggled. "I'm just giving you the look, silly. Thanks. It's a great poem."

"There's more." He handed her the other envelope with the Dixie Chicks tickets.

This time he did look at her, confident she would be thrilled. But her chin was dimpled with emotion as she shook her head. "No, Joey."

"What do you mean? Those are great seats."

"Don't you see we can't? I'll be seven months pregnant. We can't be seen together."

"I have a plan, Mallory." He clasped her hands and pulled them close to him so she had to look at him.

"Of course, you do. One of your lists. A ten-step program to solve our problems?"

People were always making fun of his lists. "It's only two steps, actually. No, three. Ready?"

"Do I have a choice?" she said.

"First, I start working at Blade after school. Every day. We can keep the install center open longer. I can get forty hours in easy."

"That's a lot of hours. You still have schoolwork."

"It's the final semester. It's a cakewalk to graduation. That's step one. The next step is I apply to ASU."

"So, you'll play football for the Sun Devils? They could use you. Their offense stinks."

"No," he said. He shifted on the bench so he could look in Mallory's eyes. "I'm applying to the night school program. I'll be full time at Blade. Work on building the install center. Become Dutch's right-hand man. I can make fifty grand a year, maybe more."

Mallory frowned. "But you hate working there."

"It's work. You're not supposed to like it. It's not that bad."

"That's a two-point plan. And I don't like it. You need to go to a real school, not college for old fogeys."

Joey waved her off. "The third part is we get married. I'll take you to the Chicks concert as part of our honeymoon."

Mallory sighed. "What am I going to do with you, Joey Blade?"

"Marry me?" he asked. He wrapped his arms around her and kissed her like she had kissed him that first time.

She gently separated them. "Go home, Joey."

Joey snuck in one more kiss and then jumped up from the bench and headed for home. He was almost skipping. She didn't say no.

CHAPTER 20

Terry Quinn called Joey the day after Valentine's Day. "We have a pre-trial conference with the prosecutors on March fifteenth. It's at three o'clock."

"That's a month away," Joey said. He wanted to complain that everything was taking too long and nothing seemed to be happening, but he knew it was pointless. To the rest of the world this wasn't a big deal. "What happens then?"

"They'll probably offer a plea. Lay out the options. The cops who got shot at are being hard-asses. I'm not sure why 'cause they look pretty shitty in this deal. But maybe they think a good offense is the best defense."

"I didn't shoot at them. I tried to stop the shooter." Joey took a breath. He realized he was shouting. "Sorry. Didn't mean to yell. I'm not pleading guilty."

"It's just a meeting. We need to hear what they have to offer. It will tell me how much confidence they have in their case. I know you don't want to take a plea, but if they offer something like probation or community supervision, you need to think about that."

"I'd have a criminal record." Joey had watched enough crime shows to know that.

"Not necessarily. But you're getting ahead of yourself. We listen and learn. That's all."

"Maybe TJ Grimes will show up before this meeting." Joey hadn't heard anything from Chico Torres, but the gang leader seemed confident they could find TJ.

"You never know," Quinn said. He didn't sound like he thought it was likely.

Joey figured Quinn wouldn't want to know about the Chico connection. He would have to tell Joey not to do that, but finding TJ was the only way Joey could restore his reputation. His dreams of football glory had been shattered like those asshole cops' windshield. He hardly thought about playing anymore. But restoring his reputation, especially now that he was going to be a father, was important to him.

Mallory hadn't said no, but she hadn't said yes either, so the only part of the three-part plan Joey could talk to his father about was working more hours at the shop. Once Mallory agreed to marry him—and Joey was convinced she would—then he could tell his parents about his plans for marriage and night school. They'd be upset—another Joey fuck up—but they'd come around. With the baby situation, this was now a family matter, and for Callie and Dutch, nothing trumped family.

Dutch was an easy sell. He wanted to expand the hours for the install center and keep it open during the week until eight p.m., and he needed someone trustworthy to run the operation when he wasn't around. He proposed that Joey start by working all day Saturday and evenings from four to eight Tuesday through Friday. That would give him over twenty hours a week.

Joey still needed to get Callie's approval, and she always resisted Joey working during the school week. But Joey had become more strategic since his life was turned upside down. Before he told her about the plan to work more hours, he told her about his meeting with Quinn and how frustrated he was with his situation and the unfairness of the legal system. He figured his mother would conclude that the extra work would keep his mind off a problem he couldn't do anything about. She agreed to let him work, but with conditions as usual. "You have to keep up your grades, Joey. Have you completed your college applications?"

"I will, Mom, and I'm working on the applications. Don't worry about that." Not exactly the truth, but close. He had submitted his application to ASU's night school program.

Saturday was his first workday. He rode down with Dutch and planned to drive the S-10 home. Dutch told him that would be his assigned company vehicle. When he was the big football hero, he was embarrassed by the beat-up old truck with the Blade Engine logo plastered on the doors. He remembered how Wendy turned up her nose at it. Now he saw that truck as his first tangible sign of moving into the working world. Next year he would have a wife and a kid and be working full time to support his family. Six months ago that would have been a nightmare scenario, but now the idea of starting a life with Mallory where they could be together all the time sounded wonderful.

"You listening to me, Joey?"

Dutch was reciting all his rules for running a successful operation. Joey had heard them a thousand times and he tuned out Dutch as he thought about his future with Mallory. "Yeah, I'm listening. Who's the lead today?"

Dutch grunted. "Donny Stewart. He volunteered. Must be trying to get his act together. He never volunteers for extra work."

Stewart was the last person Joey wanted to work with on the first day of his new career. However, business was brisk and he didn't have time to think about Stewart. Before Joey knew it, the mechanics were shutting down for the day. He was sorting the daily invoices when he heard the door open behind him.

"Good day for the Blades. We finished twelve installs. Must have cleared twenty grand." Donny Stewart, with a cheek full of Skoal, ambled into the office spitting a stream of tobacco juice into a raggedy paper cup.

Joey's face must have revealed his disgust.

"What? You don't like my chaw? Too low-class for you?"

"What do you need, Donny?" Joey asked. Stewart didn't look like he was in his joke-telling mode.

"My daughter's not too low-class for you, is she?" A squiggle of brown juice trickled down Stewart's chin. There was a tremor in his hand as he swiped it away. Beads of sweat dotted his forehead despite the cool temperatures.

Joey stared hard at him. He wouldn't let Stewart bait him.

Stewart worked his jaws and spit another stream into his cup. "You knocked up my slut daughter and now I've got to take care of it. I need ten grand. And I need it now or I'll tell your old man. He ain't gonna be too happy with his golden boy."

Joey's heart pounded. "What do you mean you're going to take care of it?"

"What the fuck you think? She ain't gonna have that baby. For Chrissakes she's just a baby with big tits. Stupid cunt. Spreads her legs for—"

Joey's right hook caught Stewart flush on the jaw. His knees buckled and he fell sideways into a display rack of Valvoline engine oil. The crash of the cans hitting the floor was shockingly loud, but not as loud as Stewart's bellow as he regained his footing. "You son of a bitch!" He lunged at Joey and launched a wild roundhouse at Joey's head.

Joey easily dodged the punch and snapped Stewart's head

back with a straight left hand to the nose. He fell backwards like someone pulled the plug on him. Choking on the tobacco chaw and gushing blood from his nose, he puked. He was on his hands and knees gasping for breath, his face inches from a puddle of blood and brown vomit.

Joey stood over him, not sure what to do. Just then Dutch burst through the doors of the service center, followed closely by fat Frank Ross, who was puffing like he might have a heart attack. He hadn't moved that fast in a decade.

"What the hell's going on?" Dutch glared at Joey and then at Stewart, who had managed to finally stagger to his feet with blood still dripping from his nose.

Stewart picked up a rag from the counter and patted his face. "Son of a bitch broke my nose."

Dutch looked at Ross. "Take him over to first aid. Get an ice pack. It don't look broke." The way Dutch said it made clear he wasn't interested in any discussion.

Stewart whispered at Joey as he passed, "Remember what I said. I ain't joking."

The two men left, Stewart leaning heavy on Ross.

"What happened here?"

Joey knew it was time to come clean. "I got Mallory pregnant. Stewart wants ten grand to get her an abortion. He can't do that, can he? We can't let that happen."

"Little Mallory? Isn't she like twelve?"

"Sixteen."

Dutch pressed his lips together. He was disappointed, not angry. Joey wasn't surprised. Little things could send him through the roof, but when the shit hit the fan, Dutch stayed cool. "Well, I'm glad she's not twelve."

"We're getting married. She's having the baby, and I'm

enrolling at ASU for night school and working here full time. He can't make her get an abortion, right?" A sob escaped from Joey's chest. It surprised him more than his father.

Dutch wrapped his arms around Joey and bear-hugged him like when Joey was freed from jail. "One thing at a time, Joey. Don't worry. We won't let that happen. You go home. I'll take care of Stewart."

CHAPTER 21

Joey drove straight to Mallory's house. She was right about her father. They needed a new plan. Dutch could delay Stewart, but sooner or later he'd be coming home and Joey didn't want Mallory to be there when he did.

She wasn't home. He walked around the house, ringing their doorbell, knocking on the backdoor, looking into the backscreen porch where they first made love. No sign of her or any of her stuff. At the house next door, a man was washing his car in the driveway. His boy and girl were helping him.

Joey approached the man while the kids were scrubbing the tires of his Chevy van. "That's a good work crew you got," he said.

The man beamed. "They work for gummy bears."

"Have you seen the girl who lives next door?"

"Mallory? Yeah. She got in a cab about an hour ago. Had a couple backpacks like she was going on a trip. You a friend of hers?"

Joey stared down at his shoes, trying to look embarrassed. "Uh, she was supposed to help me with my math homework. Guess I'm out of luck." Funny thing about lying: the more you did it, the easier it got.

The man nodded sympathetically. "I sucked at math too. I

hope she comes back soon. She's the best babysitter we've ever hired. Kids love her."

"She's good with kids," Joey said. He sighed. No way to contact her. He'd just have to wait until she called him. At least she was out of her father's house.

When Joey got back home, Callie was in the kitchen waiting for him. Dutch had called her from the hospital where he took Stewart and told her about Mallory and the fight with Stewart and his threats. She was in full-bore Callie-action mode. "We need to get Mallory out of that house. She can stay here for now until we find a safe place." Like Dutch, Callie was focused on the number one problem: protecting Mallory and the baby. She wasted no time lecturing Joey or telling him she was disappointed.

"She's gone, Mom. Neighbor saw her take a cab."

Callie pursed her lips. "Where could she go? Does she have family?"

"I don't think so. I don't know where she went. She warned me her dad would be a problem."

Callie grimaced, her hands on her hips. "Stewart's always been an asshole. And a creep. We should have fired him long ago."

CHAPTER 22

Every time the phone rang in the house, Joey jumped to answer it. But Mallory didn't call and Joey was going out of his mind as his imagination worked overtime inventing awful scenarios.

She's been abducted from the bus station.

Some sicko nabbed her when she tried to hitchhike.

She's lost in the desert.

Stop thinking like that, Joey. Face the facts, She's run off because she doesn't want you to be part of her life or the baby's.

He was disgusted with himself for feeling worse about the possibility that she was out there and just didn't want him than he felt at the prospect that she was in danger. He couldn't make himself stop thinking about her.

It was time to tell Quinn about Mallory. He called and got an appointment for Wednesday afternoon. On Tuesday he started his job on the afternoon shift, running the install center. He welcomed the work, as they were busy and that kept his mind off Mallory. The only good news was that Donny Stewart had quit. Didn't have the balls to tell Dutch to his face, just called on Monday morning and told the receptionist he was working at Challenger Engine.

As Joey was wrapping things up on Tuesday, Frank Ross

plodded into the service center with the paperwork on the install he had just completed. Joey thought Ross, who was Stewart's drinking buddy, would be standoffish, but he greeted Joey with a broad, conspiratorial smile.

"You did a number on old Donny. About time someone knocked that son of a bitch on his ass."

"I hear he's working at Challenger," Joey said.

Ross snorted. "He won't last a month. Their engines are for shit and Donny knows it. He'll tell him what he thinks—man can't help himself—and they'll fire his ass. Dutch was the only guy in the Valley who could handle Stewart."

It was true. Dutch could tolerate a lot of personality defects if the man or woman could do a superior job. But he should have never tolerated Stewart.

"How's Mallory getting along?" Ross asked.

Joey frowned. Did Ross know Mallory was pregnant? "What do you mean?"

"Stewart told me she took off. I had a beer with him over at the Holly. Can't blame the girl. Donny was always bitching about her, but now that she's run off, he's bouncing off the wall. Watch your back with that guy. He's trouble."

The next morning at breakfast, Joey was pouring himself a glass of orange juice when he glanced at the front page of the *Arizona Republic*. In the corner below the fold was a small headline that read: "Chandler Slaying 'Gangland-Style' Hit." Now that he was on a first-name basis with a drug lord, Joey read all the gang-related articles.

"The body of Edward "Peanut" Grimes was found on the south bank of the Salt River near the Thirty-Fifth Avenue Bridge. His hands and feet were tied, and the coroner estimated he had been in the water for several days. Grimes had a history of drug offenses in California, but nothing in Arizona. Sources indicated he moved to the Valley in 1998."

Joey had a cold, sick feeling in the pit of his stomach. The kitchen was warm, but he was trembling. Edward must be TJ's brother. Chico Torres told Joey he did business with TJ's brother. He assured Joey that no harm would come to TJ, but he didn't say anything about his brother. Could this murder possibly be the result of Joey's asking Chico for help? Fernando said Chico would be surprised about TJ's activity. Chico didn't seem like a man who liked surprises.

Joey dropped down into his chair and held his head in his hands. He squeezed his eyes shut and tried to pray, but he didn't even know what to pray for. The phone rang and he grabbed it, grateful for the distraction.

"Joseph Blade, please."

Joey recognized the voice of Quinn's receptionist, Arnelle. A soft, clear voice designed to soothe the jangled nerves of Quinn's clientele. "Hi, Arnelle. This is Joey."

"Hello, Mr. Blade. Mr. Quinn would like you to see if you could get your parents to accompany you to today's appointment at four o'clock."

Joey wanted to ask her why, but he knew that was pointless. If Quinn wanted her to tell him, she would have done so. *Goddamn lawyer always holds his cards close to his vest.* "We'll be there at four," Joey said.

CHAPTER 23

Joey felt worse than that night he spent in the Durango Jail. That was a nightmare, but one he was convinced he'd wake up from and everything would be okay. The truth would set him free and he would go on with his life. But TJ's brother was dead and that couldn't be undone. Joey wanted to believe the murder had nothing to do with his reaching out to Chico Torres, but he couldn't. As he sat in Quinn's reception area waiting for his parents and his lawyer, he didn't know what to do.

Should he come clean and tell his folks and Quinn that he'd gone to Chico? That could backfire. What if Chico found out? He might be putting his parents at risk. Truth didn't seem like the best option. He told himself not saying anything wasn't a lie, but he couldn't make himself believe that either.

At 3:55, Dutch and Callie arrived. Dutch was squeezed into his blue blazer. His face was tight and Callie was freckle-flushed again. They were seriously not talking to each other.

A few minutes later, Terry Quinn entered the reception area and greeted his parents warmly but didn't try to engage them in small talk. Something was clearly different. At earlier meetings with Joey, he acted casual, like this was not his main event. Today he was clearly focused. For a guy who was supposed to be Mr. Cool, he seemed tense.

They sat down at the same table they had used for their

first meeting in January. Quinn studied his yellow notepad and tapped his pencil on the pad. He gave Joey his patented stare. "You feeling okay?" he asked.

Joey hoped he didn't look as bad as he felt, but he wasn't a good poker player. Quinn could probably read him, no sweat. "I'm okay."

Okay for someone facing a felony charge, whose girlfriend is pregnant and missing, and who may be responsible for a gangland hit.

Quinn stared at him an uncomfortably long time, wanting more elaboration, but Joey wasn't going to hang himself. Quinn scanned the table like a searchlight, pausing to make serious eye contact with Callie and Dutch.

"I don't know if you saw the paper this morning, but TJ Grimes's drug-dealing brother was killed last night." He paused to let that sink in.

Callie and Dutch both frowned. Callie started to ask the obvious question. "How does that—"

"The feds have TJ Grimes in protective custody."

Joey gasped. That was the first good news he'd heard in two months.

"Have they talked to him?" Callie asked. "Has he told them Joey didn't do anything?"

From Quinn's expression, Joey could tell his joy at TJ's capture was premature. Quinn took a deep breath. "The feds are investigating the gangs. They're not interested in our case, and they're not granting access to Grimes. He's a material witness and they want his help on their cases against Vatos Locos."

At the mention of Chico's gang, Dutch's eyes narrowed.

"But you can make him testify, can't you?" Joey asked.

Quinn bit down on his lip. "I can try, but they'll fight it. Not a sure thing at all. But it could work to our advantage." He put down his pencil and did the searchlight thing again with his eyes to make sure he had everyone's attention.

Joey's heart was pounding. It felt like his whole life might be decided in these next few moments.

"The feds are after whoever killed that drug dealer, Edward Grimes. They know it's gang-related. Our case is a distraction. Which means they will put pressure on the prosecutor to settle. It might be our best opportunity to get a favorable deal."

"What's favorable?" Dutch asked. His frown creased his face. He was staring at Quinn like the man was trying to sell him the Brooklyn Bridge.

"Maybe a suspended sentence. Community service. We won't know until we talk to them. I think it's time."

Two weeks ago, when Quinn brought up the idea of pleading guilty, Joey was incensed. He had his name to protect and he was innocent. Now he didn't feel so innocent. Community service? No jail time? He'd take that. He could be with Mallory and they could get on with their lives. His name would be trashed, but if he was responsible for TJ's brother getting killed, he deserved it. And he'd have a whole lifetime to rebuild his reputation. And maybe someday TJ Grimes or Wendy Chang or Lawrence Darville would decide to tell the truth.

"That sounds okay to me," Joey said. He had been planning to tell Quinn about Mallory, but now he wouldn't have to.

Callie jerked her head around and stared at Joey. "You need to tell Mr. Quinn about Mallory," she said.

Dutch's face darkened, and he puffed up like he was about to explode. This was probably what they were fighting about. Dutch didn't trust lawyers.

"What about her?" Quinn asked. He directed his question at Joey and locked on him with his lawyer stare.

"She's pregnant and she's run away from home," he said.

Callie leaned across the table. "Tell him about the fight," she said.

Joey sighed. "I got in a fight with her father. He wanted ten thousand dollars to take care of the problem." Joey's voice quavered. It made him angry just saying those words.

Quinn rubbed his hand over his face. "Fuck," he said softly.

It was the first time Joey heard him curse. The first time he actually looked rattled.

"We're getting married," Joey said.

"Let's not get ahead of ourselves," Dutch said.

Quinn waved his hand as though he wasn't interested in Joey's marital plans. "How old is she?"

"Uh, she'll be sixteen next month," Joey said.

Quinn turned to the side, his face blank as he gathered his thoughts. Then he clasped his hands together and leaned across the table, staring hard at Joey. "She's a minor. Technically you could be charged with statutory rape."

"Rape?" Dutch pounded the table, rattling their water glasses. "That's bullshit. Half the kids in that school are having sex. No different from when we were that age for Chrissakes."

"Dutch," Callie said firmly without raising her voice. She put her hand on his sleeve. Dutch sat back in his chair.

Quinn, unfazed, almost oblivious to Dutch's outburst, continued. "This makes it even more imperative we settle this case now. If this comes out in the trial it could really hurt us. Even if you got married, which I'm not advising."

"So, what should we do?" Callie asked.

Quinn clicked his tongue. "First, I'm saying a special prayer that Joey's girl stays missing until this thing is over. She's a serious complication we don't need right now. And her father sounds like really bad news." He tapped his pencil on his notepad. "Then I'll tell the feds I want to interview Grimes and

I'll reach out to the prosecutor. What's his name . . . uh, Clark. He's green. I should be able to convince him we want to move up our plea agreement without arousing his suspicions. The feds will resist my request, but they'll put pressure on Clark to settle. Nobody wants a trial."

Not getting Mallory involved sounded like a great idea to Joey. It was a measure of how much his life had changed that he almost felt hopeful about having a meeting to discuss pleading guilty to a felony he didn't commit.

CHAPTER 24

Working every day, even if it was only four hours, was more tiring than Joey expected. But it was a good tired. It took his mind off all the bullshit he couldn't control and it gave him a temporary reprieve from thinking about Mallory. He had helped out at the plant for years, but never enjoyed it. Employees were polite to him but distant. But now, maybe because this was a real job, or maybe because he had decked Stewart, or maybe because he had baggage like most of them, they accepted him. At school, he felt like everyone was judging him even though they didn't say anything. At Blade Engine, there was no judgment.

He liked the work. When there were customers, he enjoyed the challenge of selling them on the Blade Engine installation. He had never thought of himself as a salesman; he thought they were just bullshit artists. But he was straight with all the customers, never tried to sell someone something they didn't need, and he was getting great results. When there were no customers, he would help the mechanics by pulling parts or checking engine inventory in the parts warehouse. If the job required something special, like a steel crankshaft or a performance cylinder head, Joey would schedule the work with the proper department.

Just before he closed up, Frank Ross walked into the service center. "Hear about Donny?" he asked.

"No," Joey said. He tried to sound disinterested, but Ross loved to gossip about Stewart. Joey needed to know what was happening, but he got a sick feeling in the pit of his stomach when he thought about Mallory's father.

"Challenger fired him. Told you he wouldn't last."

"What's he up to now?" Joey asked.

Ross hunched his shoulders. "Nothin'. He just sits at home getting shitfaced, living off his unemployment. Fucker's gonna drink himself to death."

o o o

The next day as Joey was walking home from school, he spotted Fernando's red Corvair parked at the corner of Mountain View and Thirty-Second Street. Fernando was sitting on the hood waiting for him. It was the first time Joey could remember him not smiling.

"Hey, Joey, get in the car. We need to talk."

"I've gotta get to work," Joey said. He was remembering the scene from *The Godfather* where that poor schlub who beat his wife got strangled with piano wire by the mobster in the back seat. Luckily the Corvair had an almost nonexistent back seat, which appeared to be empty.

"Not going nowhere, just talking." Fernando held out the passenger door and his serious demeanor convinced Joey he needed to listen to what he had to say.

The car was roomier than it appeared from the outside and immaculate. It had a fruity peppermint smell to it, like Fernando found a pink deodorizer to match the interior.

"You hear what happened to your boy's brother?" Fernando

asked. He stared straight ahead and talked in a whisper even though there was no one on the street.

Joey swallowed hard and bobbed his head. His mouth was dry. He was afraid if he tried to talk it would come out like a croak.

"We can't help you find Grimes. The heat's really on. We gotta keep a low profile."

So Chico didn't know that the feds had TJ?

"Okay." Joey's voice was croaky, but he didn't sound terrified.

"Sorry, man." Fernando acted sincerely contrite. Then he brightened. "Hey, I saw your lady the other day. Congratulations!"

"What?"

"Blondie. Why didn't you tell me you're having a baby?"

"You saw Mallory? Where?"

"You didn't know?" Fernando said. "She's at Agnes Calloway. You know. That home for knocked-up chicks. I made a delivery to someone there. I seen her in the yard. It's sort of like a prison, but they can leave if they want. It was definitely Blondie. I'd know that rack anywhere. No offense, man."

"Where is it?"

"Seventh Avenue. Just south of Mariposa."

Joey imagined that Mallory, desperate to escape her father, had run far away. At least to another state. But she was only five miles down the road. He wanted to run over there right now, but he knew that would be a mistake.

"Thanks, Fernando. I appreciate the tip."

"No problem, holmes. You're familia."

He still wanted to believe that Chico and Fernando and the Vatos Locos gang had nothing to do with TJ's brother getting whacked, but he knew he was just fooling himself. He had made a deal with the devil and now he must deal with the consequences.

CHAPTER 25

4:30 P.M. – SATURDAY – MARCH 4, 2000
AGNES CALLOWAY SCHOOL

Agnes Calloway looked more like prison than a school. Chain link fence surrounded the building and the exercise "yard" was basically a parking lot with a couple of basketball hoops with the nets missing and a tetherball pole. But there was no razor wire on the fence and there were no guards in towers with shotguns.

As soon as his shift ended, Joey drove over to Agnes Calloway. When he asked the receptionist if he could see Mallory, she told him visiting hours were from 10 a.m. to 3 p.m. She wasn't rude, just lacking in that faux receptionist friendliness. It was a home for unwed mothers and he wasn't family, he was one of the impregnators.

Two months ago he might have just left, or he might have gotten pissed at her disdain, but Joey had changed. Through four years of high school his football heroics had defined him. He was Joey Blade – everybody's All American. He enjoyed playing the game, and the fact that he was good at it made it even more fun. It would have been cool to play college ball with seventy thousand fans cheering him on, but now he knew that was never going to happen and it didn't bother him all that much. In an odd way, that fall from grace freed him. He didn't have to meet anyone's expectations. He didn't have to play by the rules. After the receptionist's curt dismissal he parked himself on the bench across from the school. Maybe they would let the inmates out again for late afternoon exercise.

At five o'clock, the gymnasium door opened, and a line of pregnant girls filed out into the yard. Joey had imagined the girls in uniforms, like convicts. But this was not a prison. It was just a place where pregnant girls with no other options could live. They seemed happy. At least they sounded happy—chattering and giggling just like the girls at Shadow Mountain. But unlike high school, Agnes Calloway was a true melting pot—white and black and Hispanic and Asian—all hanging out together. It was easy to spot Mallory. She was the only blonde in the pack. She showed more than the last time he saw her. She was two weeks more pregnant and there was definitely a bulge in her belly. Maddy was growing! Joey did the math—the baby was conceived the week before Thanksgiving, so Mallory was now more than three months pregnant.

Mallory and a small Hispanic girl were trying to play catch with a Frisbee. The girl, who couldn't have been more than twelve, didn't know how to throw the disc. She flung it hard, but it nosedived and rolled like a manhole cover, stopping at Mallory's feet. Mallory giggled and demonstrated the proper form as she flung the disc back to her friend. Gripping the Frisbee the way Mallory instructed her, the girl reached back and flung the disc toward Mallory. It soared high and wide and over the chain-link fence, landing on the curb, ten yards from where Joey was sitting. A heaven-sent opportunity.

Joey jumped up from the bench and picked up the Frisbee. He brought it over to the fence where Mallory and her friend were waiting for him. Mallory had her what-am-I-going-to-do-with-you expression, but she was smiling. Sort of. Joey flipped the Frisbee back over the fence. "Hi, Mallory," he said.

The girl picked up the Frisbee. She glanced at Mallory and then Joey, her face serious. "You cool, Mal?"

Mallory peeked over her shoulder. "Give me a minute, Nita."

"No problem." She grinned, revealing a full mouth of braces. "He's cute."

Mallory walked over and laced her fingers through the chain-link fence. "We're not supposed to have visitors now."

Joey gripped her fingers through the fence. It felt so good to see her again, to touch her, to hear her voice. He was afraid he might start crying.

"Breathe, Joey."

"You look great."

"I'm getting fat. I'll be a blimp by the time this baby is born."

"Maddy."

"Right, Maddy. Great name, because her daddy is poco loco." She gave his fingers a gentle squeeze. "My dad opened a letter from the clinic. He knew about the baby so I had to run. I didn't want you to know. How'd you find me?"

"Fernando. He saw you last week. Did you hear about TJ's brother?"

She stared down at her feet. "That's bad, isn't it?"

"I shouldn't have asked Chico for help. This is on me."

"You don't know that. Drug dealing's a dangerous job. It could have been anyone," Mallory said, but she didn't act like she believed it any more than Joey.

"Can I visit you next week?"

Mallory's face darkened and she lowered her voice to a whisper. "My counselor said someone in social services wants to talk to me. She acted like it was no big deal, but the girls said they only do that when they think it's a rape or some kind of incest thing."

"Damn." Joey stomped the ground and turned away from Mallory. He didn't want her to see his face. Rape. Quinn was right. Mallory needed to stay missing. If those prosecutors found out about her, they could make serious trouble.

"Don't worry, Joey. I'm not telling them anything." A buzzer sounded through the yard. "It's time for dinner. I'll call you on your cell after they talk to me." She air-kissed him and then turned and walked back toward the school.

"I love you, Mallory."

"You're crazy, Joey Blade. Seriously poco loco."

Joey hung on to the fence, watching until she was back in the building. His heart ached.

CHAPTER 26

Joey and his parents were ushered into a windowless room on the second floor of the district attorney's office. Terry Quinn waited in the reception area so he could talk with the young assistant D.A. who was handling the case. The room reminded Joey of the place where he met with Detective Carnes—the same battleship-gray table and utilitarian metal chairs, and the same stale air smell, not quite so heavy on the BO, but unpleasant enough. They had been waiting thirty minutes for their 3:00 meeting.

Quinn walked hurriedly into the room and sat down at the table. "They're cooking up something," he said. "They took the kid off the case and assigned it to Glen Cooper."

"What's that mean?" Joey asked.

"It means something has happened we don't know about. Cooper's a pro. He's one of the heavyweights in the District Attorney's office."

"Shit," Dutch said. He said it softly under his breath, and that worried Joey more than if he pounded the table and turned purple.

Callie chewed on her lower lip, waiting for Quinn to explain.

Quinn spread his palms over the top of the table like he was trying to calm the waters. "Remember, this is just a meeting where we listen to what they have to say. We don't have any obligation to do anything but listen. Our position is we have a winning hand and are ready to go to trial. I don't think they are, so let's stay cool. Remember, I don't want any of you to say a word. No reaction. No swearing, pounding the table, cheering. Nothing." He stared pointedly at Dutch. "Understood?"

"How long they going to keep us waiting?" Dutch asked.

Quinn smirked. "This is typical Cooper bullshit. He does it all the time."

At that moment, there was a knock on the door. "Come in," Quinn said.

The door opened and a receptionist asked them to follow her down the corridor to the meeting room. It was far from impressive, just a standard room with a gray table, but with a nice view of Central Avenue. The air-conditioner was running full blast and Joey shivered as he took his seat next to Quinn. Too hot, too cold, too stinky. The government had all sorts of ways to keep him uncomfortable.

A few minutes later, a pudgy, bald man in a rumpled blue suit lugging a beat-up leather briefcase joined them, followed by the young attorney who had handled Joey's arraignment. The rumpled man reached across the table. "Good to see you, Terry. It's been awhile." Friendly words, but delivered flat, like he was reading from a cue card.

Quinn smiled slightly more sincerely and said, "Hello, Glen." He introduced Joey and his parents, and Cooper introduced his assistant, Lonnie Clark.

After they settled at the table, Cooper pulled out a sheaf of papers from his briefcase. He flipped through them briefly and then looked at Joey. "I'm sure your attorney has explained the purpose for this meeting. This is a pre-trial conference. You've been charged with a serious crime, and we're prepared to prosecute your case at trial." He paused to let that sink in. "And we are confident we will prevail."

Quinn scowled. "Glen, please spare us the posturing. We're more than willing to stipulate that both parties are prepared to go to trial. If you have something to offer, we're prepared to listen."

Cooper frowned. "Okay. I guess I need to start with the bad news. We're prepared to amend the indictment for the additional charges of statutory rape and criminal racketeering under the state's RICO Act." He pulled out a document with a blue cover and pushed it across the table to Quinn.

Quinn showed no emotion as he read the document.

Cooper looked at Joey. His stare wasn't as penetrating as Quinn's, but it was close. "Mr. Blade, those are serious charges. Add them to the attempted murder of two police officers and you are looking at decades of imprisonment. Maybe life."

If Cooper was trying to scare him, he was doing a great job. Joey wanted to follow his attorney's instructions and not show any emotion, but it felt like all the blood had drained from his face.

Cooper turned his gaze back to Quinn. "I don't need to discuss all the details. You know how it works, Terry. I'll be taking these additional charges to the grand jury and we'll get an indictment." He paused. "But maybe we don't have to go down that road."

"We're listening," Quinn said. His tone was neutral. His face revealed nothing.

"Mr. Blade had a sexual relationship with a fifteen-year-old. That's rape. Consent, no consent, it doesn't matter. And the girl is pregnant, so paternity won't be hard to prove. But let's put that aside for the moment. Let's talk about Chico Torres."

Quinn stared at Cooper, giving Cooper no indication as

to whether he recognized the name. Cooper pulled out another folder from his briefcase and flipped through the pages and then began to read. "Chico Torres runs the Mexican na-tional gang, Vatos Locos Sinaloenses, which means, 'crazy guys from Sinaloa.' After a decade of gang warfare with the assimilated Chicano gang Mexican Brown Pride, Vatos Locos has consolidated its grip on the drug trade in the west, south, and north sides of the city. Lately they have been moving east into Paradise Valley and even Scottsdale. There were over three hundred and thirty incidents of gang violence in 1998, including over a dozen murders. Many of them can be linked directly to Vatos Locos."

Cooper stopped reading and stared around the table. Dutch and Callie were stone-faced, and Joey tried not to react, but his stomach was churning. Quinn merely shrugged, refusing to be Cooper's straight man.

The prosecutor put away his gang report. "Chico Torres is a bad man. We want to get him and his gang off our streets." He paused and stared at Joey. "We know you have a relationship with Torres."

He pulled out another folder and Joey could see it was full of photographs. He picked off the top one and placed it in front of Joey. It was a shot of Joey and Chico talking in the back of Graham's Central Station. From the angle of the shot, it must have been taken by one of the bartenders who Joey watched serving all those twenty-nine cent longnecks.

"Graham's is Chico's office. Where he meets his colleagues," Cooper said, spitting out the word. He reached across the table and tapped the photo with his index finger. "That's underage Joey Blade sitting next to a notorious gang leader. What were you talking about, Joey? The Super Bowl?"

Quinn put his hand on Joey's sleeve to remind him not to say anything. Joey didn't need any reminding.

Cooper slapped another photo down in front of Joey. "Lighting's not so good, but this is taken at Shady's, a coffee shop on Van Buren. Now you're talking with one of Torres's capos. Fernando Lopez. He's a major dealer. Discussing lattes, Joey?"

Joey thought capo seemed like a serious exaggeration. Fernando was more of a gofer. Cooper fanned through his folder and grabbed another photo. "Here you are with your buddy Fernando again. This is just a block from your house. Lopez had just come from Shadow Mountain High School. He was looking for new drug markets for Vatos Locos. Is that what he's talking to you about?"

Quinn picked up the photo and slid it back across the table to Cooper. "What do you want, Cooper?"

"I'm glad you asked. I hate it when I have to do all the talking. Let me tell you, I feel a little like Monty Hall today. I want to make you a deal, Joey. Three choices." He held up his fingers. "Go to trial. If you lose, you're going away for a long time." He uncurled his ring finger. "If you don't want to take a chance on a trial, I'm in a generous mood today. I'll knock the attempted murder down to felonious assault and we won't press for an indictment on the rape or the racketeering. You plead guilty on the assault and we'll recommend five to seven years. With good behavior you could be out in three to four years."

Joey's stomach convulsed and a flame of bile burned his throat. Four years in prison? He looked at Cooper, who seemed to be waiting for an answer. Despite Quinn's orders, he said, "That's only two choices."

"Very good, Joey. Glad you've been listening because this

is the grand prize." He unclenched his middle finger and held
the three fingers aloft. With his voice animated, he said, "I'll
give you a full walk. Drop all the charges. Even get your record
expunged. You can have your life back. Play football. Marry your
girlfriend. We just want you to help us nail Chico Torres. Get
him to admit he had Peanut killed." Joey must have appeared
confused because Cooper added, "Edward *Peanut* Grimes, the
older brother of your friend, TJ."

Quinn leaned forward over the desk and stared hard at
Cooper. "You spend fifteen minutes telling us what a vicious son
of a bitch Torres is, and now you want my client to put his life
at risk?" He paused. "And everyone in his family. Jesus, Cooper.
Great sales job."

Cooper continued to smile, but with less abandon than
earlier. "We can protect him. He won't have to wear a wire. He
can meet in a public place, like Graham's. We'll have people
listening."

"What if he's unsuccessful?"

"Oh, I think he'll succeed. Like those football coaches are so
fond of saying. 'Let's not plan for failure.'"

Joey wanted to ask what football coach ever said that, but
he knew better. It seemed like Monty Hall had just offered him
three shitty choices: prison, prison, or death. For him and his
family.

"That's it, Monty?" Quinn asked.

"That's all I got. I'll give you some time to talk it over. But
we need an answer today."

CHAPTER 27

Cooper, as part of his charm campaign, told the group that they could stay where they were and he would go back to his office while they discussed his proposal.

They all stayed seated at the table. Callie's jaw was set and her eyes burned with a fury Joey had rarely witnessed. The look on Dutch's face was the same as when Joey asked him about Chico Torres. That day Joey wasn't certain what he'd seen, but now it was clear—Dutch was scared. And more than any of Cooper's threats, that scared Joey.

Quinn dropped his poker face. He wasn't trying to hide what he was feeling. It was like he had dialed down the setting on his icy blue eyes and now his gaze was warm, empathetic. He actually felt compassion for Joey's plight. Three months ago, Joey had thought choosing Arizona over USC was the biggest decision of his life. Now he would have to make a decision that could cost him his freedom, and he would have to make it on his own.

Quinn leaned forward, scanning the table like he always did before he spoke. But his tone was less businesslike. He sounded like a friend, not a dispassionate lawyer. "Let me go through the options. I can strip out Cooper's exaggerations. Okay?" He looked at Joey, who nodded. "Option one is we take this to trial.

Cooper will get those added indictments—the grand jury will give him whatever he wants. I'm not too worried about the rape charge. I think we can convince any jury that this was not rape in any true sense. I'm more worried about the racketeering charge. Why did you meet with Torres?" He sounded almost sad or disappointed that Joey hadn't told him all the truth.

Joey stared down at his hands, clenching and unclenching his fists. Why hadn't he told Quinn? Or at least talked to Dutch? Maybe his feelings for Mallory were clouding his judgment. Or maybe it was just that after the New Year's Eve debacle, he didn't trust anyone. Whatever his reasons, he had made matters worse trying to go it all alone.

"I met Chico in the jail on New Year's Eve. Some of his gang were hassling me and he saved my ass because he knew Dutch. Later, I got the idea that he might be able to help me find TJ because they are both in the drug business."

Quinn bit down on his lower lip. "What did he tell you?"

Joey took in a deep breath and let it out. "He said he would take care of it." Saying it out loud, Joey knew it sounded bad. "I told him I didn't want anything to happen to TJ, and he told me not to worry. He said they did business with TJ's brother and they weren't going to hurt TJ. They made it sound like they would persuade TJ's brother to help them find TJ."

Quinn breathed deeply and looked up at the ceiling, processing what Joey told him. "Okay," he said. He didn't have to say that it made things look very bad for Joey. "We can mount a vigorous defense. Character witnesses, Mallory's testimony as to hearing Grimes confess to the shooting. I'll make Grimes testify, and we will make it clear he's a badass who carries a gun and so it couldn't have been high school hero Joey Blade who fired those shots. We'll go for reasonable doubt with a jury."

Joey studied his parents. There was a glimmer of hope in

Dutch's eyes, but he was always more of a dreamer than Callie. His mother wanted to believe Quinn, but Joey could tell she didn't.

"Option two is Cooper just playing games. Five to seven years is a scare tactic. If you plead, I think I can get him to take two or three years. With those cowboy cops and Cary Chang's meddling, and the feds hassling, I think he'll want to settle if he can't get you to go after Torres."

Three years. Prison instead of college.

Quinn cleared his throat. "Cooper's grand prize. Everything you could want. If you can just get Chico Torres to admit he had Peanut Grimes killed." He paused to clear his throat again. "You need to know that this gang is vicious. They kill without—"

"I want a trial," Joey said. "I'm not pleading to something I didn't do, and I'm not putting my family at risk. If the cops want Chico Torres, they can use their own men."

"Okay, Joey," Dutch whispered. His chin was trembling.

Callie buried her head in her hands and then stared at him, her eyes shiny. "No, Joey. Don't be hasty. Maybe they'll go for two years. I know that sounds bad, but it would be over before you know it and you can have a life. If you lose at trial . . ." Her voice broke and for the first time in Joey's memory his mom cried.

Dutch wrapped his arm around her. "It's okay, Callie."

Callie's sobs tore at Joey's resolve. But he had made his decision. He wanted to be free to be with Mallory and his new baby and he wasn't giving up years of his life for something he didn't do.

Quinn, who watched silently as the family grappled with Joey's decision, said, "I hear you, Joey. But how about letting me see if we can get a better number from Cooper. Maybe he'll go for something less than two years. I know you're the one who has to do the time, but two years or something less and you'll get your life back. If we lose at trial, you'll get serious time. Will you let me try?"

"Please, Joey," Callie said.

His mom was begging him. He couldn't say no. "Okay."

Quinn stood up quickly, like he was afraid Joey might change his mind. "You all stay here. I'll go talk to Cooper and see what we can do. Sit tight." He stuffed his yellow pad back into his briefcase and left.

Joey walked over to the window. Commuters heading for the expressway clogged Central Avenue. Everyone anxious to get home and get on with their life while Joey waited. Ever since that New Year's Eve it seemed like much of his life was spent waiting. Hard to believe so much had changed in less than ninety days. *Ninety days.* If he went to prison, ninety days would be just a drop in the bucket. Four years in jail would be fourteen hundred days. Even if Quinn got a deal and Cooper agreed to two years, that would be seven hundred days. Maddy would be over a year old. She wouldn't know him. He didn't dare think about what would happen if he got a longer sentence.

Dutch and Callie sat at the table, not talking. Waiting, like Joey. They were great parents. It killed Joey that he was putting them through this hell. They deserved better. When this was all over, he vowed to make it up to them.

An hour later, Quinn returned. He was back to his poker face, which Joey figured meant bad news. He didn't waste any time trying to soften the blow. "Cooper wouldn't go for two years. I tried to get him to go with thirty months, but the best he would offer was three years, and you have to accept it now. He actually thought you would go for the grand prize, so he wasn't very accommodating."

Callie got up from the table and sat down next to Joey. "Take the deal, Joey. Mallory can move in with us. We'll help her with the baby. I know it's not what you want, but three years and you will have your life back."

Joey had been convinced when he made his decision, but now his resolved wavered. "Dad?"

His father, who always knew his mind and was never reluctant to share it, was lost. He gazed at Joey with eyes that were so sad it broke Joey's heart. He opened his mouth to speak, but no words came out. Finally, he whispered brokenly, "I don't know, Joey. I don't know."

Joey had always counted on Dutch to tell him what to do. But his father couldn't help him now.

It's your decision, Joey. If you go to prison, you'll lose Mallory and your baby.

"I'm sorry, Mom. I can't take a deal. I don't want to go away for three years for something I didn't do. I want to be free, so let's play to win. Let's go to trial."

CHAPTER 28

After he left Quinn's office, Joey called Mallory to tell her about his decision to stand trial, but the operator refused to put his call through because he still wasn't on her approved caller list. He would have to wait for her to call, and if she didn't call tonight, he would drive over after school and try to talk to her during visiting hours.

He was confident Mallory would support his decision. She didn't want him sitting in prison for three or four or five years. Maddy might be in kindergarten before he got out. That was no good. And now there was an actual trial date they could plan for. Glen Cooper, miffed that Joey refused to take his "get out of jail free" offer, asked the court for an immediate trial. Quinn resisted, suggesting a fall date, and the court compromised, setting the trial to start on May 15.

Frustrated that he couldn't talk to Mallory, Joey started working on Quinn's first assignment: preparing a list of character witnesses. They had two months to get ready for the trial. That felt like an eternity to Joey, but Quinn insisted it was a very tight timetable and he would need Joey's full cooperation.

He also needed more money. Ten thousand dollars just to get to the starting line. More if the trial dragged on. The O.J. Simpson trial went on for over a year, but Quinn was confident this trial wouldn't take more than three to five days. Joey wondered how many Krugerrands Dutch had stored in that safety deposit box. He didn't even blink when Quinn asked for ten grand.

Quinn didn't want a long list of character witnesses. He wanted folks who would make a good impression on a jury. "We don't need more than three witnesses. Our goal is to sell Joey Blade, not put the jury to sleep listening to your second-grade teacher telling us how you cleaned the blackboards."

When Joey jokingly asked him what a blackboard was, Quinn actually smiled.

Joey quickly compiled his list: Mr. Coots, Coach Klein, and Lua. They were all strong personalities who oozed sincerity. They would make a great impression on the jury.

Joey had just finished writing mini-profiles on his choices when his cell phone rang. It was Mallory and she was crying.

"The district attorney has subpoenaed me! What's going on?"

"I tried to call you. The trial starts May 15. They've added new charges. Rape and racketeering."

Mallory's voice broke as she choked back a sob. "Rape? That's crazy! I swear I didn't tell that investigator anything about us, Joey."

"It's okay, Mallory. I'll tell Quinn about the subpoena. How are you feeling? The baby all right?"

"How can they charge you with racketeering?"

Joey didn't want to burden Mallory with all the bad news, but he didn't want her to hear it from someone else. "They think I'm working with Chico Torres. They offered to drop all the charges if I would help nail him."

"Oh my god! Don't do that, Joey." The fear in Mallory's voice was palpable.

"I told them no. That's why we're going to trial. Their other offer was for me to confess and they would recommend three to five years."

"Five years?" Mallory whispered.

The line went silent except for the sound of Mallory sniffling.

"Mal? Are you there?"

"Joey, can you loan me three hundred dollars?"

"Sure. I can bring it to you tomorrow."

"I have an aunt in Seattle. She said I could stay with her. If I'm up there they won't be able to keep asking me about you."

Joey didn't want to lose Mallory again, but at least this time he would know where she was. If she wasn't in town the DA couldn't keep hassling her. "I'll stop by tomorrow after school," he said.

"I have classes all afternoon. Put it in an envelope and leave it with the receptionist. She'll make sure I get it."

"When are you leaving? Can I see you before you go?"

"As soon as I have the money. It's better for you not to be seen with me right now."

"I want to say goodbye."

"It's not goodbye. Focus on the trial, Joey. You can't lose."

Confident or desperate? Joey couldn't tell. But he wouldn't lose and soon they would be together. Forever.

CHAPTER 29

Terry Quinn was wrong. The time did not pass quickly. For the last eight weeks, Joey imagined his trial a thousand, maybe ten thousand times. Mostly he saw himself standing before the jury with the foreman shouting, "Not Guilty," and everyone in the courtroom cheering, Mallory in the front row running to hug and kiss him, and the two of them walking out hand-in-hand. Joey didn't let himself imagine the other possibility.

Today would be his last meeting with Quinn before the trial started. His lawyer was sitting at his office table where they had all sat at the first meeting in January. He smiled warmly as Joey stepped into his office. That worried Joey. Quinn's smile, like his penetrating stare, was just one of his lawyer tools. He used it sparingly.

"Sit down, Joey. Let's get started."

"Why are you smiling?" Joey asked.

Quinn stopped smiling. "There've been some developments." He paused. "Complications, but nothing we can't handle."

"Mallory?" It must be something to do with Mallory. She left Agnes Calloway the day after Joey left the three hundred dollars for her with the receptionist. He didn't tell Quinn or anyone else about the money or that Mallory had an aunt in Seattle. The prosecution wanted to call her as a witness, but no one knew where she was. The district attorney interviewed Donny Stewart, but he claimed to have no idea where his daughter was.

"That's one of them. The DA's located her and she's back on their witness list. I think overall it's a plus for our side."

Joey felt a swarm of conflicting emotions. He was desperate to see Mallory but hated the thought she would have to testify at this trial. "How is it a plus?" he asked.

Quinn leaned forward, clasping his hands. "They'll put her on the stand and she'll testify that you and she had sex. I'll cross-examine her and make it clear it was consensual. I don't think any juror will want to convict you on the rape charge. I'm surprised they haven't thrown it out."

"Do they ever do that?"

"You bet. Happens all the time. They don't like to lose any more than we do. Here's the plus. Now that they've found Mallory, we can call her to testify that she heard TJ confess he was the one who shot at those cops. They'll try to discredit her testimony, but I don't think that will be effective. I can object that if they want to impeach her testimony, they'll need to produce TJ Grimes, who remains hidden away in some witness protection program."

"What's the other complication?"

"I don't know how this will affect us. The feds have charged Fernando Lopez with just about everything they can find: extortion, drug dealing, assault, murder."

"But not Chico Torres?"

Quinn shook his head. "Not yet. But it looks like they're getting close." He leaned back in his chair. "Let's get started." There were two piles of papers on his desk. He plucked the top three pages from one pile and pushed them across the table to Joey. "Here's the latest list of witnesses from the prosecution. As you can see, they've added Mallory."

There were over fifty names. The only names Joey recognized were Gordon Smith who was in lockup with him, the two cops who arrested him, and Officer Carnes, who had questioned him. A couple of the witnesses were simply listed as "undercover officer," their identity protected.

"That's a lot of people," Joey said, flipping through the pages, trying to imagine what each witness might have to say. "This will take a long time."

"They won't call them all." He pulled another sheet off his pile. "The trial will start at nine a.m. for the jury selection. I want you in my office by seven thirty. I'll have breakfast brought in. You can bring your folks. I'll give you complete instructions to take home for you and your folks. First thing is appearance. Your parents need to dress like the good, solid citizens they are. Nothing flashy or trashy. Your dad's sport coat is fine. Do you have a suit?"

"Not a suit, but I've got a blue blazer."

"No. That looks too preppy. Buy a new suit. Dark. Blue or black. Not brown. Black shoes. No boots. White shirt and dark tie. No fancy patterns."

"Okay."

"All right . . . demeanor. This is important. You pay attention and look at anyone who is talking. The judge, the DA, me, the witness. No facial expression. No shaking your head. Just look like you're looking at me now, taking it all in. I don't care if the witness is lying through his ass, you don't react. And make sure Dutch and Callie get that message. The first half of this trial is all the State's version of the story, so you just have to suck it up. We will get our turn."

"I can do that," Joey said.

"I know you can." Quinn grabbed the next page from his pile. "Jury selection. It's not like on television. The judge will bring in about fifty prospective jurors and he'll take fourteen at a time. He'll ask them a bunch of questions about job, marital status, kids. Could ask anything, it depends on the judge. If we don't like a juror we can challenge them. Judge keeps calling more jurors until we get twelve."

"Who do we want on the jury?"

"You'll be testifying so we want ladies. Mothers. You come across well. You're sincere and good looking. You don't look like a gangster. We might like some young athletes who will identify with you, and maybe some young women who will be attracted to you, but Glen Cooper is unlikely to let us keep either of those. We want to stay away from religious zealots who might want to punish you just for having sex."

"How long will that take?"

Quinn tilted his head from side to side, doing the mental arithmetic. "Jury selection will take all day. The trial will start on Tuesday with opening statements. Cooper will lay out the case as he sees it and then I'll have my say. The statements won't take long. After that they'll start calling their witnesses.

"They have three charges to prove. Attempted murder, statutory rape, and racketeering. I suspect they'll start with the joyride incident, as that's how this all began. Then they'll probably call Mallory. I'm guessing they'll finish with those undercover cops who were taking pictures of you at Graham's and Shady's. That's more or less their case."

"Can I see Mallory before she testifies?"

"No!" Quinn came halfway out of his chair. "Come on, Joey. You know you can't. She's a witness for the prosecution. If you talk to her that will look like witness tampering. Check that. It *is* witness tampering. You stay miles away from her. Do you hear me?"

"Yeah, I hear you." Joey knew Quinn would say no, but he had to ask.

Quinn settled back into his chair and tried his smile again. It didn't really work. "I'll be cross-examining all the witnesses and I'm confident I'll leave a few marks. Definitely score some points against those cowboy cops who started this mess."

"How long will their case take?"

Quinn tapped his pencil on the desk. "I think the prosecution will be finished on Wednesday and we'll start first thing on Thursday. We don't have a long list of witnesses, but they'll be effective, especially with Mallory added. We could be done in a day. I'll finish with you and they'll want to cross-examine you. After that, closing statements and then the jury gets to decide."

"So it could be done by Friday?"

Quinn chuckled. "Nothing goes as planned, Joey. Should be done early the week after."

"What are you going to ask me?"

"The same questions I've been asking you all along. I don't want to rehearse it. You tell the truth, simply, with as few words as possible. If I want longer answers, I'll ask another question. Trust me to see when you need to expand and when you've said enough. You're a sincere, credible person. I don't want you to sound rehearsed. Just be yourself, Joey. You'll be fine."

Joey wished he could feel as confident as Quinn sounded.

CHAPTER 30

The salesman at Dillard's convinced Joey to buy a complete package: suit, shirt, tie, and dress shoes. "You never get a second chance to make a first impression," he said. "Go for quality. You can wear a good suit for ten years if you lay off the beer." He winked and grabbed his gut. "Should have followed my own advice. I was a stud athlete just like you ten years ago."

Ten years. Where will you be in ten years, Joey? Married to Mallory? Working at Blade Engine and coaching Maddy's soccer team? Or . . . He wouldn't let himself think about what would happen to him and everyone he cared for if he lost. He couldn't lose. He selected a Calvin Klein navy blue suit, an Arrow white shirt, a burgundy silk tie, Florsheim black loafers, and black nylon socks that stretched over his calves. When he showed up in Quinn's office with Dutch and Callie for their pre-trial breakfast, Quinn beamed.

"Damn, Joey, you're better dressed than your lawyer."

Joey frowned, "I, uh—"

"Relax. You look great. Perfect. Better take off that coat and tie while we eat. No food stains allowed."

Joey grimaced. "It took me twenty minutes to tie that tie."

"Just loosen it and slip it over your head," Dutch said. "That's an old army trick."

The courtroom was freezing. "They crank up the a/c on jury selection day," Quinn said. "It's the only day when the courtroom's packed. All those prospective jurors generate a lot of heat."

Joey took a seat next to Quinn at the defense table on the right side of the small courtroom. The courtroom furnishings and paneling were champagne-colored, with the same Scandinavian-modern look as Quinn's office. Joey was cold, but his armpits were damp with sweat. The collar on his starchy shirt was choking him, the calf-length socks were itchy, and the shoes pinched his feet.

Quinn squeezed his neck. "Relax, Joey. The game is about to begin."

Dutch and Callie were the only visitors in the gallery and the officious deputy ordered them to the far corner away from the pews where the potential jurors would be seated. Inside the low railing that marked the space for the real players, the courtroom was empty except for Cooper and his assistant, the bailiff, the court stenographer, and a couple of bored deputies. One of the deputies opened the doors and a phalanx of jurors entered. Quinn told Joey there would be about sixty prospective jurors on the panel. They took seats in the gallery and as soon as they were all settled, the bailiff snapped to attention and said, "All rise. The Honorable Judge Thomas Squires, presiding."

Judge Squires reminded Joey of one of those TV judges. Jowly, with a ruddy face and a full head of white hair and what appeared to be a considerable belly under his robe.

"He was a cornerback for ASU about twenty years and a hundred pounds ago," Quinn whispered. "When he introduces you to the jurors, just nod at them respectfully."

Judge Squires leaned forward and peered at the jurors over his glasses. "Ladies and gentlemen, you have all been called to serve as jurors in the trial of Joseph Blade. He has been charged with attempted murder of a police officer, statutory rape, and a violation of Arizona's racketeering influenced corrupt organization statute."

Joey's face burned as the judge read the charges. He was thankful he wasn't facing the panel of jurors. The judge introduced the bailiff, the court clerk, the stenographer, and Glen Cooper and his assistant. Cooper turned and smiled at the jurors.

The judge said to the panel, nodding in Joey's direction, "And this is Mr. Blade and his attorney, Mr. Terrance Quinn." Joey nodded in what he hoped was a respectful and humble manner. His face felt like rubber.

After the introductions, the judge asked all the jurors to stand and be sworn to tell the truth as they were questioned. After the swearing in, which took less than a minute, he delivered what Quinn called "the pep talk." He lectured the jurors about the importance of serving on a jury. He told them it was a privilege and a responsibility for everyone living in a free society. He didn't want to hear any complaints about the inconvenience.

The jurors stared blankly at the judge. They didn't have any more idea what to expect than Joey. The judge shuffled all the juror questionnaires and picked fourteen. He called out their names and each juror called came up from the gallery to take a seat in the jury box.

Joey studied the prospective jurors who would decide his fate. In this first draw, there were eleven women and three men. The judge questioned each juror on a variety of things: occupation, marital status, spouse's occupation, kids, experience with the criminal justice system, as a defendant or a victim, etc. He wanted to know if anyone had served on a jury before. It took an hour to interview the first panel and then the jurors were given a ten-minute break while the attorneys made their challenges. Quinn rejected a Black woman who was a Jehovah's Witness and a no-nonsense insurance adjustor. Cooper challenged a Hispanic short-order cook. At the end of the day, they had gone through four sets and arrived at a jury. Four men and eight women. The men included a retired banker, a Black hospital orderly, a shoe salesman from Nordstrom's, and a Mexican waiter who worked at Red Lobster. Of the eight women, three were white housewives about Callie's age, a Black customer service rep for the phone company, a librarian, a Hispanic nurse, and a middle school music teacher. They seemed like fair people to Joey.

He was counting on that.

CHAPTER 31

Quinn warned Joey it would be a tough morning. The trial would begin with Cooper's opening statement to the jury. "Remember," Quinn said, "no reaction, no doodling, no whispering to me. No smiling. He is going to make you look like a serious badass, and you just have to sit there and take it. We'll get our chance."

The courtroom was nearly empty. Dutch and Callie were in the first row behind the defense table. There were less than a dozen visitors in the gallery. Dutch looked uncomfortable in his blue blazer and khaki Dockers that Callie bought for him last week when he discovered he could no longer fit in his other "dress" pants. Callie wore a simple blue dress, and her red hair was pulled back into a tight ponytail so she would look more like a concerned mother than a fading beauty queen.

Judge Squires wasted no time. After a short conference with Cooper and Quinn, he instructed the bailiff to bring in the jury. After a brief explanation as to what to expect, he asked Cooper to make his opening statement.

Cooper stood up and buttoned his suit jacket. It was stretched tight across his belly so he unbuttoned it again. "Your Honor, ladies and gentlemen of the jury," he said, nodding at the judge and then turning to face the jury. "Thank you for your time. As Judge Squires has explained, you have an important job to do.

It's a serious responsibility and your community is counting on you. My first job is to give you an overview of the case. Since the evidence will come in at different times from different witnesses, sometimes in a disjointed way, I want to explain how it all fits together, sort of like how we need the cover of a jigsaw puzzle box to help us put together the puzzle."

Cooper paused and pointed at Joey. "Joseph Blade has been charged with three serious offenses. Seeing him there all cleaned up with a nice suit, he doesn't look like a bad guy." He looked intently at the jury. "But appearances can be deceiving! Your job is to weigh the evidence in this case and make your decision not on appearances, not on testimonials from friends and family, not on sympathy or emotion, but strictly on the facts." He paused, his face tight with concern. "The facts!" he repeated. "The facts in this case are very clear. On the night of December 31, 1999, Joseph Blade participated in a raucous, alcohol- and drug-fueled party at Shadow Mountain High School that resulted in over twenty thousand dollars of damage to school property. As police arrived, Joseph Blade jumped into the back of one of the trucks that was leaving the scene of the crime.

"Moments later, as that vehicle was heading north on Highway 51, it was approached by two off-duty police officers. Joseph Blade fired three shots at those officers from a Smith & Wesson .38-caliber revolver, knocking out their windshield and causing their vehicle to skid off the road into a highway sign on the Squaw Peak Parkway. The two officers were fortunate to escape with their lives. We have the gun, and you will hear testimony from those officers."

Cooper looked directly at the jury.

"So, was this a case of a good kid doing something reckless under the influence of alcohol or drugs? A serious crime, but one where there might be some reason for leniency? Who is this Joey Blade? Football star? Golden boy? As the evidence will show, Joseph Blade is not the All-American boy that the defense will try to portray him as.

"First and foremost, Mr. Blade is not a boy. He's an adult who has been having a sexual relationship with a fifteen-year-old girl. In the state of Arizona, and most any other state, that is rape. Mr. Blade was a high school football celebrity. Someone younger kids looked up to. He used that reputation to take advantage of a girl who was not old enough to give consent.

"His conduct was reprehensible. A moral outrage for which he must be held accountable.

We shall present evidence that will, without any reasonable doubt, prove that Joseph Blade is guilty of this charge.

"Joseph Blade has also been charged with racketeering. What does that mean? In Arizona, if an individual is part of, or participates in, an illegal organization—one that is involved in activities such as homicide, robbery, kidnapping, forgery, theft, bribery, gambling, extortion, drug trafficking, money laundering, or prostitution—then that individual is in violation of Arizona's racketeering statute even if that individual is not directly involved in any of those activities.

"I'm sure you all read the papers. Gang violence in our city is out of control and getting worse. Police departments are under siege. These gangsters don't always have a string of tattoos or shaved heads. Sometimes they're disguised as a handsome, clean-cut young man. We will present evidence that will prove that Mr. All-American Joey Blade has in fact been working with the notorious Vatos Locos gang. In the last twelve months, members of Vatos Locos have been charged with seven murders, twenty-seven assaults, one hundred and forty-two drug trafficking offenses. Without question, the Vatos Locos gang is a criminal enterprise.

"It is my job to present the evidence. You, as jurors, must evaluate the evidence and not be swayed by appearances. Joseph Blade is not the innocent, clean-cut, boy-next-door you see sitting at that table. He is, in fact, a gunslinging, sexual predator who is part of a vicious criminal enterprise that is destroying our community. If you believe the evidence we present—and I am confident you will—then you must convict him. Thank you for being here today. Thank you for helping us bring justice to your community."

Joey sat at the defense table, his hands folded. *Don't react. Try to breathe normally. Don't act like a gunslinging sexual predator.* His stomach churned and he was afraid he might get sick. His mouth was dry, but he didn't dare pour himself a glass of water—his trembling hands might betray him.

Cooper remained standing, staring at the jury, milking the moment for as long as he could. Joey stared blankly at the jury box, unable to bring himself to make eye contact with any one juror. Finally, Cooper sat down and Quinn immediately stood up, like the two men were on a teeter-totter.

"Your Honor, ladies and gentlemen of the jury. My name is Terry Quinn and I am representing the defendant, Joey Blade." He patted Joey on the back. "I'm proud to be his attorney. He's a fine young man." Quinn paused and gave the jurors his blue-eyed stare, making eye contact with each juror so they would feel like he was talking directly at them and them alone. "Plain and simple, the district attorney's case is a house of cards. A flimsy house.

"On the evening of December 31, 1999, Joey Blade, along with dozens of other Shadow Mountain High School students, attended a bonfire to celebrate the millennium. After the bonfire, he planned to attend a party held at Lawrence Darville's home.

"The evidence will show that there were at least fifty students at the bonfire. It was a typical high school pep rally. Joey Blade didn't build the bonfire. You will hear from witnesses who will testify that Joey Blade was not drinking. He was not taking drugs. If he were doing any of those things, surely the prosecutors' investigators would have found at least one of those kids who could testify to that. The district attorney doesn't have any witnesses. Why? Because there was nothing to witness. No one will claim Joey Blade was drinking, doing drugs, or even throwing a log onto that fire. So the first leg of this flimsy case doesn't hold up.

"Now let's go to that alleged shooting. The evidence will show that Joey Blade was in the back of a pickup truck driven by Lawrence Darville, who was heading toward his home for the millennium party Joey Blade was also planning to attend. Seated next to Lawrence Darville was Wendy Chang. In the truck bed with Joey Blade was a sophomore named TJ Grimes. Grimes was a pot supplier who sold marijuana to Wendy Chang. He never sold to Joey. Joey is an athlete who doesn't use drugs. Wendy Chang was a witness to this shooting, but the prosecution will not be calling her as a witness. You might ask why the prosecution is not calling her as a witness. The evidence will show that the gun fired at those officers belonged to TJ Grimes, and Grimes was the shooter. Joey Blade tried to take the gun away from Grimes. Unfortunately, he wasn't successful. When the police stopped Darville's truck, Grimes escaped and the police have been unable to locate him."

"Mr. Cooper says you're not supposed to be swayed by appearances. That's a convenient argument when all the appearances in your case look so bad. Who are you going to believe? A drug dealer with a half-dozen arrests who had been drinking heavily at the bonfire, or an honor student with a clean record? A boy who had just earned a full scholarship to the University of Arizona? Mr. Cooper is asking you to believe that a sober, decent young man with no criminal record and a bright, bright future just decided to throw it all away for no reason. Joey Blade wasn't drinking. He wasn't 'drug fueled' as Mr. Cooper has suggested. But TJ Grimes was. Who are you going to believe?"

After a few moments of meaningful eye contact, Quinn continued. "Joey Blade is a popular student at Shadow Mountain High School. He didn't take advantage of anyone. He certainly didn't rape anyone. The prosecution case is not weak, it's nonexistent."

Quinn stared at Cooper. "Gangster? Racketeer?" He shook his head and his mouth twisted with contempt. "Really?" He took a couple of steps toward the jury. "The evidence will show that the police made a mistake. They let the shooter, TJ Grimes, get away and arrested the wrong man. As jurors, all you can do is find Joey Blade 'not guilty.' Unfortunately, that won't be enough. Where does Joey Blade go to have his reputation restored? Thank you."

Joey took a deep breath and slowly released it. He looked at the jurors but couldn't read their faces. He wished he had studied them after Cooper's statement so he could see if there was any change in their expression. All Joey knew for certain was that Quinn made them pay attention.

Quinn had done a good job. Joey wanted to thank him, but he remembered Quinn's caution. Joey reached for his glass of ice water. His hand was steady.

Judge Squires turned his attention back to Cooper. "Is the State ready to proceed?"

"Yes, Your Honor. We call patrolman Thomas Waldham."

Joey recognized Waldham, with his seventies-era bushy sideburns and beefy tattooed forearms, as the cowboy who hurled the can of piss at their vehicle. Even dressed in his uniform he looked more like a gnarly biker or a porn star than a cop. Quinn wasn't planning to bring up the piss can in his cross-examination because as shitty as it was, it also implied there was a motive for the shooting. The piss can was what set off Grimes. Cooper spent a few minutes getting Waldham to describe his history as a police officer. He'd been on the job for five years.

Cooper walked back to his table and glanced down at his notes. "Officer Waldham, can you tell us where you were at approximately nine p.m. on the evening of December 31, 1999?"

"I was on the Squaw Peak Parkway. Highway 51."

"Driving?"

"No sir. I was a passenger in a truck driven by Johnny Coyle."

"Mr. Coyle is also a police officer?"

"Yes sir."

"Were you on duty?"

"No sir. We stopped for a late dinner and were driving home."

"You were involved in an accident on the Squaw Peak?"

"Yes sir."

"Can you describe what happened?"

Waldham leaned forward in his chair and licked his lips. "Johnny started to pass this Toyota Tacoma. The driver swerved into the passing lane and cut him off. Johnny slowed down to avoid an accident and this kid in the back of the Tacoma fired a gun at us and blew out the windshield. We skidded off the highway and hit a sign."

"Who fired the gun?" Cooper asked, staring at the jury as he asked his question.

"The kid in the truck bed."

"Is he here in the courtroom today?"

Waldham pointed at Joey. "That's him. The defendant."

"Your Honor, may the record reflect that Officer Waldham has identified Joseph Blade?" Cooper asked.

"The record will so reflect," said Judge Squires.

"Thank you, Officer. No more questions at this time."

Quinn leaped to his feet. "Mr. Waldham. How fast were you driving when you were fired upon?"

"I wasn't driving."

"Oh yes. Your friend Johnny was driving. How fast was he driving?"

Waldham smirked. "I don't know."

"What's the speed limit on the Squaw Peak?"

"Fifty, I guess."

Quinn took a step back. "Really? My experience is that cars usually drive faster than that. Do you think Mr. Coyle was driving over the speed limit?"

"It's possible."

"So you were moving pretty fast, I guess. Were you drinking?"

Waldham sat back in his chair, looking suitably insulted. "No."

"Where were you coming from?"

"A diner. We stopped for supper."

"What's the name of the diner?"

"I don't remember."

Quinn picked up his yellow pad and flipped a few pages. "Let me refresh your memory. Could it have been Staley's Bar and Grill on Seventh Street?"

Waldham shrugged. "Possible. We eat there sometimes. Yeah, we did eat at Staley's."

"Did you have anything to drink?"

"Maybe a beer."

Quinn flipped a few more pages. "I talked with your waitress and she said—"

Cooper rose from his seat. "Objection. Hearsay!"

The judge nodded. "Sustained."

Quinn stared hard at Waldham. "Would it surprise you that the bill for your meal included eight beers and two shots of Royal Crown?"

"Objection."

"Move on, Mr. Quinn"

Quinn took a few steps closer to the witness. "Okay. You had something to drink before you and Officer Coyle got into his truck. Is that a fair statement?"

"I didn't have eight beers."

Cooper glared at Waldham, like he'd spoken out of turn, but he remained seated. He was frowning, which Joey thought must mean Quinn was doing okay.

"It was dark, you were in a speeding vehicle, you might have had a drink or two or three. Is it possible you could have been mistaken in your identification of the shooter?"

Waldham sat back, his arms folded, like he had just pulled Quinn over for a violation. "Someone points a gun at you, you remember that. We're trained to ID suspects."

"Right," Quinn said. "Because you are a law enforcement professional."

"Yes."

"Mr. Waldham. In the accident report you filed right after this incident, you described the shooter as a 'skinny, long-haired hippie.'"

Waldham unfolded his arms and licked his lips. "Okay," he said. He sounded wary. Not so certain anymore.

Quinn tilted his head to the side like he was confused by the answer. "Do you know a boy named TJ Grimes?"

Waldham frowned. "No."

Quinn stepped back and glanced at the jury. "Are you sure? Let me show you a photo of him."

"Objection," said Cooper. "Witness has answered the question. There is no relevance. The witness can't be asked about anything in a book not in evidence."

"Your honor, I will have Joey authenticate this Shadow Mountain Yearbook and Mr. Grime's photo when he testifies, but may I ask Mr. Waldham about the photo now, subject, of course, to tying it up later?"

Judge Squires paused, considering Quinn's proposal. "The photo may be shown but any testimony regarding the book is subject to being stricken if you fail subsequently to get the book admitted into evidence."

"Thank you, your honor."

One of Joey's tasks during the trial prep was to find a photo of TJ. He didn't think a kid with no legit activities would be in the yearbook, but there he was, leaning against the wall at a high school dance.

Quinn grabbed the yearbook and stepped over to the witness stand. "Do you recognize this boy leaning against the wall, Officer Waldham?"

"No."

"How would you describe him?"

"Objection," Cooper said, not bothering to get out of his chair.

"Get to the point, Mr. Quinn," the judge said.

"He has long scraggly hair. He's skinny. Sort of looks like a hippie, wouldn't you say?"

"Objection."

"Move on, Mr. Quinn," the judge said.

Quinn stepped back from the witness stand. "That's TJ

Grimes. Is it possible that he's the skinny hippie-looking guy who shot at you?"

"Objection."

"I withdraw the question." Quinn marched past the jury box, flashing the photo of TJ to the jury. "Joey, please stand up."

"Objection."

"I just want to tighten up the identification."

"Overruled."

Joey stood up, ramrod straight and stared at Quinn.

"Okay, Officer Waldham. Does Joey Blade look like a skinny, long-haired hippie?"

Waldham glowered at Quinn. "He's cleaned up his act."

Quinn rubbed his chin, acting perplexed. "He must weigh close to two hundred pounds. He doesn't look skinny to me. Do you think he's gained forty pounds?"

"Objection."

"Withdrawn. No further questions for this witness."

Cooper announced that his next witness would be Randy Parker, the DPS officer who escorted Joey to the Durango Jail. It was close to noon, so the judge called for a recess and asked everyone to be back at one p.m.

Quinn ordered sandwiches and they had lunch with Joey's parents in the room next to the courtroom that was designated for the defense team.

"How did you find out how much those guys had been drinking?" Joey asked. They hadn't discussed it during the trial preparation.

"I was bluffing. I know those guys were drinking. Nobody goes to Staley's for the food. Especially cops. I doubt he could remember what he drank. He fell for it. That's a lesson. When you testify, if they ask you a question, you always pause and give me a chance to object."

"Got it," Joey said. Quinn had told him that lesson at least a dozen times.

"Cooper's decided not to call Johnny Coyle, the driver," Quinn said. "Drunk driving cops is not the image he wants to project to the jury. He's moving on. Calling that rookie cop, Parker, who brought you to the jail I'm surprised he's leading with the rookie instead of the veteran."

o o o

DPS trooper Randy Parker appeared as nervous on the witness stand as he had when Joey first encountered him on New Year's Eve.

Cooper stood up and cleared his throat. "Officer Parker, you responded to an accident call on the evening of December 31, 1999?"

"Yes sir."

"Could you describe the incident?"

"We were looking for a dark blue Toyota Tacoma involved in a shooting incident on the Squaw Peak Parkway. We spotted the vehicle just before the canal. The man in the back of the truck tossed a gun out of the truck as they crossed over the canal."

"Okay. What happened next?"

"Luis, my partner, ordered them to stop the car. They pulled over. Luis talked to the driver while I secured the man in the back of the truck."

"Who was that man who tossed the gun?"

"It was Joseph Blade. The defendant."

"Was there anyone else in the back of the pickup?"

"No sir."

"You're sure of that?"

"Yes sir."

"After securing Mr. Blade, what did you do next?"

"While Luis questioned the driver of the Tacoma, I questioned the passenger. Wendy Chang."

"The driver was Lawrence Darville?"

"Yes sir."

"And what was Miss Chang's relationship to Darville."

"She said he was her boyfriend."

"When you questioned Mr. Blade, didn't he say he was Miss Chang's boyfriend?"

"Yes sir."

"But he was in the back of the truck?"

"Yeah. I think he was fantasizing."

"Objection." Quinn stood up and stared at Parker.

"Sustained," the judge said.

"Move to strike." Quinn returned to his seat, still drilling Parker with his eyes.

"The answer will be stricken and the jury is instructed to disregard the answer. Officer, you are to listen to the question and make your answer responsive," The judge said it as if he'd said the same thing a thousand times before.

"Okay. Did Miss Chang explain what Joey Blade was doing in the back of Mr. Darville's truck?"

"She said they'd all been at a bonfire and Mr. Blade hitched a ride with them."

"Was she aware that shots had been fired?"

"No sir. She was surprised. She said the radio was loud."

"Thank you. No further questions at this time."

Quinn flipped through his pad, shaking his head slowly.

"Mr. Quinn, do you have any questions for this witness?" the judge asked.

Quinn rose slowly. "Yes, Your Honor." He again stared at

Parker for an uncomfortably long time. "Did you ask Miss Chang if there was anyone else in the back of the truck with Joey Blade?"

Parker scrunched up his face, confused. "No. There wasn't anyone else in the truck."

Quinn took a step toward Parker. "Okay. The Tacoma pulled over to the side of the highway?"

"Yes."

"And your car stopped," he paused, "twenty yards behind them?"

"Yeah. About twenty."

"Okay. When you got out of the car, you must have diverted your eyes from the vehicle in order to open the door. Correct?"

Parker shrugged, still perplexed. "I guess that's possible."

Quinn pulled out a photograph from his stack of exhibits. "Your honor, Mr. Cooper and I have stipulated that this is a photo of Mr. Darville's truck, the truck he was driving that night. I move to admit it as Defendant's Exhibit 1."

"No objection."

"It may be admitted."

"Mr. Parker, showing you Exhibit 1, the truck Mr. Darville was driving has especially big wheels, correct?"

"Yeah, it's a high rider."

"When you're sitting in your vehicle you can't see into the bed of the Tacoma, can you?"

"I guess not."

"Someone could have been in the bed of the Tacoma and when you turned to open your door they could have slipped out of the truck and escaped, undetected. Isn't that correct?"

"Objection. The witness can't testify as to what he didn't see."

"Overruled."

"I don't think so," said Parker. "Where would he go?"

Quinn ignored the question. "The gun recovered was a .38?"

"Yes sir."

"Same kind of firearm you carry?"

"Yes sir."

"Have you practiced firing your weapon?"

"Of course. We shoot at the range every month."

"Good. At the range do you wear sound protection?"

"Yes sir. It's required."

"I imagine a .38 caliber police special is pretty loud."

"Yes sir."

"But you can't hear it when you wear those sound muffs, right?"

"Oh no. You can still hear it plenty."

Quinn stopped and rubbed his chin, acting surprised. "Are you able to explain to the jury how come Wendy Chang did not hear the gunshots as she claims?"

"I don't know. You'd have to ask her."

"I'd love to. Do you know where she is?"

"Objection. Irrelevant."

"It's not irrelevant since the officer just told me I need to ask her why she didn't hear a gunshot fired just feet from her ears."

"Overruled."

"So, Officer, where is she?"

"Um, Switzerland."

"How long has she been in Switzerland?"

"A few months."

"So she left for Switzerland immediately after the shooting?"

"I guess so."

"You guess so? It is true, isn't it, that you know that her father sent her off to school in Switzerland just three days after she was at the scene of the shooting?"

"Okay."

"Okay? Is that your way of saying yes?"

"Yeah."

"And the father who sent her off to Switzerland, that would be Cary Chang?"

"Yes."

"You told me that I should ask Wendy Chang whether she heard gunshots, so let me ask you, did you ask her about hearing gunshots?"

"No."

"You didn't ask her because she was shipped out of the country, right?"

"Yeah."

"And you also couldn't ask her whether TJ Grimes was in the back of Lawrence Darville's truck, correct?"

"We didn't even hear about TJ Grimes until Mr. Blade told us about him."

"So you never asked her about TJ Grimes, either at the scene or in your investigation, right?"

"Yeah, we couldn't."

"Well, you could have before she was driven away from the scene, correct?"

"Yeah."

"And I could ask her about TJ Grimes and about who shot the gun were she not in Switzerland instead of here in this courtroom, couldn't I?"

"Yeah."

"I could ask her whether, in fact, it was Wendy Chang who told Joey Blade to throw away the gun?"

"Okay, yeah."

"But, Officer, neither you nor I can ask her anything the jury might like to know about what happened on the highway that night because you didn't ask her then and she fled to Switzerland just days later, right?"

"I guess."

"Sir, neither I, Mr. Cooper, the judge nor the jury needs your guesses, so let me ask you again. Neither you nor your partner, either at the scene or later, asked Wendy Chang the questions you now say I should ask her. So none of us know what she would testify about the shooting. Don't guess, just tell me if what I said is accurate."

Parker's cheeks were rosy, like he'd been slapped. "Yes," he said, staring down at the floor.

"I'm sorry, I couldn't hear you, Officer," Quinn said, even though he must have heard him.

Parker took a deep breath and looked up at Quinn. "Yes sir," he said.

Quinn shook his head dismissively "No more questions of this witness, Your Honor."

"Redirect, Mr. Cooper?" the judge asked.

Cooper shook his head. "No redirect, Your Honor."

The judge turned to Parker. "Witness is excused."

Parker, still flushed, stood up and nearly stumbled as he stepped down from the witness stand. He walked quickly out of the courtroom, his head down like he didn't want to look at anyone.

Cooper entered the gun into evidence after having it identified by the cop who recovered it from the canal. He called Detective Carnes who testified that Joey admitted to him that he tossed the gun out of the pickup truck. In his cross-examination Quinn asked Carnes if Joey told him TJ Grimes was the shooter and Carnes acknowledged he had.

At the end of the day, they reconvened in the defense room.

"We had a good day," Quinn said. "We want the jury to have questions the prosecution can't answer. Questions lead to reasonable doubt. The jurors have to be wondering what the deal is with TJ Grimes. Where is he? Where's Wendy Chang? Or Darville? Why isn't the prosecution calling them?"

"What will happen tomorrow?" Callie asked.

"I'm not sure. The strongest part of their case is the gang association, so I think they will go with that last. If I'm right, they will be calling Mallory to the stand tomorrow. But she's a wild card for them so I don't know what Cooper will do."

Joey hadn't seen Mallory in weeks. He desperately wanted to talk to her before she testified but he knew better than to ask.

"Where is she?" Joey asked.

"Nobody knows," Quinn said. He looked pointedly at Joey, choosing not to remind him that he couldn't talk to her.

"Cooper must know where she is," Dutch said. "I hope she's not back in that house with Donny."

Quinn held up his hand to quell debate. "She's not at home, but we don't know where she is. Cooper said she contacted his office last week and said she would testify. She wouldn't talk to them in advance so they don't know what she will say. If she were to deny that there was any relationship with Joey, they can compel a paternity test on the baby, which will, in their mind, prove their statutory case."

"Can they do that without her permission?" Joey asked.

"They won't need to unless she doesn't tell the truth. If she testifies as to your relationship, they've made their legal case, but I don't think the jury will be persuaded. And then we get to call her to testify about TJ's confession. So, all in all, I think her testifying is a good thing."

CHAPTER 32

L ast night Joey couldn't sleep. He kept thinking about Mallory—desperate to see her, but not up in the witness stand. She was the prosecution's witness, Quinn had said, so Cooper wouldn't be hard on her, unless she didn't cooperate. If she didn't cooperate, he could treat her as a hostile witness. Joey wasn't exactly certain what a hostile witness was, but he was pretty certain Mallory wouldn't cooperate. Quinn thought she would be the first witness called, but Cooper surprised them by announcing a new witness—Donny Stewart—whom he planned to call as his first witness of the day. Quinn objected and the judge had the jury taken out while Quinn and Cooper argued about the issue. Quinn's main objection was that they didn't have any time to prepare for Stewart and he had nothing to do with this case. Finally, after Quinn and Cooper exhausted their arguments, the judge ruled that Stewart could testify and the jury was brought back in.

Stewart was wearing jeans and a Blade Engine polo shirt, untucked. His complexion was pasty, like he'd spent the last two months indoors. Joey wondered if he was wearing the Blade polo to make a point, or if it was simply the best shirt he owned. Cooper questioned him about his work history. After establishing that Stewart had worked at Blade Engine for over ten years, Cooper zeroed in on the reason Stewart was testifying.

"On Saturday, February nineteenth of this year, were you working at Blade Engine?"

"Yeah. I was heading up the mechanics in the install center."

"While at work that day, did you have an altercation with the defendant?"

Stewart smirked. "Kid sucker punched me. It was a cheap shot."

"What was the reason for this encounter with Mr. Blade?"

"He got my daughter pregnant. I wanted him to do the right thing by her."

"Objection," Quinn said, half rising from his chair. "Lacks foundation. And I renew my objection to this witness. His testimony has no purpose."

"Overruled."

Cooper turned his attention back to Stewart. "When did you learn your daughter was pregnant?"

"A few days before. She told me."

Joey stared down at the table so the jury couldn't see his face. There was no way Mallory would have told her father. Stewart was lying.

Cooper took a few steps closer to Stewart and leaned in as if he wasn't sure he had heard him correctly. "Your daughter told you she was pregnant?"

"Yeah."

"Were you made aware of who the father was?"

Stewart's mouth twisted into a frown. "Everybody knew. I told her to stay away from Joey Blade. But she's only fifteen. She don't listen to her old man."

"Objection."

"Sustained. Jury will disregard Mr. Stewart's comment about what he thinks everyone knew."

"No further questions, Your Honor."

Quinn tapped his eraser on the table as he stared at Stewart. Stewart swallowed hard, and sweat beaded his forehead. "Just to be clear, Mr. Stewart, your daughter did not say, 'Joey Blade is the father of the baby.' Is that correct?"

"Everyone knew—"

"Just yes or no, Mr. Stewart. Did your daughter tell you that Joey Blade got her pregnant?"

"No."

Quinn pulled a folder from the stack of documents on the table. "Mr. Stewart, on May fifth of last year, your daughter was detained by Tempe Police when they raided a fraternity party at ASU. Is that correct?"

"Yeah, they called me. I picked her up."

Joey stared at Quinn, but his lawyer wouldn't look at him.

"According to the report, it was, and I quote, 'a drunken orgy with underage girls.' The police wanted to pursue a case against the frat boys, but none of the girls would file a complaint. Do you recall that?"

"I don't remember nothing about any complaint. Had to spend six hours down there with a bunch of social workers buzzing around. Cost me a day's pay."

Quinn nodded almost sympathetically. "And then two months later, on July twelfth, your daughter was picked up by Scottsdale police when they answered a complaint of a group playing naked water volleyball. The police report notes there were six men and two underage girls. They issued a citation to the homeowner and detained the two underage girls. Do you recall that incident?"

"Yeah, I picked her up," Stewart said. He folded his arms, disgusted.

Quinn started to pick out another folder and Joey clapped his hand down on top of the pile. Quinn stepped back from the pile like he hadn't intended to reach for another case. "No further questions of this witness, your honor," he said and sat down. He thumped his eraser on the pad, trying to conceal his anger.

They broke for lunch and Joey hustled back to their conference room, not waiting for Dutch or Callie. "Why do you have to trash Mallory?" Joey said as soon as Quinn stepped through the door.

Quinn held up his hand for silence as he held the door for Joey's parents.

"Don't ever mess with my cross-exam, Joey," Quinn said. His cheeks were flushed.

"You made her sound like a whore. Why didn't you go after Donny? He's fucking lying about everything."

Callie walked over and put her arm around Joey. "You have to calm down."

Quinn took a deep breath and composed himself. "I know he's lying. But attacking him doesn't help us. You hitting him because he wanted Mallory to get an abortion just makes you look guilty."

"Why do you have to make her look bad?"

"Come on, Joey. Reasonable doubt. Stewart admitted she didn't tell him you were the father, so maybe it was one of those party guys. It doesn't help us with the law, but it helps us with the jury. If the jury thinks you're not the guy who got her pregnant, and if they think she's sexually active, then the likelihood that they'll convict you of statutory rape goes down."

Dutch picked up the tray of sandwiches. "Try the roast beef. It's really lean."

Joey waved him off. "Not hungry."

Dutch stood behind him and squeezed his neck. "You gotta eat, Joey. This is a fifteen-round fight. You need to stay strong."

He plucked a sandwich from the tray and set it on a plate next to Joey. "How about a Coke?"

Joey shook his head. "I'll stick with water." He was too upset to eat, but he knew the only way to get Dutch to back away was to take the sandwich. He took a bite, but his mouth was so dry he almost choked on it.

Quinn pushed away from the table. "I don't know what will happen this afternoon. Neither does Cooper really. Mallory hasn't allowed him to talk to her in advance, so he's flying blind. That's usually dangerous, but in this case, I don't think it can hurt him. We'll just have to see how it goes."

○ ○ ○

Everyone but Judge Squires was back in their seats by 1:30. Joey sat next to Quinn, neither of them talking. Joey's mouth was dry and there was a knot in his stomach, like he had swallowed that shitty roast beef sandwich whole.

Quinn broke the silence. "I'll be extra nice to Mallory in my cross. But remember, you have to stay focused. No emotional disturbances or reactions. Got it?"

"Yeah," Joey said. He felt angry, but not at Quinn. He didn't know what he was angry about. Maybe at the world that judged Mallory without knowing her?

Finally, the judge emerged from his chambers and took his seat. The bailiff called them all to order and Cooper said, "Prosecution calls Mallory Stewart."

The courtroom doors opened and Mallory walked up the aisle. Joey wanted to turn and look at her but he was afraid he wouldn't be able to control his emotions. As she passed, he realized he was holding his breath. Mallory was wearing a navy-blue tent dress and a large blue cardigan. Her short blonde hair was not so short any more. It was dull, like she'd been washing it with soap, and her complexion was sallow. She looked sick, but she was probably just nervous about having to testify. Who wouldn't be?

After she was sworn in, Cooper stood up. "My name is Glen Cooper. I am an assistant District Attorney for Maricopa County."

Mallory stared at him, her expression blank.

"Are you the daughter of Donald Stewart?"

"Yes," she said. Her voice was soft, barely audible.

"How old are you, Mallory?" Cooper asked. He used his friendly tone, like he was talking with a child.

"Sixteen."

"When did you turn sixteen?"

"April 17th."

Joey grimaced. He had forgotten her birthday.

"So you just turned sixteen last month, correct?"

"Yes."

"Do you know the defendant, Joseph Blade?" Cooper was halfway between his table and the witness stand. He pointed at Joey. Joey tried to keep his expression blank, but his whole body was churning with emotions and he was certain it showed in his expression.

"Yes," Mallory said.

"What is your relationship with Mr. Blade?" Cooper asked.

"He's a friend." Mallory's voice was low, almost a whisper.

"I'm sorry, but could you speak up, please?" the judge asked. "The jury needs to hear your answers."

"He's my friend," Mallory said, louder this time.

Cooper's mouth twisted sourly. "He's more than a friend, isn't he?"

Mallory stared at him, not answering.

"Objection, Your Honor. Asked and answered," Quinn said.

"Sustained."

"Isn't it true that Joseph Blade has had sexual relations with you?" Cooper continued.

Mallory stared hard at Cooper. Killing him with her eyes. "No," she said.

Joey held his breath. *Don't do this, Mallory.*

Cooper seemed frozen in his tracks. "Miss Stewart, I need to remind you that you are under oath. Do you realize that a paternity test will reveal the identity of the father of the child?"

"I'm not pregnant," Mallory said.

Joey gasped. *What is she talking about?* Mallory was all wrapped up in a bulky cardigan, but there was no baby belly evident.

Cooper, flustered and confused, stalled for time. "One moment, Your Honor." He almost ran back to his table and started flipping through files. "Isn't it true, Miss Stewart, that on February twentieth you were admitted to the Agnes Calloway School for unwed mothers?"

"Yes."

"Do you recall being interviewed by a social services counselor at the school on March sixth?"

"Yes."

"The counselor asked you who the father of your child was, and according to her report you answered all of her questions. Her report is confidential, but we can have it unsealed if we have to prosecute you for perjury. So, I'll ask you again. Is Joseph Blade the man who got you pregnant?"

Mallory stared at Cooper and she no longer looked pale or sick. "I had an abortion. It was my father who got me pregnant."

"Holy shit," Quinn whispered.

Joey felt sick to his stomach. *An abortion? Her father? No.*

That couldn't be true. She's making up that story to protect me. Or to take down her father. Or both.

Cooper's jaw dropped as he stared at Mallory. He didn't even try to hide his surprise. "No further questions," he said. He walked back to his seat, shaking his head.

Quinn stood up. "Your Honor, I move that the charges of statutory rape be dismissed. The prosecution has proven that Joey Blade is not guilty."

"Mr. Cooper? Any rebuttal?" the judge asked.

Cooper stared down at the table as if he was weighing the pros and cons. "No objection, Your Honor."

"Okay, charges of statutory rape are dismissed. Miss Stewart, you're dismissed."

Mallory stepped down from the witness stand. As she walked past Joey, their eyes met, but he couldn't read her. She seemed a different person.

Judge Squires appeared almost as drained as Cooper. He ran his hand through his thick mane of white hair. "I think that's enough for today. Let's reconvene tomorrow morning at nine."

CHAPTER 33

Joey sat slumped at the table, across from Quinn in the defense room, his hands clasped like he was praying.

Why Mallory? Why did you do it? I know you made up that story to try and save me. But I didn't want that. That was our baby.

His parents had driven on home, but Quinn wanted to meet with Joey. More bullshit strategy and tactics to discuss. Joey was sick of it.

"Joey, are you listening to me?" Quinn seated across from him, was saying something about Mallory. He wasn't going to be able to use her as a witness.

Joey clasped and unclasped his hands. He continued to stare down at the table. "Why can't you use Mallory as a witness?" he said, his voice weak and broken.

Quinn reached across the table and took hold of Joey's hands. "Listen, son. I know what you just heard was a shock. I'm sorry. Sorry that happened to Mallory. Sorry they had to put her through that. Sorry there are people like her father in this world. But now we need to regroup. I need you to focus, okay?"

Joey took a deep breath. Quinn's I'm-your-friend look was almost convincing. "That wasn't her father's baby," Joey said, his voice breaking. "It was mine. She made that up to protect me."

Quinn sighed. "Okay. You know better than me. But that's my point. She lied on the witness stand. If not about the father of the baby, she lied when she said you didn't have a relationship. She's perjured herself. I can't put her on the stand as a witness to TJ's admission and then have Cooper cross-examine her and allow her to perjure herself again. As an officer of the court I can't do that. She succeeded in getting the rape charge dropped, but now she can't help us on the attempted murder of those cops. And that's the heavyweight charge here."

Joey was tired. He felt physically crushed. It was hard to breathe, harder to talk. Or even think about talking. He'd lost the baby he never got to know. He'd lost the girl he would love forever. And now he would probably lose his freedom. Right now, he didn't care about that. Or anything else. He tried to speak, but he didn't even know what he was supposed to say.

Quinn sat down in the chair next to Joey. He put his arm around him. "You're a good man, Joey. You didn't deserve this. Any of it. What Mallory did there on the stand, that took real guts. I believe you. She did that because she loves you and you deserve that love. I will do everything in my power to help you."

If Quinn had just called him an asshole or told him to suck it up, he might have been able to keep it together. But his kindness, which Joey knew was from the heart, not part of his lawyer bag-of-tricks, broke him. He started to sob and he couldn't stop. It was like when he had the wind knocked out of him—his lungs convulsed trying to suck in air and he made awful whooping sounds as he buried his head unashamedly in Quinn's shoulder. Finally, he stopped and let go of Quinn. He wiped his eyes with the back of his hands and sat back in his chair. He actually felt better.

"Sorry," he said.

"Nothing to be sorry for, Joey. It's been a long day. Get your coat and I'll drive you home. One more day of defense and then we get the ball."

CHAPTER 34

Quinn called late in the evening and told Joey he would like to meet with Joey and his parents tomorrow at his office. He said Everett Blainey would also be there. He didn't say why Blainey would be there or what the purpose of the meeting was and Joey was too tired to ask.

The next morning while Joey was tying his tie, he could hear his parents talking softly in the kitchen. That was unusual. Both of them normally spoke loud enough to be heard over heavy machinery. Five minutes later when he walked into the kitchen they had stopped talking altogether.

"Why do you think Everett's coming today?" Joey asked.

His mom looked sideways at Dutch, but Dutch acted like he didn't hear Joey. "I can't believe Clinton's letting Janet Reno send that kid back." He thumped the paper and showed it to Joey. "Look at the poor kid."

The boy, Elian Gonzales, had been rescued from the Atlantic Ocean last month when his mom and twelve others tried to escape from Cuba. His mother drowned. Elian was the only survivor and his father, who had not been part of the escape, sued the U. S. government to return his son to him in Cuba.

Dutch had ignored Joey's question because he was so incensed about Elian Gonzales? *No way. Something isn't right.* "Do you know, Mom?" Joey asked again.

Callie looked unsettled. "No," she said. "Let's get moving so we can beat the traffic."

o o o

When Joey and his parents arrived at Quinn's office and saw Everett Blainey sitting at the table, Joey knew something was up. Blainey had handled Blade Engine's legal matters for over a decade. Quinn's greeting was forced. "Welcome, Blades. I brought in coffee. Black, black, and black. As far as coffee ordering, you're the easiest clients ever."

They settled down around the table. Blainey sat next to Dutch and Callie on one side and Joey took his usual spot opposite Quinn.

Quinn handed Joey's parents a legal form. Blainey said, "This is an engagement letter making Terry your attorney of record. I want both of you to sign it. This way, anything we discuss in here is protected by attorney-client privilege."

Callie pulled out her reading glasses and read the one-page document. Dutch picked up a ballpoint and signed it without reading it. He didn't act surprised by the request. Callie signed her copy and pushed it across the table to Quinn.

Quinn countersigned the document. "There's been a development in the case." He scanned the table. "As you know, the feds arrested Fernando Lopez. Cooper told me that Lopez is being offered full immunity to testify against the Vatos Locos gang, including Chico Torres."

Joey glanced at his parents. Dutch's jaw was set and his eyes narrowed when Quinn mentioned Chico's name. Callie looked grim, stone-faced. Her poker face was as good as Quinn's.

"They have Lopez stashed away in one of their safe houses. Their plan is for Lopez to testify to the grand jury in secret and then they'll round up the gang. They expect to grab all the bigshots."

"How does this affect my case?" Joey asked. He had an uneasy feeling that everyone knew more about what was happening than he did.

"They don't want to pin their whole case on Lopez. They're willing to offer you full immunity if you will testify for the grand jury, corroborating what Lopez will be telling them about the Peanut Grimes hit."

Joey winced. "I didn't ask them to kill TJ's brother. I didn't even know the guy."

Quinn waved off his protest. "You had a conversation with Chico. You can testify as to that conversation, and Lopez will testify as to what happened to Grimes after you talked to Chico."

"They will drop all the charges against Joey?" Callie asked. "All of them?" She didn't believe him.

"It's not the feds' case, but the DA will drop the charges without prejudice. Meaning, if you were to renege on the deal, they could refile. But if you don't, they'll drop the charges for good and you can get on with your life."

"But is it dangerous for Joey to testify?" Callie asked, looking from Dutch to Blainey to Quinn.

"Most of the bad actors will be locked away," Quinn said. "Joey's not ratting out anyone. He's just testifying about a conversation. The feds are being overly cautious—they want belt and suspenders and the DA is willing to do them a favor because their case is falling apart."

There were no smiling faces at the table. Dutch and Callie were both stone-faced, and Everett Blainey looked like someone had kicked him in the balls.

"What's the catch?" Joey asked.

Quinn gave a sideways glance toward Blainey. "If they give you immunity, you have to tell the truth about everything. If you lie or cover up and they catch you, you lose your immunity and those charges against you will be refiled."

"I won't lie."

"Right. The problem is they'll almost certainly ask you about Blade Engine's connection to the Vatos Locos gang."

"What?" Joey said. He looked at his father. "The turbochargers?"

Dutch started to say something, but Blainey put his hand on Dutch's sleeve. "It's a little more involved than that," said.

Callie's face was ashen. "Chico Torres controls Encore Supply, Joey."

Encore was Blade's major core supplier. Blade bought at least a hundred thousand dollars of engine cores from Encore every month. Encore's prices were ten percent lower than the competition.

"I don't get it," Joey said.

Dutch sat like a statue, staring down at his hands. Callie leaned forward, her hands pressed into the table. "We didn't want you involved in this. In any way. Chico uses his drug money to buy cores and then he sells them to us."

"Money laundering?" Joey asked.

Blainey held up his hand as if to stop the discussion. "That's an assumption the Feds might make."

Dutch leaned forward, his fists clenched. "We paid good money for those cores. They gave us a fair price. It's not our business how they buy the cores."

Blainey looked at Dutch liked they'd had this discussion before. "That's the position we would take, but it is not a strong hand. President Clinton is in his last year and his justice department is loaded with hotshots looking to make their mark before the party's over. Money laundering with a notorious gang is a headline and those federal prosecutors love that publicity. So does Janet Reno."

"Janet Reno." Dutch waved his hand dismissively. "She's too busy shipping little kids to Cuba."

"What are the risks, Everett?" Callie asked.

"You could lose the company. You could both go to jail. I'm not trying to be alarmist. You're the finance person, Callie. You're as much at risk as Dutch."

"What if they don't ask about Encore?" Dutch asked.

"Well that's the win-win," Quinn said. "Joey gets his life back and you keep the company. And your freedom. But that's a big unknown."

"But if I don't take the deal and we win our trial," Joey said, "then we don't have to worry about losing the company. They've already dropped one of the charges."

"That's true," Blainey said.

Quinn shook his head. "You can never predict what a jury will do."

His parents worked their whole lives to build Blade Engine. If Joey could help save the company and keep his parents out of jail, then Mallory would have sacrificed their baby for something more than just Joey's freedom. Something truly worthwhile.

"It's too big a risk, Joey," Callie said. She stared at her husband. "Tell him to take the deal, Dutch. He shouldn't have to pay for our mistakes."

Dutch took a deep breath. "You're right," he said. "You shouldn't have to pay the price either, Callie. I'm sorry." He had a heartbreaking smile as he said to Joey, "I love you, son. And I'm proud of you. You're standup. But I made a bad choice and that's on me. You need to take the deal."

Joey had a lump in his throat and for a moment he couldn't

speak. He breathed slowly and then pushed himself back from the table and stood up. He had lost his reputation. His football scholarship. The girl he thought he loved and the baby he knew he would have loved with all his heart. Now because of him, his parents could lose their company. They could go to jail. He couldn't let that happen.

Joey glanced at the yellow pad Quinn had furnished him. He hadn't made any notes. "My parents aren't going to jail," he said softly. He stared at his attorney. "No deal. Let's win this thing."

CHAPTER 35

Quinn told Joey that Cooper had been super-pissed that Joey again rejected his offer. "I think he'd already marked this one up in the win column," Quinn said as they headed down the long corridor to their courtroom.

"But if I'd taken his deal, they would have dismissed the charges."

"The case would be cleared and he'd get major points with the Feds. That would have been a win for him," he said. "Looks like our character witnesses are here."

Lua, Coach Klein, and Mr. Coots were all seated on a bench outside the courtroom. Mr. Coots was finishing one of his stories. ". . . apparently you don't know my wife," he said and then slapped his knee as the other two men groaned. Mr. Coots was about to start another story when he spotted Quinn and Joey.

Quinn shook hands with Mr. Coots. "Keeping everyone loose, eh Danny?" he said. He flashed the group his lawyer smile. "You men ready?"

"When will we be called, Mr. Quinn?" Lua asked.

Quinn scratched the back of his neck. "Prosecution should wrap up their case at some point today. My plan is to call Coach

Klein first. We'll talk about Joey's decency, his accomplishments. Just be yourself."

"You mean bossy?" Lua said, winking.

"Exactly," Quinn said. "And then I'll have Danny talk about Joey's academic side. How he related to the other kids in school, not just the jocks and superstars."

"I can do that for sure," Mr. Coots said.

"Don't tell those awful jokes, Mr. Coots," Joey said.

"Ha! I've got some real zingers for the jury."

Quinn turned his attention to Lua. "You'll be up last. I'll ask you about the bonfire, how Joey saved TJ from the flames, how TJ was a jerk, and how you saw them ride off in the back of that Toyota Tacoma. Then I'll want you to talk about the conversation you had with Joey the next day. The DA will cross-examine you, but that won't be a problem for you. Just tell him what happened."

"We really have to stay out here?" Lua asked. "We can't watch the trial?"

"Sorry, bud. That's the rules," Quinn said. "Hope you have a good book to read. Today will be a lot of sitting."

Cooper called the undercover cop who was the coffee barista at Shady's the day Joey came looking for Fernando. Quinn didn't question her. Next up was Darlene, one of the blonde escorts from Graham's. She was dressed in a prim white blouse and black skirt. She looked like a teacher, which in fact she was —second grade at one of the primary schools in the city. Joey figured she was probably a really fun teacher. Again, Quinn declined to question her.

At the break, Quinn explained, "None of these contacts hurt us. I want to spend as little time as possible on them."

Cooper's final witness was the bartender from Graham's who took the photos of Joey sitting next to Chico Torres. He testified that when Joey sat down next to Chico, all the other folks who were sitting with Chico got up and left. He estimated they were seated together for ten minutes.

Quinn did have questions for the undercover bartender. "Did you hear their conversation?" he asked.

"No. I was twenty feet away and it's pretty loud in there."

Quinn picked up the photo of Joey and Chico and studied it. Both men appeared to be staring off into space. "Did you even see these men actually talking to each other?"

The bartender paused and thought about what he should say. "I don't remember. I was busy filling drink orders. I think they were talking to each other."

"But you don't really know?"

"That's correct."

"No further questions, Your Honor."

As Quinn was headed back to his seat, Cooper stood up. "Your Honor, we have one more witness to call. Because of special circumstances, he was just added to our list."

Quinn's face hardened. He was pissed, but he couldn't show it. "Objection, Your Honor. We haven't had an opportunity to prepare for another witness."

"Counsels, approach." The judge beckoned Cooper and Quinn to step up to the bench.

For ten minutes, the two lawyers argued in slightly hushed voices. Finally, the judge called a recess for lunch and to reconvene in an hour.

"No spectators or press will be allowed in the courtroom for the afternoon session to protect the identity of the witness. Defense will begin tomorrow morning."

While Joey and his folks made their way back to the defense room for lunch, Quinn went out in the hallway and told Lua,

Coach Klein and Mr. Coots that they wouldn't be needed until tomorrow.

"Tuna and chicken salad today," Dutch said. "What do you want, Joey?"

Joey had lost his appetite. He had that ominous feeling another shoe was about to drop. *A last-minute surprise witness? This has to be bad news.*

Quinn walked briskly into the room and grabbed a tuna sandwich and a bottle of ice tea. "They're planning to call Fernando Lopez. Feds have loaned him to Cooper."

"Will that hurt us," Callie asked.

"I don't know," Quinn said. "He'll be able to add narrative to those photos. All depends on what he says. Anything more I need to know about your contacts with Fernando?"

Joey shook his head. "You have the full story." He was pretty sure he'd told Quinn about all his meetings with Fernando.

"Okay, then," Quinn said. "I'll do my best to discredit Mr. Lopez in my cross."

o o o

The courtroom was eerily quiet without the murmur from the spectators and press. When Cooper called for Fernando, he was brought into the courtroom from a room in the back, surrounded by dark-suited men who scanned the court room like Secret Service agents. Fernando was wearing a garish purple, polyester suit. He looked like a pimp, and acted like the men guarding him were part of his entourage. He was still missing his front teeth, which always made it hard for Joey to take him seriously.

After establishing that Lopez worked for Chico Torres as his "executive assistant" for the last five years, Cooper began his questioning. "When did you first encounter Joseph Blade?" he asked.

"Jail."

"Was that the Durango County Jail on New Year's Eve?"

"Yeah. It was crazy in there."

"How did you meet Mr. Blade?"

"I was admiring some dude's cufflinks and Blade took them away from me."

"What happened then?"

"I was about to straighten him out when Chico Torres told me to lay off. Said Blade was family."

"Chico Torres, the head of the Vatos Locos gang?"

"Yep. El grand *jefe*."

"When did you next encounter Mr. Blade?"

"A couple weeks later at Shady's."

"The coffee shop on Van Buren. Is that correct?"

"Yeah. He comes in all secret agent-like and tells me he wants a sit-down with Chico. Won't talk to no one else."

"Did he say why?"

"Nah. He thought he was too important to parley with me."

"Was a meeting arranged?"

"Yeah, Chico told me to have Blade meet him at Graham's."

"Graham's Central Station on Indian School. Is that correct?"

Fernando smirked. "Yeah. Redneck cowboy bar. Chico thought it was the perfect place to do business."

"Did they have that meeting, to your knowledge?"

"Yeah. Later that day."

"Do you know why Mr. Blade wanted to meet with Mr. Torres?"

"Chico said he wanted our help to find some high school homie," Fernando said, grinning. "Turns out the dude's brother was Peanut Grimes."

"Were you able to find the person Mr. Blade was looking for?"

"Nah. But we found out Peanut was cheating us."

"What happened to Peanut?"

"He's dead."

"Isn't it true that Peanut Grimes was murdered?"

Fernando shrugged. "Dude stole from Chico Torres."

"So Mr. Blade's inquiry—"

"Objection. Counsel is attempting to testify."

"I haven't asked my question yet," Cooper said.

"Sustained. Save your recap for your closing arguments," Judge Squires said.

"No further questions, Your Honor."

Quinn stood up and quickly stepped over to the witness stand, standing directly in front of Fernando.

"Objection, your honor. I can't see my witness."

"Step back, Mr. Quinn," the judge said.

Quinn took a small step back. "Mr. Lopez, you have been granted immunity by the district attorney, is that correct?"

"Yeah."

"You are aware that if you lie your immunity can be revoked."

"I ain't lying, holmes."

"Have you ever been arrested for taking sexual liberties with a boy?"

"Objection!" Cooper jumped to his feet. "Irrelevant!"

"Where are you going, Mr. Quinn?" the judge asked, his brow furrowed.

"Prisons are particularly difficult for gay—"

"I ain't no fag," Fernando yelled, jumping out of his chair.

"Mr. Lopez! Sit down and remain silent," Judge Squires said with enough authority that Fernando actually sat down.

Quinn continued. "My point is, Your Honor, that Mr. Lopez is facing serious jail time, so he is highly motivated to seek an offer of immunity, which makes his testimony unreliable."

The judge wrinkled his nose. "Sustained. Move on, Mr. Quinn."

"Your Honor, since we just learned this afternoon that Mr. Lopez would be a witness, we need time to prepare. Could we adjourn for the day to allow us more time to develop our cross-examination? We don't want to waste the court's time."

The judge, disgruntled, stared at Quinn. "Thank you for your consideration, Counselor."

It didn't sound to Joey like he really meant it.

"We'll adjourn and resume at nine tomorrow morning. I expect the defense to be ready to present their case as soon as you are done with Mr. Lopez."

"Thank you, Your Honor."

o o o

"Fernando's gay?" Joey asked as he walked with Quinn to his car.

Quinn laughed. "Queer as a three-dollar bill."

"Oh," Joey said. "And that made him unreliable?" He didn't understand.

"Look. I don't care if he likes men, women, or animals. But the jury might. They might give his testimony less credence, especially if they think he's a pedophile."

"Is he?"

"Doesn't matter. We got the message to the jury. Not sure I have anything more I want to ask him."

Joey took off his suit coat and slung it over his shoulder. Summer had arrived. His white shirt was damp with sweat.

Quinn sniffed. "We're about the same size. I'll bring you a fresh shirt tomorrow. Want you looking good for our defense. That shirt's starting to walk on its own."

"Thanks, boss," Joey said. "Will it be over tomorrow?"

"Yeah. Everything but the waiting."

CHAPTER 36

When Joey walked into the kitchen for breakfast, Dutch was standing at the kitchen counter talking on the phone, his face lined with concern. "He just came down. You can tell him yourself." He handed the phone to Joey. "It's Quinn."

Joey took the phone and stretched the cord so he could reach the orange juice in the refrigerator. "Hi, Mr. Quinn. Do you have my shirt?" he asked.

"Someone blew up the safe house where Fernando was staying. Picture's on the front page of the Republic."

The pitcher of orange juice almost slipped from Joey's hand. His hands were shaking as he closed the refrigerator and picked up the newspaper from the table. The headline read, "DEA Agents, Gang Leader Killed in Mesa House Explosion." The photo below the headline showed the smoldering ruins of what had been a ranch house at 8452 Coyote Drive in Mesa. In the driveway there was a burned-out red sports car that could have been a Corvair. "Holy shit. Fernando?" he whispered.

"Yeah. And the two agents who were protecting him. It happened about ten last night. Just in time to make the morning edition, I'm afraid. I'm asking for a mistrial."

Joey sank into the kitchen chair.

That whole week for nothing?

"Why?" Joey said. He immediately felt bad that that was his first reaction. People had died.

"First, because I didn't get a chance to finish cross-examining Lopez."

"I didn't think you had any more questions to ask him."

"The court doesn't know that," Quinn said. He sounded annoyed that Joey was questioning him. "It's grounds for a mistrial."

"What happens then?"

"They can decide to re-try you, or maybe they'll pass. They've already lost one count."

"I don't want to have to go through this again," Joey said.

"The other problem is that this kind of thing is highly prejudicial. Jury sees that the witness who testified against you gets blown away—that could make them look at you differently."

"They're not supposed to be reading the papers."

"It's pretty hard to miss a front-page photo in the *Republic*. Trust me, at least one of them has seen it, and that's all it takes. I'll meet you in the defense room at eight thirty. I've got to prepare my motion now."

Joey sat at the kitchen table and stared at the carnage on the front page.

First Peanut, now Fernando and those two agents. All dead because of me.

CHAPTER 37

T he mood in the courthouse was subdued. Everyone knew about the bombing. The jury was kept in the jury room while Quinn presented his motion for a mistrial. Cooper, who looked devastated, was opposed, but he seemed distracted. He wanted the case to be over too. The feds had done him a favor, loaning him Fernando for this trial, and he had to believe that exposure got Fernando and those agents killed.

When the two attorneys finished making their arguments, Judge Squires leaned back in his chair, took off his bifocals, and cleaned them on the sleeve of his robe. He sighed wearily. "I don't believe this tragedy will have a prejudicial effect on the jury. Chances are they know nothing about it, and if they do, they will have no reason to connect it to this case. Motion denied. Bring in the jury."

When the jury returned, the judge explained the situation. "Yesterday, defense counsel was in the process of cross-examining Mr. Fernando Lopez. Unfortunately, Mr. Lopez is no longer available. Since the defense counsel can't cross-examine this witness, I am excluding Mr. Lopez's testimony. The jury must not consider Mr. Lopez's testimony when they deliberate this case. For your purposes it never happened. Mr. Cooper, call your next witness."

"Prosecution rests, Your Honor."

Joey thought about the impossibility of trying to forget something you just heard. Being told to forget something made it more memorable, not less.

"Mr. Quinn, are you ready to proceed?"

"Yes, Your Honor. Defense calls Fred Klein."

It only took ninety minutes for Quinn to present Joey's three character witnesses. Coach Klein was solid with his just-the-facts approach. Mr. Coots was heartfelt as he expounded on Joey's relationship with other students. Lua described TJ Grimes as a skinny, scraggly-haired freak who sold him a dime bag of pot at the bonfire. He told how TJ sprayed the bonfire with lighter fluid and managed to catch himself on fire. And he vividly described how Joey chased down TJ Grimes and saved his life. Most importantly, he told the jury that he saw Joey and TJ ride off in the back of Lawrence Darville's Toyota Tacoma. Cooper tried to make it appear that Lua might be some kind of a pothead, but Lua remained respectful and steadfast. He didn't let Cooper bait him, and it looked like the jury believed him.

Now it was Joey's turn. Quinn smiled confidently and adjusted his tie. "Defense calls Joseph Blade."

It took forty-five minutes for Quinn to walk Joey through the events of December 31, 1999. With the rape charge dismissed and Mallory no longer a witness, Joey didn't have to testify about meeting her on New Year's Eve. He told the court about meeting Wendy at the bonfire, how TJ and Lua went off to buy pot, how TJ ran screaming, on fire, through the parking lot. He told how he tackled him and put out the fire and then how the bonfire got out of control and he, at Wendy's request, jumped into the back of Darville's pickup. He described how he discovered TJ's gun, and how he tried to stop TJ from firing at the men in the Silverado. He told them how TJ escaped when Darville stopped his truck on the highway. And that was it. Quinn didn't ask him any questions about Chico Torres. Or Fernando.

"No further questions, Your Honor."

As Quinn returned to his seat, Cooper stood up, buttoning his jacket. "Mr. Blade, you testified that Mr. Tupola was smoking pot, is that correct?"

"Yes sir."

"Were you smoking with your friend?"

"No sir."

"You testified that Wendy Chang was smoking pot, is that correct?"

"Yes sir."

"But you weren't smoking with her?"

"No sir."

"You testified that TJ Grimes was drinking Southern Comfort. Is that correct?"

"Yes sir."

"Were you drinking along with Mr. Grimes?"

"No sir."

"So let me be sure I have this correct. You are at this wild party with all your friends who are smoking and drinking, but you, Joey Blade, are not partaking. Is that your position, Mr. Blade?" Cooper looked at the jury, his mouth twisting as though Joey's answers were preposterous.

"Yes sir."

"You have testified that after you saved Mr. Grimes. . ." Cooper put a special emphasis on "saved" as though he didn't truly believe that Joey had saved TJ. ". . . you and he jumped into the back of Mr. Darville's Toyota Tacoma. Is that correct?"

"Yes sir."

Cooper rubbed his chin and pretended to be puzzled. "But

didn't you tell the arresting officer that Wendy Chang was your girlfriend?"

"Yes sir."

"So why were you relegated to bed of the pickup? There was room for you in the cab. Why weren't you sitting up there with the girl you claim is your girlfriend?"

"Wendy wanted me to keep an eye on TJ."

"Ah yes, the mysterious TJ Grimes." Cooper glanced down at his notes. "Do you like to show off, Mr. Blade?"

"Objection. Relevance, Your Honor."

"Sustained."

"Yesterday we heard from Miss Darlene Crosby who testified that she was with you at Graham's Central Station."

"Do you recall her testimony?"

"Yes sir."

"Miss Crosby said that you were being hassled by someone in one of those bell ringer games. Do you recall her saying that?"

"I wasn't being hassled."

"Okay. Isn't it true that you challenged another man to see who was stronger at that game?"

Joey looked over at Quinn. That wasn't really what had happened but Quinn had told him to avoid arguing with the questioner. Now Quinn waved his hand as if to say it didn't matter. "Yes," Joey said.

"Were you showing off for the young woman, Mr. Blade?"

"Again, objection, Your Honor. Relevance."

"Sustained."

"Isn't it true, Mr. Blade, that when you discovered Mr. Grimes's gun, you decided to show your quote unquote girlfriend, who had you riding in the back of her real boyfriend's pickup truck, that you were a tough, macho guy? And that's why you fired at those police officers."

"Objection."

Joey wanted to say that was ridiculous, but he followed Quinn's orders and kept his mouth shut while Quinn objected.

"Sustained."

Cooper chuckled like he said something funny. "All right. You know a man named Chico Torres?"

"Yes sir."

"Where did you first meet Mr. Torres?"

"At the Durango County Jail on New Year's Eve."

"That would have been after they arrested you for shooting at those police officers, correct?"

"Objection."

"Withdrawn." Cooper glanced down at his notes. "Did you subsequently meet with Mr. Torres at Graham's Central Station on the night of January 29, 2000?"

"Yes sir."

"What was the reason for meeting with Mr. Torres?"

"I thought he might be able to help me find TJ Grimes."

"Why did you think that?"

"Because TJ sold drugs, and I heard that Chico Torres had a lot of drug connections."

"You heard that he had a lot of drug connections? Had you heard that he was the head of the Vatos Locos gang?"

"Yes."

"Did you know that in the last year members of the Vatos Locos gang were charged with seven homicides, twenty-seven criminal assaults, and one hundred and forty-two drug trafficking violations?

"Objection, counsel is testifying."

The judge sustained the objection but it didn't matter. Cooper was testifying and Joey didn't have to answer. The jury was being reminded that Joey Blade was hanging out with Chico Torres, and Chico Torres was a bad man. Cooper picked up a paper from his table, nodding like there was something exceptionally interesting on the document. He glanced at the gallery and then directed his gaze back to Joey.

"Are you familiar with Encore Core Supply."

"Objection. May we approach, Your Honor?" Quinn had told Joey that if Cooper brought up Encore, he would try to persuade the judge that it was clearly irrelevant but highly prejudicial.

Judge Squires gestured to the two counsels. "Approach."

Joey couldn't hear what they were saying. It was a short discussion with no dramatics. Quinn didn't want the jury to hear about Encore, but if he made a big deal about it and lost his objection, that would be a signal to the jury that this was important.

The attorneys returned to their table and the judge said, "Overruled." He turned to Joey. "You may answer the question."

"I am familiar with the company."

"Isn't it correct that Encore Core Supply sells auto parts to Blade Engine, a corporation owned by your family?"

"They sell engine cores."

Cooper stared at Joey and then picked up another sheaf of papers. He fanned through the pages. "Isn't it correct that they also sell used parts, like carburetors and turbochargers?"

"I don't know."

"Are you familiar with the term 'chop shop'?"

"Yes."

"Is it your understanding that a chop shop is a place that takes stolen cars and tears them down and then sells those parts?"

"I'm not sure. It sounds right."

"Isn't it true that Encore Auto Parts is owned by—"

"Objection," Quinn said loudly as he stood.

"—Chico Torres, the same man—"

"Your Honor, Counsel is testifying!"

"—who met with Joey Blade on the evening of January twenty-ninth of this year."

"Sustained. Move on, Counsel."

Again, Cooper didn't need Joey to answer the question. He had made his point. Now he took a few steps toward Joey. "Did Mr. Torres mention that TJ Grimes had a brother who worked for Mr. Torres?"

"Yes."

"Was that brother Edward Grimes? Also known as Peanut?"

"I don't know. I think so."

"Were you aware that Edward Grimes's body was found in the Salt River on February twenty-third of this year, twenty-five days after you met with Mr. Torres?"

"Objection."

"Sustained."

Cooper stared at Joey, his arms folded. His smile was sly, smug. "No further questions, Your Honor."

Joey walked back to the defense table, trying his best to not look defeated, but that was how he felt. Cooper had landed punch after punch and Joey was defenseless. When he sat down, Quinn whispered in his ear, "You did great. Just nod your head and keep looking sincere."

Judge Squires called a recess for lunch. He told the jury to stay in the jury room and their lunch would be provided. Closing statements would commence after lunch.

Quinn had ordered a pizza from the cafeteria.

"This crust tastes like cardboard," Dutch said. He pushed the plate away. "Can't eat pizza without a beer." Dutch had been uncharacteristically silent ever since they learned about the bombing.

"It's not that bad," Callie said, taking a second slice. "Are they sequestering the jury?"

"No. They only do that for high-profile cases like O.J.'s. Too expensive and inconvenient for the jurors."

"Do they know who did the bombing?" Joey asked.

"It's either Vatos Locos or someone who wants us to think it's them," Quinn said.

"A rival gang?" Joey asked.

"Or the cartel. It's an effective message. A warning and a demonstration that no one can be protected." He frowned at the pizza. He hadn't touched his slice. "Okay. Here's what will happen this afternoon. Cooper will reprise his opening statement, but now he has to omit all the comments about Joey being a sexual predator. He can't use Fernando's testimony, so all he really has is the testimony of those drunk cowboy cops and a bunch of photos with Joey and Chico Torres. When's he finished, I'll make my statement. I'll keep it short and sweet. The judge will give his instructions to the jury and then we can all go home and wait."

Go home and wait. That was all Joey had been doing for the last six months. Maybe there would be a decision tomorrow, but Joey didn't believe it would ever be over, no matter what the jury decided. Everything had changed.

○ ○ ○

The courtroom was empty when they returned after lunch. Joey shivered. The a/c was working overtime. Cooper's assistants entered. One was lugging an easel and the other a stack of poster boards. Jocy didn't want to think about what was on those posters.

Cooper strolled confidently down the aisle as the bailiff brought in the jury. The judge was announced and this time there were no motions or discussions. It was game on. The judge told Cooper to proceed with his closing arguments. Cooper had the photos of Joey blown up to poster-size and arrayed on easels in front of the jury. He had a lot of statistics about what an evil force Vatos Locos was. He described the situation in the valley as a war between vicious drug lords and brave police officers like the ones who were shot at while defending the community. He described Joey Blade as "a wolf disguised in an Armani suit." Cooper was passionate. The jury listened raptly but stone-faced. Joey couldn't read them.

Quinn remained seated while Cooper's assistant removed his array of photos and exhibits. Quinn was wearing his "closing suit"—a navy blue pinstripe and his lucky tie, a dark green speckled with the Notre Dame logo. As they cleared away the last exhibit—an easel with the photo of Joey seated next to Chico Torres—Joey could feel his heart racing like it always did in the moments before the kickoff.

He closed his eyes and thought about Mallory. After this was all over—if he was free—what would happen to them? He loved Mallory and he had believed that she would grow to love him, but without the baby to tie them together maybe that would never happen.

Quinn stood in front of the jury. Tall, straight, shoulders back like a soldier. "Your Honor, ladies and gentlemen of the jury. It's been a long week. I thank you for your service and attention. The judge will soon give you instructions. He will tell you that you can find Joey Blade guilty or not guilty of those charges. As I said in my opening statement, not guilty is not good enough."

Quinn patted Joey on the back. "Joey Blade is innocent. Not just 'not guilty.' He is totally one hundred percent innocent of all of these charges. He's a victim. You all heard the testimony of Lua Tupola. Joey Blade is a hero. A student who wasn't even a friend of his was in peril. TJ Grimes was on fire. In a panic, Grimes ran, and Joey Blade, without any thought to his own safety, pursued the boy and managed to catch him and extinguish the flames.

"Mr. Tupola has testified as to what Joey Blade told him the very next day. TJ Grimes, angry at someone in a pickup truck who tossed a can of urine at them, took out his handgun and fired at the vehicle. Joey Blade disarmed TJ and kept him from taking any more shots. If not for his heroics those men might have been killed.

"And then, as the police ordered the Toyota Tacoma to pull over, TJ Grimes escaped into the night. It was TJ Grimes who shot at the off-duty police officers driving home after an evening of heavy drinking. One of those officers described the shooter as a skinny hippie. Joey Blade is six foot two and two hundred pounds. You have heard Mr. Tupola describe TJ Grimes—he is no more than five foot eight and weighs less than one hundred forty pounds." Quinn stopped and pointed at Joey. "That's Joey Blade, and this is TJ Grimes." He held up the yearbook photo of Grimes. Which one of those guys looks like a 'skinny hippie'?

"Joey Blade had just signed a letter of intent to play football for the University of Arizona. He had a bright, bright future. He has a stellar academic record. No arrests. He's never even been to detention. There was no possible reason why he would fire a gun at random strangers.

Quinn walked back to the desk and took a sip of his ice water.

"Because the arresting officers didn't do their job. Because they allowed the actual shooter to escape, Joey spent a terrifying night in jail.

"There has been absolutely no evidence presented that Joey Blade belongs to a criminal gang. Joey Blade has never been part of any gang. Not ever. It is ludicrous to even consider that a possibility. This is clearly and simply a game of guilt by association. Not everyone who Chico Torres says hello to is a member of his gang. To use the state's RICO clause to trump up a charge against Joey Blade is unconscionable.

"Joey Blade is innocent." Quinn paused and stared at the jury. "Let me say it again: innocent! We can't protect our community by destroying the reputations of good people. Joey Blade is a good man. End his nightmare. Find him innocent of all charges. Thank you."

Joey's face burned. It felt like everyone was staring at him and they probably were. The judge took an hour to give the jury their instructions, and by the time he finished it was nearly five o'clock so the jury was sent home. His last instruction was that they were not to talk to anyone about the case and not to read any newspapers or watch any news on television. They were to return to the courthouse on Saturday morning to begin their deliberations.

"How long will it take the jury to decide?" Joey asked Quinn as he, Dutch, and Callie crossed Central Avenue toward the parking lot.

"It's a simple case. Not much evidence or testimony to consider. I think we'll have a verdict tomorrow. I'll call your mobile phone as soon as I hear anything."

After all the days and weeks of waiting, Joey couldn't quite make himself believe that this nightmare would finally be over. One more day.

CHAPTER 38

At 5 a.m. Joey was awakened by the buzzing of his mobile phone. It was charging on his desk and Joey jumped from his bed and almost face-planted as he ran to his desk to get the phone. It was Mallory.

"Joey. Can we talk?"

"Sure. Where are you?"

"Can you meet me at Roadrunner Park in thirty minutes?"

"You're not back home, are you?" he asked.

"No. Thirty minutes. Okay?"

She hung up before he could reply.

Joey put on shorts, a T-shirt, and his Nikes so he could run over to the park. It was only ten minutes away if he ran at a decent pace. The temperature was already into the eighties and the sun was still just below the horizon. It felt comfortable running. That was the danger of dry heat. Your body didn't notice the heat like it did when there was humidity. Sweat quickly evaporated, making the body feel cool. But stay out there too long and the dry heat would kill you before you knew what hit you.

Mallory was sitting in the same swing as she had been in last November when this all started. She was wearing another Dixie Chicks tee-shirt, which reminded Joey of the concert that he had given her tickets for. Maybe they'd be able to go.

Mallory smiled sadly as Joey approached. She still looked drained. Beaten. He wanted to take her in his arms and tell her it was okay. But he wasn't sure it was okay. For either of them.

"Hi, Joey. Thanks for meeting me."

Joey stood in front of her swing. There was a lump in his throat. He didn't know what to say.

Mallory stood up. They were face to face less than a foot apart. She studied his face. "I'm sorry about the baby, Joey. It was yours. I lied about my father. He's a creep, but he never touched me."

"I'm sorry you had to go through all that because of me."

"They have to let you go."

"My attorney says we should know today."

Mallory took a deep breath. "I'm leaving, Joey. I'm going to live with my aunt. She drove me down here so I could testify. She lives in Seattle. I can start over. No bad reputation. No nothing."

Joey couldn't look at her. His legs were trembling. "What about us?" he said, his voice hoarse.

Mallory shook her head. "We're star-crossed, Joey. It was always going to be a struggle, and now with what I did to our baby, we would never make it. You need a fresh start too."

Joey took a deep breath. He stared at Mallory and it hurt. In his chest. His heart. He knew she was right, but that just made it hurt more. He closed his eyes. "I will always love you, Mallory."

Mallory wrapped her arms around him and buried her face in his chest. She sobbed softly. "Be free, Joey Blade."

CHAPTER 39

I t was the longest day of Joey's life. He seldom got any calls on his mobile phone—nobody other than Quinn, Mallory and Lua knew the number. But the house phone seemed to ring every twenty minutes. Insurance salesmen, charities, opinion pollsters. Finally, Quinn called late in the afternoon. "They have a verdict. Meet me at the courthouse at six. You don't have to wear the suit again. Just be casual and comfortable."

The courthouse was nearly deserted and their footsteps echoed through the empty corridor as they made their way to the courtroom. Joey joined Quinn at the defense table. His folks and Everett Blainey were the only people in the gallery. Cooper arrived a few minutes after them. The two lawyers whispered to each other. Joey couldn't hear what they were talking about.

His palms were sweaty and his mouth was dry. He poured a glass of water from the pitcher. It was tepid, left over from the day before. Judge Squires entered. Joey could see that he was wearing tennis shoes under his robe. Probably shorts, too.

The bailiff brought in the jury. Joey watched them. It was supposed to be a good sign if they looked at him. Some of them did and some didn't. He couldn't tell what their looks meant.

"Madam Foreman, have you reached a verdict?"

The jury had chosen the Black customer service rep from the phone company as their leader. "We have, Your Honor."

"Please hand the verdict forms to the bailiff for the reading of the verdict."

The bailiff took the paper from the forewoman.

"Will the defendant please rise?"

Joey and Quinn stood up. Quinn squeezed the back of Joey's neck.

"Bailiff, please read the verdict."

"In the matter of the State of Arizona versus Joseph Blade on the charge of attempted murder of a police officer, we the jury find the defendant not guilty."

Joey exhaled slowly. It felt like a nail had been pulled from his chest.

The bailiff flipped to the next page. "In the matter of the State of Arizona versus Joseph Blade on a violation of Arizona statute, A.R.S. 13-2301, the racketeering influenced and corrupt organization statute, we the jury find the defendant guilty."

Joey closed his eyes. Quinn was saying something to him. The judge was thanking the jury for their service and behind him he could hear Callie sobbing and Dutch moaning. Holding on to each other.

Joey's nightmare was finally over. His long night was just beginning.

PART 2

Joseph

CHAPTER 40

Seventeen years later...

Joseph had built his cabin on a platform with an overhanging flat roof lined with solar panels. The solar cells generated enough electricity for the refrigerator-freezer, water pump, coffee maker, and a couple of lamps. That was all he needed—he had a wood-burning stove and oven, but he didn't cook much and it never got that cold. With a cup of coffee in one hand and his logbooks tucked under his arm, he dragged his rocking chair around the corner of the porch to the east side of the cabin to catch the morning sun. He had spent the last two hours birdwatching at the west end of Sutter Lake. It was cool in the mountains, low fifties, but the sun warmed him enough that he was comfortable rocking on the porch in his work jeans, flannel shirt, and insulated vest. Lua would be arriving soon.

He flipped open his Books Read log and on page 33, line 45, he wrote: *"Light in August* / Faulkner / pregnant girl trying to find father of her child." He rated it four stars and then changed the four to a five. He couldn't give Faulkner less than five stars. This was the seventeenth Faulkner novel he'd read this year and there was something about it that troubled him. But still it deserved five stars.

He picked up his Bird log and noted: "Vermilion flycatcher / west end of Sutter's Lake / 11-20-17 / dawn." He flipped back through the pages. He hadn't spotted a flycatcher since last February.

In the distance, Joseph could see a cloud of dust rising over the steep mountain road that led to his cabin. He heard the faint whine of a truck engine downshifting. Moments later Lua pulled up to the cabin in a white Ford dually with **TUPOLA LUXURY HOMES** painted on the passenger door panel.

Lua eased himself out of the truck. He walked stiffly across the lot and handed Joseph the Sunday *Arizona Republic* and another book package from Amazon. His brow was creased. Something was on his mind.

"What?" Joseph asked.

Lua pointed to the paper. "Wendy Chang's dead. Obit's in the back."

"How?" Joey Blade hoped Wendy or Darville would someday come clean and tell the truth about what happened that night. Joseph knew better. He stopped thinking about Wendy years ago. Darville was gone too—drug overdose the year after Joey went to prison.

"Drowned in her pool in Malibu. It wouldn't have made the papers if her old man wasn't such a bigshot. Just another poor-little-rich-girl suicide."

Joseph tucked the paper under his arm and opened the Amazon package.

"You finish reading all that Faulkner shit yet?" Lua asked.

"This is the last one," Joseph said. "Why you walking like an old man?"

"My back's killing me. Unloaded a couple tons of concrete blocks yesterday."

Joseph frowned. "That's my job."

Lua raised his palms to the heavens. "If you owned a cell

phone, I'd have called you. But you wouldn't have had it turned on, so what the fuck." He shrugged. "I couldn't wait."

Joseph's lack of a cell phone was the one thing that tested their friendship. The whole world seemed to depend on cell phones now. "Thanks for the book."

Lua twisted, trying to stretch his back. "You could order it yourself if you had a cell phone. I could even pay you by phone. Save all the wear and tear on my truck. And me."

Joseph grinned. "You know you'd miss me." He held up the used paperback Lua ordered for him. "*The Sound and the Fury.* Supposed to be Faulkner's best." He flipped to the end. "Good. It's only three hundred pages. I'll be able to finish Faulkner before the end of the year."

"Who's up next?" Lua asked.

"James Joyce. I'll give you my list."

"Jesus, Joseph. Why don't you read something fun like Stephen King?"

"Hmm. I think I have Stephen King on my list." He flipped to the back of the Books Read Log where he made the list of authors to read. "Yeah. He's right behind Toni Morrison."

"What'd he write?"

"Toni's a woman. I haven't made a list of her books yet." Whenever someone recommended an author Joseph would put the writer on his list. One of his co-workers in the prison kitchen, Jamal, had recommended Morrison.

When he was preparing to read his next author, he would go to the library and make a list of all their books. He used to take them out of the library or try to find them in used bookstores, but four years ago he started having Lua buy the books on Amazon. He got every book he wanted on Amazon without hunting all over town. And unlike the library, he could make notes in the margin and keep the books. "Let's go inside. There's still some coffee left."

Lua followed Joseph into the sparsely furnished one-room cabin. There was a board and brick bookshelf along the far wall filled with all the books Joseph had purchased. It was organized alphabetically by author. Joseph made room on the F shelf and inserted *The Sound and the Fury* between *The Reivers* and *The Town*.

Lua sat down at the small table in the center of the room and Joseph poured him a mug of coffee. He handed him a sheet of paper he'd ripped from one of his spiral notepads. "Here are the Joyce books I want. I'd like to start with *A Portrait of the Artist as a Young Man* and finish with *Ulysses*. Other than that, I don't care what you order. Stick with the used books."

Lua tucked the paper into his shirt pocket. He handed Joseph his weekly pay—ten one-hundred-dollar bills—and his work schedule for the week. Lua had been building luxury homes for the last twelve years. As a lucrative supplement to his construction business, he started a maintenance company that most of his new home customers used. It provided a steady stream of income even when new house construction was slow and it kept him close to his wealthy clients. When Joseph got out of prison in 2009, Lua hired him as an all-purpose handyman for the maintenance business.

Joseph lifted the floorboard next to the bookcase and pulled out a small toolbox. He peeled off eight of the hundreds and added them to the stacks of bills that were rubber-banded together in sets of five. With those eight bills, he now had eleven sets of five hundred dollars. His expenses were minimal, so with his excess cash he bought Krugerrands just like Dutch used to. He counted out ten sets and handed them to Lua. "You stopping at the bank this week?" he asked.

"This afternoon. How many of those gold coins you got now?" Lua's banker kept Joseph's Krugerrands in a safe deposit box along with any excess cash.

Joseph recorded the entry in his Krugerrands book. "Three hundred and seventy-seven. It'll be three eighty-one after this purchase." Krugerrands were trading for just over twelve hundred dollars.

"Cool. Close to half a million. Might need to hit you up for a loan once of these days."

Joseph put back the cash box and replaced the floorboard. "Any time, brother. Any time." Joseph could never repay Lua. The man had always been there for him.

Lua refilled his coffee mug. "Mrs. Landis has another job for you. Problem with the garage door." He looked at Joseph with his sideways glance, like he was trying to see through him.

"What?" Joseph asked.

"That lady has a lot of special maintenance for that house. Didn't you fix the garage door a few months ago?"

Joseph shrugged. "It's a three-car garage."

Lua gave him another look but let it drop. "Your mother called me."

"Why?"

"She wanted to remind you to get your haircut so you don't show up for Thanksgiving looking like Jesus."

"She didn't say that." Joseph's hair was down to his shoulders. He trimmed it on the first day of the month. He visited Callie every other Tuesday after work and she never said anything about his hair.

Lua smirked. "She wants you to come early for Thanksgiving. No later than ten. She said she wanted some time with you before Solita and Garth show up with their horde."

When Solita met Garth Lynch, he was playing golf on

the Nike tour, trying to make it as a professional golfer. They were married one month after 9/11 and had three babies in five years. For a decade, Solita was a stay-at-home mom active in all of Amber, Madison, and Rebecca's school and after-school activities. When her youngest, Rebecca, entered first grade, Solita got her real estate license, and last year she was named the top agent in Sotheby's Scottsdale office. Garth was laid-back and easygoing. Solita was a tornado.

Joseph picked up another pad from his table. "Callie 10 a.m. Thanksgiving," he said as he wrote the note on his schedule pad.

"Do you make a note every time you take a dump?" Lua asked.

Joseph frowned. "Not in this book. This is my schedule. That would be in my diary," he said, deadpan. Lua never tired of busting balls about Joseph's list-making. He flipped back through the pages of his schedule pad. "Hey. Last year at this time we were playing golf with Garth." Garth had invited Joseph and Lua to play at his country club with his oldest daughter, Amber, who was a junior league champion. It was a humbling experience for both of them.

Lua groaned. "I lost every ball in my bag. That course is insane."

Five years ago, Garth built a sprawling ranch house in north Scottsdale. He applied for admission to the exclusive Troon Country Club, and because of his hotshot golf credentials, managed to jump the long waiting list. He entertained customers and suppliers there almost every weekend. With Solita using it for networking and Amber and Madison active in the junior golf and tennis activities, the club had become an integral part of their lives.

"It's a little more challenging than Encanto," Joseph said.

Encanto was a municipal course in central Phoenix where Lua played in an after-work league.

"And dangerous," Lua said. "I don't like rough where you have to fight the rattlesnakes for your ball." He took a last swig of coffee and stood up. "Okay, Joseph. I've gotta take off. You be sure to make Mrs. Landis happy. She's my best maintenance customer."

"I'll do my best, boss."

CHAPTER 41

9: 30 A.M. – MONDAY – NOVEMBER 20, 2017
8790 N. ARROYA GRANDE DRIVE, PHOENIX, AZ

Anita Landis's house was on the edge of the Phoenix Mountains preserve. Her late husband had been a big-time developer in Missouri and hired Lua to build the house he designed for his new wife. He spared no expense. Five bedrooms, six baths, a projection room, a great room, marble-tiled patio, an infinity pool, and a three-car garage.

It was a forty-mile drive from Joseph's cabin to Mrs. Landis's house. When he steered his pickup into the driveway, her Mercedes convertible and Lexus SUV were parked in front of the garage. A Subaru hatchback that belonged to Mrs. Landis's daughter, Kristi, was behind the Lexus. Kristi, as Mrs. Landis explained it, was in the sixth year of a four-year undergraduate program at ASU.

Joseph pulled up behind the landscaper's truck at the end of the driveway. Miguel, who was high above him trimming the top of a tall palm tree, saw him and yelled, "Hey, Joseph!" He quickly scooted down the trunk. "Thank you. Thank you. Thank you."

"Uh, you're welcome," Joseph said. He hadn't seen Miguel in weeks.

"You talked to Carlos. Got his head straightened out."

Carlos was Miguel's oldest son. He had been working for his father for the last month since he got out of Sheriff Joe Arpaio's tent city where he had spent six months on a minor drug charge. Last week he had been trimming bushes while Joseph was replacing loose patio stones. Carlos knew Joseph had been in prison, and they talked for over an hour about getting out and staying out.

"Carlos? He's a good worker. Must've picked that up from his old man. How's he doing?"

Miguel beamed. "He's working a property over in Scottsdale on his own. Said he didn't need any supervision. I don't know what you told him, but he's got a whole new attitude. So, thank you, Joseph. God bless you."

"Not sure I earned any blessings." Joseph closed the truck door and started walking up the driveway to the garage.

"When you buying a new truck?" Miguel asked.

"Can't afford one," Joseph said. He peeked back over his shoulder at Miguel who was grinning at him. He'd been asking Joseph that question ever since he replaced his twenty-year-old truck last year. "I'm not a rich landscaper like you."

Joseph still drove the 2003 Silverado four-wheel drive Lua furnished him when he started work in 2009. He declined repeated offers from Lua to swap the truck out for a newer model. There was no need to change—he kept the Silverado running smooth, and the body was cherry without a mark on it. He washed and polished it every Sunday afternoon. Joseph figured the odometer would turn past a million miles in April or May. That was important to him. He wasn't sure why.

Joseph had installed new door openers on two of the garage bays a month ago. He pushed the button to open the third door, which was seldom used, as the garage was empty except for the two cars. The door rattled and clanked as it rolled up the track. A minor chain adjustment and some lube was all that was needed.

Joseph headed back to the Silverado to get his toolbox. The mid-morning sun was warm on his back. He grabbed his toolbox and discarded his vest and over-shirt.

The door was a quick fix. He adjusted the chain, tightened the brackets, and cleaned and lubed the track and chain. When he tested it, the door rolled up and down the track as smoothly as the other two doors. As he was putting away his tools, Kristi, backpack in hand, strolled out to the Subaru. Mrs. Landis was a forty-something, six-foot blonde who could have been a *Sports Illustrated* swimsuit model. Kristi was a miniature version of her mother. She was wearing a white halter top and patched, ratty-looking cutoff jeans that Mrs. Landis said were from Gucci and cost a thousand dollars.

"Hi, Joseph," Kristi said. She gave him a coy finger wave. With an impish grin, she set her backpack down and walked over to the open garage door. "I see Mom's keeping you busy with another of her projects."

Joseph pressed the button and the door moved smoothly down the track. "Works great now. Just needed a minor adjustment."

Kristi studied him, her head tilted. Joseph knew better than to ask her what she was looking at. "I love your hair," she said. "And those eyelashes. You should try modeling."

Joseph laughed. "Yeah, I don't think so."

"I'm serious." She lightly touched his forearm. "You're ripped. With that body and your long, curly hair and that sexy scar, you'd get noticed."

Joseph reflexively patted the two-inch scar on his right cheek. He'd been slashed over ten years ago, but the skin was still numb to his touch. He picked up his toolbox. "Do you want me to move my truck or can you get by?"

Her smile faded as she picked up her backpack and climbed

into the Subaru. "Don't worry, Joseph. I won't hit your precious truck."

Miguel had finished trimming the palm trees and moved on down the road to his next client. Joseph drove his truck to the front of the garage door he had just repaired. He pressed the remote gadget over the visor and the door glided open. He parked the Silverado and entered the kitchen from the door at the back of the garage.

The kitchen area opened on to the great room. The far wall of the great room was all glass for an impressive view of the mountains. Sliding glass doors opened onto the patio and infinity pool. The master bedroom was accessible from the great room and it too had an all-glass wall and a door to the patio. Tucked away in a corner of the patio, just outside the master bedroom, was a Jacuzzi.

Joseph unlaced his work boots and set them on the welcome mat in the kitchen area. He stepped quietly across the great room and into the master bedroom. The door to the patio was opened and he could hear the whoosh of agitated water. He stepped out on to the patio. Mrs. Landis was in the hot tub, smiling at him. Her bare breasts, which had been surgically enhanced, seemed to float on the excited bubbles streaming from the Jacuzzi jets.

"Come on in, Joseph. The water's perfect."

Joseph stripped off his clothes and slipped into the water, hip to hip with Mrs. Landis. She leaned over and wrapped her arms around his neck, her bullet-shaped breasts poking his chest as she kissed him. "I am so horny. Did my daughter hit on you again?"

Joseph shifted sideways, lifting Mrs. Landis so she straddled him. He gently kissed her breasts. "She said I should try modeling."

"And what did you say to that?"

"I told her that wouldn't leave me any time to fuck her mother."

Mrs. Landis whooped, throwing her head back violently. Joseph called it her donkey laugh. "I almost wish you had," she said between whoops. "I would have paid money just to see her face."

Joseph kissed her hard, hoping to prevent Mrs. Landis from going off on a rant about Kristi. It worked. She grabbed his cock. Her sex moans were almost as loud as her donkey laugh, and Joseph was tempted to cover her mouth so the neighbors wouldn't hear, but there were no neighbors. She came easily and often and loudly.

It had started three years ago when Mrs. Landis had asked Lua to install custom blinds on all her windows. It was a three-day job, and by the end of the second day Mrs. Landis' friendly chitchat had escalated to obvious flirtation, which Joseph had done his best to ignore. When he showed up for work on the third day, she was naked in the hot tub, and Joseph stopped ignoring her. After that, she would come up with one or two projects for him to work on every month. She was Lua's best maintenance customer.

After the sex, when Joseph tried to get dressed, she grabbed his boxers and jeans and ran into the bedroom. "Here." She tossed him a terrycloth robe with "Phoenician" embroidered on the front. "Wear this. I told Lua I needed you for a full day of projects. You have to stay."

"Come on, Anita." He lunged for his boxers, but she pulled them away and he lost his balance and toppled onto the bed.

"Hey, we're making progress. You called me Anita. Won't be long before you're taking me home to meet your mom." She straddled him, grinding into his pelvis.

"Damn, you're heavy," he said.

She pressed her hands down on his ribcage. "I think you're getting carried away with your vegan diet. I can count your ribs."

"Kristi said I was ripped."

"Yeah, you are. But I don't like my man weighing less than me."

Joseph cupped her breasts. "Your implants probably weigh ten pounds."

Anita pressed her hands on top of Joseph's, squeezing her breasts. "Best investment I ever made."

That first time in the hot tub, she told Joey her boob transformation story. "I was a gawky six-foot Amazon with no boobs. When my good-for-nothing, long-time-missing Daddy died and left me five thousand dollars, I spent three grand at Dr. Gupta's New You Clinic in Rolla, Missouri, and went from an A cup to a D. Then I got a shag cut and color and went from mousy to platinum. I spent the rest on clothes. Two years later I was Mrs. Ted Landis, wife of the richest man in Howell County." She said the last line with a serious hillbilly twang.

During their next hot tub rendezvous, after she had had a few drinks, she confessed that she had a husband who was fighting in Iraq, and two children—Daniel and Kristi—when she started fooling around with Ted Landis. She hadn't planned on cheating. She thought the boob job would make her more desirable to her husband, but it turned out he was gay. "It wouldn't have made any difference," she said. "I made the right decision for the wrong reason."

Joseph grabbed her under her armpits and rolled her on to her back. "No special projects today," he said. "I've got to buy something for Thanksgiving dinner."

He jumped off the bed and slipped on the robe. "You steal this from the hotel?"

"No. They comped me. What are you bringing for the big family homecoming?"

"This sucker's soft," Joseph said, stuffing his hands in the pockets of the robe. "I don't know. Maybe a pie from Marie Callender's?"

Anita made a face. "No good. Thanksgiving is for homemade pies. How about a nice bottle of wine?"

Joseph bit down on his lip. "I don't like buying wine. Those wine sellers are intimidating."

Anita's eyes went wide. "Oh my." She wrapped her arms around him. "You survived seven years in that awful prison. Nothing out here in the real world can be as scary."

"It was nine years," he said. "There's a lot of scary shit out here, Anita."

"Like what?"

"Making a mistake. Doing something that gets me sent back." He shuddered. "I won't ever go back again."

Anita traced his scar with her finger and then softly kissed his cheek. "You won't, Joseph. I'm quite certain you've used up all your bad luck." She kissed his forehead. "I know what you can bring." She ran into the kitchen and opened her wine refrigerator. "Here it is. A Marcassin Vineyard Pinot Noir, 2007 vintage. My dear departed husband bought a case of this. Cost a fortune. It will be perfect with turkey or whatever it is the Blade family has for Thanksgiving dinner."

"I can't take that," Joseph said.

"Yes. You. Can. Joseph Blade. You know red wine gives me a headache. You'd be doing me a favor. I insist."

Joseph knew it was pointless to argue. Anita was as stubborn and commanding as his mother. He took the bottle and kissed her on the cheek. "Thanks, Anita. I still have to go. I've got work to do."

She waved him off. "Just stay for lunch. I'll make you a quesadilla. We can have a nice meal. It will be like a real date."

Joseph handed her the robe and went back to the bedroom to get dressed. When he returned, she had just finished whipping up the guacamole and grating the cheese.

"It'll be ready in a few minutes. I'm having a Bloody Mary. Do you want me to make you a virgin?"

"I'll just have water." Joseph didn't drink. That was part of his life plan. No drugs. No alcohol. No meat. It was easy to give up meat in prison most of the meat was bad. He wasn't a vegan— he liked eggs and cheese too much. For a while he'd given up sex, too, but then he met Anita.

He sat down on one of the couches in the great room that had an impressive view of the mountains. He thumbed through Anita's latest issue of *Phoenix Today*—a glossy monthly that highlighted activities in the city and valley. He wasn't really looking for anything—he never went out at night—when he saw a photo of an attractive blonde wearing a chef's hat and standing at the entrance to McCormick Railroad Park. The woman had built a successful "family-friendly" gourmet restaurant chain in the Pacific Northwest and was now expanding into Arizona with a new location next to the railroad park.

The restaurant was called the *Dixie Café* and the woman was Mallory Stewart.

CHAPTER 42

Joseph's cellmate at Florence Correctional Center, Howard "Red Cross" Woodbine, had told Joseph he could train his brain just like he trained the muscles in his body. Red Cross, six foot six with a Fu Manchu and a shaved head, was three hundred pounds of lethal muscle and bone. The toughest dude in the prison, but neutral, like the Red Cross. All the gangs—white, black, and brown—respected him, and that saved Joseph's life.

"You can't think about that girl anymore," Red Cross told him the first day they met. "You have her in your head and you ain't gonna be able to do the time. Make your brain think about somethin' else, boy." And he had. It had been years since Joseph thought about Mallory.

Red Cross told him he needed to build barriers to keep out the bad thoughts and Joseph believed him. He thought his defense system was impregnable. But Red Cross was wrong. One lousy photo and Joseph's defenses crumbled. For the last three days, he hadn't been able to get Mallory out of his head. He tried immersing himself in the stream-of-consciousness narration of *The Sound and the Fury*, but he read the opening pages over and over again and couldn't make sense of them. On his Wednesday trail hike, he was so distracted he made a wrong turn and ended up hiking twice as far as he intended, barely making it back to the cabin before sunset. This morning he spent a half hour looking for the bottle of wine Mrs. Landis had given him. He was getting angry, and part of his life plan was to never get angry. How could he lose a bottle of wine? He stormed out of the cabin and then he remembered. His truck. The wine was in the glove box. He'd put it there so he wouldn't forget to bring it. He had forgotten to remember that. It would have almost been funny, except now he would be late getting to Callie's house. He was never late. Always being on time was part of his life plan.

He went back inside and changed into the white shirt and blue suit he wore to every Thanksgiving and Christmas dinner. They were the clothes he'd bought at Macy's for his trial. The salesmen had been right. "A good suit will last you ten years if you don't drink too much beer." The suit had lasted almost twenty years. He'd been bigger back then. His shoulders and arms muscled up from weightlifting and his diet mostly meat and potatoes. Now without all that extra muscle and fat, the shirt was baggy and the sleeves too long. One time after shower sex with Anita, he stepped onto her digital scale and discovered he weighed 164 pounds. When he entered prison he was 198.

Traffic was light on Highway 51, with most folks staying at home for Thanksgiving. He could have easily driven seventy or eighty and made it to Callie's by ten, but he couldn't risk getting a ticket. A major tenet of his life plan was to never ever give the police a reason even to question him. That trumped his punctuality goal. He kept the Silverado a few miles below the stated speed limit and pulled into Callie's driveway at 10:10 a.m.

Dutch had been responsible for the upkeep of the house, but he never wanted to pay someone to do the work, insisting he could do it himself. He put off most projects as long as he could. The place always looked a little shabby. After Dutch died in 2003, Callie was more than willing to hire landscapers and handymen. This year she had the stucco exterior refurbished and painted a salmon pink. With her well-maintained cactus beds, the property sparkled.

The driveway was empty, but Joseph parked on the street so Garth could park his Suburban in the driveway when he and Solita and their three girls arrived. Joseph was ten minutes late, but at least he remembered to bring the wine. He rang the doorbell.

Callie shouted something and a moment later flung opened the door. She shook her head. "Why do you ring the doorbell? Never mind, come here." She hugged him fiercely. She'd never been a hugger, but after Dutch was gone, it was like she inherited that trait from him. At least she always hugged Joseph whenever he showed up.

"Happy Thanksgiving, Mom." He handed her the bottle of wine.

"This looks like a fancy vintage. Are you drinking?" she asked, sounding surprised.

"Nah, not today. I like your hair."

After Dutch's funeral, Callie had cut her hair short. She'd wanted to do it for years, but Dutch loved her long, red hair. It had turned rusty gray, and today was stylishly short with a frosted look.

Callie beamed. "I tried out a new salon that just opened in Paradise Valley. Come out to the patio. We've got some things to talk about."

Joseph could smell the turkey roasting in the oven. He used to love turkey, meat of all kinds, but Red Cross had taught him how to train his brain to resist temptations like unhealthy foods and now the smell of meat almost made him sick. The kitchen, which was warm from the oven, had been dramatically remodeled. The door to the backyard was now a sliding glass entryway that led to a flagstone patio. Callie poured Joseph a cup of coffee and they settled down at the patio table.

"It should be warm enough out here with that sun." She tugged at his frayed cuff. "I'm buying you a new shirt for Christmas. Time to retire that one."

Joseph looked down at his shirt. "Clothes for Christmas? Not fair."

"You look good, Joseph. Godawful skinny, but good."

"What time are Solita and the gang arriving?"

"I told Garth to get here by noon. I'm hoping they make it by one. Garth's always late. We'll eat at two."

Solita was pregnant when she and Garth got married. There was no way Garth could support a family on his meager golf earnings, so Dutch hired him as a salesman. Garth was clever and had an easygoing, good-old-boy sincerity that served him well. It didn't hurt that customers loved playing golf with him. After Dutch died, Callie asked Garth to run customer service. Last year she retired and made Garth the CEO. She remained as Chairman of the Board.

"You still enjoying your retirement?" Joseph asked.

Callie's face darkened. It was clear she was not. "We've got serious problems."

Joseph and Solita each inherited twenty-five percent of the company. Callie owned the rest. Callie had wanted Joseph to work for the company when he got out of prison, but he knew there were too many opportunities to cross a line and get in trouble with the law. It happened to Dutch and he couldn't take that chance. He did his best to stay out of company affairs. Garth didn't have Dutch's passion for the business, but nobody did. Golf would always be Garth's first love, but from what Joseph could see he had made some good decisions. Right after he took over, he pushed the company into rebuilding specialty engines like lawn mowers, compressors, LNG vehicles, anything with an internal combustion engine. The auto rebuilding business was in serious decline so it was a smart move.

"What's the problem?" Joseph asked. "Not the specialty engines?"

Callie frowned. "Those industrial accounts are different from the garages and dealerships. They buy a lot of engines, but they take forever to pay. We needed more working capital, so Garth brought in this new banker he met at that damn country club."

Callie bit her lip and her eyes were cast down. She didn't have to tell Joseph what she thought of the new banker. "I should have said something. Dutch wouldn't have given this guy five minutes. Glib asshole named Bobby McGee. His company is RM Capital, and he's crushing us."

"What's his deal?" Joseph asked. Callie had dealt with bankers for years. There were always issues, especially with Dutch's tendency to ignore terms and conditions when they didn't suit him, but Callie never let a banker rattle her. This time it seemed different.

"He's a sleazy asset-based lender. Has a lien on all our inventory and receivables. Two of our major industrial accounts—Homko Lawn Mowers and Stauffer Chemical's LNG fleet—are having financial difficulties and they're slow-paying us. Their receivables are over ninety days so the bank declared them ineligible. This guy McGee puts the loan in default, and then charges us fifteen percent interest. He wants the loan paid off or else."

"Or else what?"

Callie hung her head. "I don't even want to tell you. I'm such a fool. I signed a personal guarantee. I'm on the hook for three million dollars."

A personal guarantee. Bankers were always trying to get

Dutch to sign a guarantee. He always refused. He didn't trust bankers.

"Why would this banker go after you? You don't have three million dollars." Joseph remembered Dutch's stash of Krugerrands. "Do you?"

She gave him a look. "Everett says it doesn't make any sense. Garth has a meeting set up for Tuesday morning at the bank. He'll tell us what that's all about after dinner today. I'm afraid he's in over his head. Everett agreed."

Joseph ran his hand through his hair. This was crazy. "When Dutch got into trouble with Thunderbird Bank, he just stopped paying them. It didn't take long for them to negotiate a new deal. Why don't you stop paying this asshole?"

Callie shook her head. "Customer payments go directly to the bank's lockbox. They have control of the cash and they take their fifteen percent interest before we get a nickel. Bobby McGee is strangling us, and he knows there's nothing we can do about it."

One of the lessons Joseph learned in prison was that there was always another play. It might cost you your freedom, or your privileges, or your reputation, but as long as you were breathing you had a choice. Joseph walked over to the edge of the patio. The Phoenix Mountains Preserve—the same mountains Anita's house bordered—loomed on the horizon. "Well let's see what Garth has to say," he said.

o o o

Solita and her two younger daughters, Madison and Rebecca, arrived at noon. Madison was thirteen and in the eighth grade. Sandy-haired, compact, and athletic like her father, she skipped into the kitchen holding an aluminum pie tin like it was an offering to the gods. "Hi, Grandma. I made a pecan pie for dinner."

She hugged Callie and then spotted Joseph on the patio. "Uncle Joseph!" She ran out to the patio and wrapped her arms around his waist.

Joseph loved his nieces but he hadn't seen them since last Christmas. That was on him. Solita was always inviting him for dinner or family events, but he knew it was best for him not to be reminded of what he couldn't have. "How's your tennis game, Madison?"

"Troon Junior league champion!" she said. "Next year I get to play with the high school kids."

Solita rushed into the kitchen and set a big casserole down onto the stove. "Here are the sweet potatoes, Mom. Amber's playing nine holes with her dad. They'll be here by one." She shrugged. Golf was one of the few things she couldn't control. "Joey!" She skipped out to the patio and hugged Joseph.

"Joseph, Mom, not Joey," Madison said.

"Hah. He's my baby brother. He will always be Joey to me." She held him at arms-length. "Still the pretty boy, aren't you? Love that hair. But goddamn, you are skinny. You start eating meat yet?"

"Hey, Solita," Joseph said softly.

Rail-thin, intense, and intelligent, Solita inherited Dutch's dark skin and hair and his penchant for offering unfiltered opinions. She was a force of nature, and Joseph couldn't imagine a better sister. Almost every week for nine years she made the hour-long drive to Florence to visit him. No one—not even Lua or Callie—visited more.

"Mom, you shouldn't say 'goddamn,'" Madison said.

Solita wrinkled her nose at her rules-obsessed middle daughter then turned her attention to her youngest daughter. "Hey, Becca, where's your pie?"

Eleven-year-old Rebecca was walking slowly through the

kitchen with her head buried in one of the Harry Potter books. She looked up at her mom and frowned. "I forgot. It's in the car."

"Well, go get it, honey. We can't eat it in the car, can we?"

Rebecca sighed and turned around, still clutching her book.

"Put the book down, doofus," Madison yelled. "You've only read it like five times already."

"Madison," Solita said, her tone serious. "I don't believe I made you the boss."

"I'll take the book, Becca," Joseph said. "What are you reading?"

Rebecca smiled shyly. She was dark, like her mom, but quiet and serious. "*The Deathly Hallows*. It's the last one." She handed him the book.

"I'll mark your place," he said. He slipped the book cover to the page she was reading.

"You still reading your way through Hemingway?" Solita asked.

"Faulkner. Working on the last one. It's a struggle."

Solita snorted. "Talk about a struggle. Did Mom tell you about the bank situation?" Solita said, attempting, but failing, to whisper.

"Yeah. Sounds bad."

She gritted her teeth. "I'd like to kill that little fucker."

"Bobby McGee?"

"Pffft. No. Garth. He should have never trusted that prissy son of a bitch."

"Solita!" Callie and Madison were rolling out crescent rolls at the counter. "We can talk about this after dinner."

Solita shuddered. "I need a drink." She grabbed the bottle of Jack Daniels from the liquor cabinet. "Still on the wagon, Joey?" she asked. She took a glass and filled it with ice and whiskey.

"Yeah, but I'll have a Coke and sit with you on the patio." He held the door for her as they walked out onto the patio table. "Remember when we used to play Crazy Eights?"

"Sunday sex day," Solita said, sipping her whiskey.

"Sex day?"

"Yeah. Mom and Dad would lock us out in the backyard with a deck of cards, a bowl of popcorn, and a six-pack of Coke so they could have their weekly sex. Didn't you know that?"

"No. Glad I didn't. Thanks for not telling me. It was fun playing Crazy Eights."

"Fun? You lost every game. You were pathetic."

"I let you win. You'd have a fit if you lost and then Dutch would have come out and you two would have a huge fight and the whole day would have been ruined."

Solita smiled wistfully as she crunched her ice. "We did have our battles. I miss that. I miss him." She swirled the whiskey and ice and drained the glass. "No way you let me win."

Garth and Amber arrived at fifteen minutes before two.

Amber, cheeks flushed and blonde ponytail bouncing, skipped into the kitchen waving her scorecard. "I shot a forty-two, Mom!"

Her father trailed behind her. Garth, his short, wheat-colored hair now flecked with gray and matted from his golf hat, was tanned and trim and with his Troon Country Club polo and white golf pants, still looked like a touring pro. That was all he ever really wanted to be. His dream hadn't worked out as planned either.

"Amber put it all together today. Forty-two on that course is awesome." He kissed Solita on the cheek and she wrinkled up her nose.

"You didn't take a shower?"

"No time, babe. Didn't want to be late for Thanksgiving. Hey,

Joseph." He winked as they shook hands and clasped Joseph on the elbow, like a politician. "You're looking good, partner."

"What'd you shoot?" Joseph asked.

"Daddy shot a thirty-six. One over par," Amber said. She showed the card to Joseph. "See. If he hadn't double bogeyed number seven, he'd have been one under."

"Coulda, shoulda, woulda. That Troon rough is nasty," Garth said. "No crying in golf. Right, Amber?"

Callie stood at the door to the patio with the bottle of wine Joseph brought. "Come on in, gang. Dinner's ready. Joseph, you want to open the wine?"

Despite the ominous situation, the dinner conversation was animated.

"Hey, Joseph! This is a great Pinot. Where did you get it?" Garth asked.

Garth was a wine snob. It wasn't part of Joseph's life plan not to lie, but he did try to avoid unnecessary lies. This was borderline. "One of Lua's clients gave it to me. She said red wine gave her a headache."

"Damn. That's a grateful client. A 2007 Marcassin? That's a hundred-dollar bottle, easy," Garth said.

That got Solita's attention. "Which client?" She considered all of Lua's luxury home customers as future clients for her business.

Joseph took another helping of sweet potatoes. "These potatoes are great, Mom."

"Solita made them," Callie said.

"Who gave you the wine, Joey?" Solita asked again, perturbed.

"Mrs. Landis over on Arroya Grande."

"Anita Landis?" Garth asked. His tone made it sound like Mrs. Landis was some kind of celebrity. "She's on the hiring committee looking for a new club pro. She's got like a five handicap."

"Oh, wow," Solita said. "That blonde babe with the silicon rack? I love her house. Can you get me an introduction?"

"Mom!" Madison said. "'Silicon rack' is not nice."

Solita squirreled up her face at her middle daughter. "Where did you come from?"

"I doubt she's looking to sell," Joseph said.

"Everybody sells eventually. I play the long game." She pulled a business card from her pocket. "Will you give this to her?" She pushed the card across the table.

Joseph slipped the card into his suit coat pocket.

"Remember when we would plan these dinners around the Dallas Cowboys kickoff?" Callie asked.

"Why did you do that?" Amber asked.

"Your grandfather was a diehard Cowboys fan," Callie said.

"Oh God, remember the time he got so mad at Joey for cheering against the Cowboys that he stopped watching the game at halftime."

"I don't think that's what happened," Callie said. "Dutch never got mad at Joseph."

"That's mostly true. Joey was the golden boy," Solita said. "But he was mad that time. I remember because it scared the shit out of my boyfriend."

"Daddy was scared?" Rebecca said, wide-eyed.

"No. This was before Daddy arrived on the scene. Oh wait. I remember. It was when you told him you wanted to take the football scholarship to USC."

"You were a football player, Uncle Joseph?" Madison asked.

His nieces all knew he had been in prison, but they didn't know anything about the life he had before he went away.

"Your uncle was an all-State running back. Right, Joseph?" Garth said.

Joseph could feel his face warming.

Rebecca, sitting next to him, stopped reading the book that was in her lap. Her eyes glistened. "But you didn't get to go to college, did you?"

"No, honey. I didn't."

Callie decided to have the girls take their dessert into the TV room—Dutch's old office—so they could watch the latest *Star Wars* movie. She retrieved the pecan pie from the kitchen counter and announced in a loud voice so the girls could hear, "We're saving the pumpkin pie to have with our leftovers tomorrow." She looked conspiratorially around the table and whispered, "I think sweet, distracted Rebecca mixed up the sugar and the salt."

After everyone had their dessert and coffee, Garth, looking grim and uncomfortable, cleared his throat and said, "I talked with Bobby on Tuesday. He has a proposal he would like to share with us all next Tuesday in his office."

"Why's he need a plan?" Solita said. Joseph had heard that strident, angry voice dozens of times growing up when Solita and Dutch were having their almost daily battles. "If that asshole would just cut his interest rate to something even semi-reasonable the company could catch up."

Callie gently rested her hand on Solita's arm. "Do you know what he's proposing, Garth?"

Garth shook his head. "He didn't want to get into it. Said it was important that all the shareholders hear it at the same time."

"That doesn't sound good," Solita said. Her jaw was clenched and her breaths were short, angry puffs.

Garth looked at Joseph. "His office is on Scottsdale Road, just north of Shea. He wants to meet at ten. Can you make it there, Joseph?"

Joseph hitched his shoulders. "Don't think I can add anything. I'll go along with whatever you folks decide."

"Bobby made a point of asking that you be there. He wasn't really asking."

"Arrrgh!" Solita threw her napkin down on the table. "I hate that little fucker. If we didn't have those goddamn guarantees, I'd tell him to shove that fucking loan up his ass."

"I think we need to have Everett at that meeting," Callie said.

"No lawyers. Bobby doesn't want to get the lawyers involved," Garth said.

Solita glared at her husband and was close to hyperventilating.

"I can make it, Garth," Joseph said. "Let's hear what he has to say." It was obvious to everyone but Garth that whatever Bobby McGee wanted wouldn't be good.

CHAPTER 43

Fourteen years earlier . . .

JUNE 4, 2003 — 2 P.M.
FLORENCE CORRECTIONAL CENTER

Joseph was mopping the A wing corridor when the prison chaplain tapped him on the shoulder. Father Brubaker conducted an all-faiths service in the Gen Pop common area every Sunday that Red Cross insisted Joseph attend with him. "It's important that those gangbangers know you're on my team. That way no one will fuck with you."

Joseph didn't mind attending church services. Father Brubaker told interesting stories and the hourlong service was a welcome break from the monotony of prison life. Brubaker was short and muscular with a buzzcut, like some badass Marine. He'd been in a gang and spent five years in some prison in New Mexico. His message to the inmates was that there was a life after prison. Joseph wasn't convinced, but for sure when he got out, he would never take a job that put him anywhere near another prison. Prison was hell. Who in their right mind would ever return to hell?

"Follow me, Joseph," Brubaker said. "Leave the mop."

Joseph didn't ask why. Red Cross had been clear about that.

Don't ask questions. If one of those COs tells you to do something, just do it. These bastards aren't your friends. And that goes double for the priest. He ain't Father Flynn and this ain't the movies. That priest is just a CO with a funky collar.

Brubaker led Joseph into his office and closed the door. There were two chairs and a small table in front of his desk. "Take a seat," he said.

The chair, unlike the bolted down benches and chairs in the dining hall and Gen Pop, was cushioned, almost comfortable.

Brubaker grabbed a folder off the top of his desk and sat down across from Joseph. "Joseph, your father died this morning. I'm sorry. It was a heart attack."

Joseph heard the words. He understood, just like when he heard that bailiff read the verdict that he was guilty. He was aware Brubaker was talking to him, but he couldn't process the words.

He had seen Dutch and Callie and Solita just three days ago. It was a cool day and they had sat at one of the picnic tables in the prison yard. Solita's baby girl, Madison, was almost two and Dutch spent most of the visit bragging about her. He had more pictures of Madison than Solita did. He and Solita even had a friendly fight when Solita suggested Madison was not actually a perfect child. It was almost like old times.

Prison visits put everyone off their game. Dutch more than most. But this time he had been more natural, more Dutch-like. And now there would be no more visits? Joey would never again be wrapped up in a bear hug by his dad? Inhale his Aqua Velva? Cringe at one of his pussy lectures? Laugh at one of his tantrums? Feel the overwhelming love Dutch had for his family?

"Joseph." Brubaker leaned over and tapped Joseph's knee. "I know this is a blow, but you need to focus. We don't have much time."

Joseph took a shallow breath. He raised his head. "Yes sir."

"You can apply for an escorted leave to pay your respects. Your family has to pay the costs for the escort. It'll run you about a grand. Is that something you're interested in?"

"Yes sir."

"Good. Here's the deal. You can't go to the funeral or the church. It's got to be a funeral home or mortuary. No home visits. No family members or friends can be present. It's a private viewing. You only get one hour of visitation and no more than eight hours total time out." He glanced at the file. "You're in Phoenix so that shouldn't be a problem."

"Yes sir."

Brubaker grabbed a clipboard off his desk. "I've got the application. We'll fill it out now and get it to the deputy warden for approval. I'm recommending you, so there won't be an issue."

The application, as Brubaker predicted, was approved. Joseph called Solita and explained the ground rules. "No one from the family?" Solita said, her voice breaking. "That sucks, Joey."

"It's prison. Everything here sucks."

"Oh, Joey." She paused and Joseph could hear her sniffling. She was trying to control her emotions, which wasn't something Solita had ever been good at. "I'm sorry to complain. Okay. Visitation is at Williams Funeral Home on Shea and 24th Street. Regular hours will be from 11 a.m. to 2 p.m. so I'll tell them to be ready for you at 10 a.m. Does that work?"

"I think so. I'll ask Brubaker. If there's any problem I'll let you know. How's Mom doing?"

"Sad. Lost. It hasn't sunk in yet."

"I know the feeling."

o o o

Joseph left the prison on Saturday morning in his neon orange jumpsuit, shackled to a seat in the prison van and escorted by two armed correctional officers. They arrived at the funeral home, with impressive prison efficiency, at 9:55 a.m. Barnes, the senior CO, unshackled Joseph from the seat. Joseph had a chain around his waist and connected to the waist chain were chains for both legs and arms. He could only move his hands and his feet about six inches in either direction. He was forced to shuffle-walk, hunched over. He was glad no one could see him.

The funeral director, a nervous little man with a patchy mustache and ill-fitting suit, met them at the door. "Gentlemen, this way." He led them into a large parlor-like room with floral drapes and a cloying funeral home smell. Rows of chairs, eight across, filled the room. Dutch's coffin was on a raised platform at the front of the hall. Around the perimeter there were photos of Dutch. His high school graduation picture; a staged football shot from the yearbook with Dutch in a leather helmet and lumpy shoulder pads growling in his three-point stance; his wedding photo; photos from the honeymoon in Hawaii; family photos: Dutch grilling steaks; hula-hooping with Solita; playing catch with little Joey; holding his precious granddaughter, smiling like the world's happiest grandpa.

A tear trickled down Joey's cheek. He brushed it aside with his shoulder. *Keep it together, Joseph. Give them nothing.*

The funeral director, uncertain of the protocol for this kind of visit, stood to the side and looked at CO Barnes, hoping he would take the lead.

Barnes scratched his neck. "I'm hitting the head. Go ahead, Blade. Pay your respects. Marty, stay here. He ain't going nowhere."

The other guard settled himself down in the last row. "Got any coffee?" he asked.

The director beamed, relieved he had something to do. "Absolutely. I'll bring it right away. How do you take it?"

"Cream. Two sugars."

Joseph shuffled up the aisle to the coffin. Dutch looked awful. Pasty and gray. His jowls sagged and his skin was waxy.

The only thing real about him was that he was scowling. Dutch would have hated everything about this scene—the room, the director, the asshole guards, being dead. And the suit they had stuffed him into.

There was a chair by the coffin and Joseph sat down. What did he feel? His father had a great life until Joey fucked it all up. Dutch loved that boy named Joey, and when he went to prison it killed Dutch. It just took three years for his body to get the message. If Dutch had survived, Joseph wanted to believe they could have had a new beginning when he got out. But now he wouldn't have that chance.

Red Cross said that you can't dwell on all the bad shit that's happened to you.

Fucking Red Cross and his fucking rules.

Joseph couldn't think about Mallory. He had to forget about football. He must never explain how he was screwed by TJ Grimes and Wendy and her snob boyfriend. Joseph had followed all of Red Cross's goddamn rules. That golden boy life he once led had been erased from his memory.

Now he must let Dutch go, too? By the time he got out of prison, he'd have nothing left. What was the point? Joseph laid his head on the edge of the coffin, and to his surprise he started to sob.

He lost track of time. Someone laid a gentle hand on his shoulder. Was his hour up already? He looked up. It was Chico Torres, as sharp as ever in a dark suit and shirt and his signature eye patch. "I hear they call you Joseph now."

"Chico? How?" Joseph looked to the rear of the hall, but the guards were gone.

"They're taking a short break. How are you holding up? Howard looking out for you?"

Joseph stared at Chico, mouth agape. "What?"

"When you went in, Dutch asked me if I could help you inside. Your old man was loyal. All the way. I made sure you got in with Howard. No one fucks with that dude."

"That's for sure," Joseph said. "He's taught me a lot. Didn't know he was part of your crew."

"He's not. Where they got you working?"

"Custodial. Mostly mopping floors."

Chico shook his head. "That ain't no good. There will be an opening in the kitchen next month. My man Felix is getting released. I'll make sure you get his spot."

The kitchen was the most coveted job in the prison. Joseph knew better than to ask how he could do that. "Thank you." He stood up.

Chico clasped him on the shoulder. "Stay strong, Joseph. Listen to Howard. You're tough, just like Dutch. Do your time like a man and you'll be out of there before you know it." He squeezed Joseph's shoulder. "I'm sorry about Dutch." He stepped back and tapped his chest over his heart then walked quickly down the aisle and out the door.

A moment later the two guards returned. "Time to go, Blade. Wrap it up."

CHAPTER 44

Joseph wanted to believe the situation with that banker wasn't as bad as it sounded. That was what Red Cross called "magical thinking."

Magical thinking must be avoided. Always. Don't plan on happy endings.

Clear-eyed pessimism was part of Joseph's defense system, but after he saw that picture of Mallory, his defenses were useless.

On Monday, Lua stopped by the cabin to give him his work schedule for the week. Joseph told him about the upcoming meeting with the banker on Tuesday, and he confirmed Joseph's suspicions.

"Bobby McGee?" His face screwed up like he was in pain. "Total bad news. What the fuck was Garth thinking?"

"Crooked?" Joseph asked.

"Worse. He thinks everyone else is a crook and he's the last honest man."

Joseph hitched his shoulders. Nothing he could do about it. "Do you have my list? I want to get to Home Depot before the meeting. Need to replace one of my solar panels."

Lua handed him the work schedule. "Hey, your boy, Grenier, is moving up in the world."

Lua had hired an ex-con named Billy Grenier to be Joseph's

assistant. The arrangement only lasted six months. Billy was a perpetual motion machine with big ambitions. But in the time they worked together, Joseph shared with him all the lessons he had learned for surviving in the real world. Billy graduated with honors.

"I heard Billy started a stone company," Joseph said.

"Mission Stone. Just added a new location over on Shea. I need you to stop there and pick up thirty cartons of pavers and then drop them at Willoughby."

"Willoughby?"

"You know. That house that looks like the Alamo. Finished it in the summer. Just off Indian Bend, near that railroad park."

McCormick Railroad Park. That was where Mallory had opened her new restaurant.

"Hey. You with me?" Lua gave him a puzzled look.

Joseph picked up his work schedule, his heart was racing. "Thirty cartons?" he said. He took a deep breath and tried to regroup.

"Billy will have them ready for you."

Joseph wrote "*Mission Stone, 30 cartons.*"

"Don't go there before your meeting. Those cartons are dusty as hell."

Joseph grinned. "You afraid I won't make a good impression?"

o o o

The new Mission Stone location was just across from Home Depot on Shea Boulevard. Joseph was disappointed Billy wasn't there. It didn't make sense to drive back and pick up the bricks after the meeting. He had plenty of time. The brick pavers were packaged in cardboard containers—twelve to a box—and it was dirty work. He had loaded half of the cartons when a shiny new silver Lexus pulled into the parking lot and a grinning Billy

Grenier jumped out of the car. With his starched white shirt, gold neck chains, and an ear-to-ear grin, Billy looked like the successful businessman he always wanted to be.

"Joseph! You longhaired son of a bitch. How ya doing, man?" He jogged across the lot and pumped Joseph's hand.

"Hey, Billy. You're looking prosperous."

Billy snugged his belly. He was at least twenty pounds heavier than when Joseph had last seen him. "Hah. Couldn't stick with that vegan shit, but everything else you taught me, it's all good, man."

"Nice place you got here."

"Opening another next month in Mesa. Business is great. You ever want to leave that crazy Samoan, give me a call." He grabbed a carton and hoisted it onto to his shoulder.

"Don't do that, Billy," Joseph said. "You're management now. You'll get that pretty shirt all messed up."

"Fuck you, Blade. We're ex-cons. We stick together. Isn't that what you taught me?"

He set the carton down in Joseph's truck. His shirt was smeared with stone dust. "When you getting some new wheels, dude?"

Joseph tried to tell Billy he could handle the rest, but Billy wouldn't hear of it. In ten minutes, they had the remaining cartons loaded. As they were finishing, Billy got a call on his cell. He was needed at his other location. He pumped Joseph's hand again and clasped him on the back. "Don't be such a fucking hermit, Blade. Come down off that mountain and we'll go barhopping, meet some ladies. I'll settle for your rejects."

"Sounds good, Billy," Joseph said. He knew that Billy knew that that was never going to happen.

Despite Billy's help, Joseph was covered head to toe with a fine layer of grit. Garth said McGee was a stickler for appearance. A neat freak impressed with the cleanliness of Blade Engine. Keeping the operation spotless had been an obsession of Dutch's. Joseph was grateful Anita recommended he keep a clean T-shirt and towel in his truck for "emergencies." Not looking like a homeless dude for the big meeting with the asshole banker probably qualified as an emergency. He stripped off his filthy shirt and poured his water bottle onto the towel. He damp-mopped his chest, arms, face, and neck, and shook the dust out of his hair. He pulled on the clean white shirt and inspected himself in the truck's side mirror. He had definitely moved up a couple of grades from homeless.

Bobby McGee's office was just a half mile west on Shea in an upscale strip mall that included a Trader Joe's, an Apple store, an LA Fitness workout facility, and a BoRics hair salon. RM Capital, McGee's company, was next to the salon. Joseph hand-combed his hair and pushed open the tinted glass door.

The receptionist—a serious young woman in a serious blue suit—glanced up from her mail sorting. "The barber shop is next door," she said. She didn't have a receptionist smile.

Joseph gave her his charm smile. "I cut my own hair. I'm here for a meeting with Mr. McGee."

Her jaw dropped and she had a worried frown as she looked at the logbook on her desk and then back at Joseph. "You are . . . ?"

"Joseph Blade."

"I don't see—"

"Garth Lynch asked me to come."

A light went on. "Oh, of course. You're with Blade Engine."

Joseph stood silently, waiting for her to figure out what to do with him.

"Come with me, Mr. Blade." She ushered him into a windowless conference room. A large table filled most of the room. "Would you like some coffee?"

Joseph took a seat at the end of the table, farthest from the white board. The woman returned with a Styrofoam cup. The coffee was lukewarm and tasted worse than prison coffee. Joseph set the cup on the table.

The door opened and a trim, fortysomething man in a charcoal gray suit and a yellow tie entered the room. He frowned and then quickly recovered into a faux smile. "Mr. Blade?" He walked over, hand extended. "Bobby McGee."

Joseph stood up and shook hands.

McGee spotted the coffee cup on the table and frowned again. Joseph thought he was about to say something about his dusty appearance, but instead he grabbed an RM Capital coaster and placed it under the Styrofoam cup.

"Joseph, you're Garth's brother-in-law?" McGee said. It wasn't really a question.

"Yes," Joseph said.

"But you don't work for the company?"

"No."

McGee asked questions he knew the answers to, expecting Joseph to add something to the conversation, but Joseph never volunteered information. Anita suggested that was a prison habit he should drop because his one-syllable answers were no good in most social settings. She was probably right, but this meeting was more like prison than a cocktail party.

McGee stopped trying. "Not a big talker, are you, Joseph?"

"It's your meeting."

McGee looked impatiently at his watch. "Yes, it is. Where's the rest of your party?" He stared hard at Joseph.

"I don't know," Joseph said. He stared back until McGee looked away, pretending to check his watch again.

The door opened and the young woman ushered in Garth, Solita, and Callie. "Sorry we're late. There was traffic on Shea," Garth said. He grinned nervously. "You remember Solita and Callie?"

McGee summoned his fake smile again. "Of course. Good to see you both. Please sit down. Would you like coffee?"

Callie attempted a smile but failed. Solita just glared at McGee, unwilling to hide what she was feeling. Joseph loved her for that.

McGee turned to his assistant. "Julie, can I have the file, please?"

She pulled a thin manila folder from the large boxy briefcase she had lugged in.

McGee took the folder and then surveyed the room. He took the seat diagonal to Joseph's and gestured to the others. "Please sit down. Garth, why don't you sit here?" He indicated the seat across the table from him. Solita and Callie sat next to Garth and McGee's assistant sat next to him. Joseph had the end of the table all to himself.

McGee cleared his throat. "No coffee takers? Well, okay. Let's begin." He flipped open the file and acted like he was reading. "Well, we have a problem, don't we?" He gazed around the table, stopping at Joseph as though he were expecting him to say something. When Joseph remained silent, he continued. "As of this morning, Blade Engine and its guarantors"—he stressed the word and stared at Callie—"owes RM Capital . . ." He nodded at the young woman and said, "How much, Julie?"

She read from the paper she was holding. "We have advanced Blade Engine three million, five hundred and eighty-nine thousand dollars. The company has eligible receivables of three million five hundred fifty-eight thousand dollars. The advance rate on those receivables is sixty percent for a borrowing base of two million one hundred and thirty-five thousand dollars. So, Blade Engine is over-advanced by one million, four hundred and fifty-four thousand dollars, sir."

"Let's call it one-and-a-half million. We're all friends here." McGee smiled, humorlessly.

Garth's face reddened like a kid who had failed to turn in his homework. "But if you count the Homko and Stauffer receivables, we have more than enough collateral."

McGee gave a palms up gesture. "Those receivables are over ninety days old. Read your loan agreement. They're ineligible. The loan is in default."

"But Homko says—"

McGee held up his hand. "I'm not interested in your opinion about those accounts. You have been telling me for six months that you would fix this problem. I don't want to hear any more about your grandiose long-range plans. We're past that. Tell me how I get paid."

Garth took a deep breath, like he was trying to steady himself over a six-foot putt. He clicked his briefcase open and pulled out a sheaf of papers. He handed copies to Solita and Callie and pushed the other copy across the table to McGee. He grinned nervously at Joseph. "Sorry, Joseph, I didn't make enough copies."

Joseph waved him off. "Not a problem. I'm just here for the coffee." McGee harrumphed, but quietly. He was one of those guys who was used to people sucking up to him. Joseph obviously annoyed him.

Garth cleared his throat. "Bobby, we just need three months." He was struggling to keep the desperation out of his voice but was failing. "If I offer Homko and Stauffer a twenty percent discount, I'm confident we can bring those accounts back into compliance in ninety days."

McGee studied Garth's schedule. His lips were pressed tight and his expression was sour. He picked up his Cross pen and made a mark on the schedule. Joseph could see that McGee had corrected a typo. He was a fastidious motherfucker.

"This is the same old, same old. Your plan is to try harder. What do I get for this?" McGee said.

Solita slammed her fist on the table. "You're getting fifteen fucking percent, asshole!"

Garth's face got tight, but he knew his wife well enough to know that nothing he could say would mollify her.

McGee pressed his hands together like he was praying. "I know this is a tense time," he said. His voice was low and he spoke slowly like Solita was a child he was lecturing. "But there's no call for that kind of language. If you want me to carry you for another ninety days, I need something. What can you offer me?"

Garth threw up his hands. "You already have our guarantees."

"We don't have Mr. Blade's guarantee." He looked to his assistant. "Do we, Julie?"

This time she didn't need to check her file. She knew she was just a prop. "No sir."

Solita leaned forward, her face as red as Dutch's used to get. She was about to explode, but Callie put her hand on Solita's forearm like she had done with Dutch a thousand times.

"Mr. McGee," Callie said, her voice calm but clear. "Joseph doesn't have any assets that could help you."

McGee had a smug, patronizing smile. "He doesn't have a house or car or a fancy country club membership, but he does own twenty-five percent of Blade Engine. And he lives modestly. I'll bet he has more assets than you might suspect."

Dutch never trusted bankers. He was convinced they all talked with each other. Joseph hadn't believed that, but now he was starting to wonder if McGee knew about his Krugerrands.

"Julie, do you have the guarantee form?" McGee asked.

The young woman pulled out a legal document with red "sign here" arrows clipped to it.

Garth leaned forward. He sensed a reprieve was being offered. "So, if Joseph gives you a guarantee we get another ninety days to fix the loan?"

McGee scoffed. "No. I'm just tidying up something we should have insisted on from the outset. Can I have the warrants, Julie?" His assistant handed him another document. More arrows. "I need warrants for one thousand and one shares of Blade Engine Common that I can exercise after ninety days for a dollar a share."

Garth's brow was knitted. He was trying to catch up with McGee's math. Callie was way ahead of him. There were a thousand shares outstanding. "That gives you control of the company in ninety days," she said. She kept her hand on Solita's arm, holding her back like a dog on a short leash.

"It gives me leverage. It's a way for me to protect my assets." He pushed the warrant document across the table to Garth and handed the guarantee to Joseph.

Joseph handed it back. "Not interested."

McGee tried to keep from scowling. Joseph wasn't playing by his rules. He wasn't used to that.

Garth leaned forward, his face tight with agitation. "Bobby, can we have some time to confer among ourselves? This is a lot to digest."

Joseph pushed back his chair and stood up. "Garth, you can confer all you want, but I'm not signing this man's guarantee."

Garth stood up. "Come on, Joseph. We need your help."

Joseph shook his head. "He doesn't give a shit about my guarantee. He wants the company."

McGee stood up. "Wait, Joseph. I'm afraid we got off to a bad start. I'm not trying to take over the company. I just want to be paid."

Joseph stared hard at McGee. "You don't want the company?" He picked up the warrant. It was simply written and there was no expiration date.

McGee waved his hand. "Of course not. I'm a banker. Getting paid is all I'm interested in."

Joseph knew that was a lie. "Then you need to put that in writing. If you get paid, then you give back the warrant." He handed the warrant document back to McGee.

McGee smiled. "I can't give an open-ended commitment." He paused as if he were sincerely trying to come up with a solution. "Tell you what. I'll give you your ninety days." He wrote something on the warrant and pushed the document across the table to Garth. "But I need your guarantee, Joseph. I have investors to answer to, and besides, it's not fair to your sister and mother who have demonstrated their good faith by providing their guarantees. You need to be reasonable."

"I'm not big on fairness," Joseph said, his voice barely above a whisper. "And I don't give a damn about your investors."

"Come on, Joseph," Garth said. It was a plea, not an order. His voice was tinged with desperation, and sweat beaded his forehead even though the room was icy.

"He doesn't care about my guarantee," Joseph said, nodding toward McGee. "Your banker just wants that stock thing. At least with ninety days you've got a fighting chance."

McGee's eyes darted around the room, as if he was a poker

player trying to decide if Joseph was bluffing. His face relaxed, and he took Joseph's guarantee and slipped it into his briefcase. "I can hold off on the guarantee for now. But I have to have the warrants."

Joseph wasn't bluffing. The banker made the right call. Bobby McGee was a good poker player, but he had just shown his cards. It was the company he was after.

CHAPTER 45

The Willoughby mansion did look like the Alamo—before the battle. It even had a ten-foot high adobe wall surrounding it. The pavers were for the landscaping crew. Apparently, unloading wasn't part of their deal, so Joseph unloaded the cartons and stacked them next to the carriage house. The temperature was near ninety degrees, and by the time he finished unloading he was twice as sweaty and gritty as when he loaded them.

He gave himself another water bottle bath and then stepped up into his truck. It was times like this he was glad he had resisted getting a cell phone. After the meeting, Garth wanted everyone's input, and they were going to meet for lunch so they could strategize. Poor Garth. He was so unlike Dutch. Joseph tried to imagine how Dutch would have handled someone like Bobby McGee. Not with a committee. Dutch always knew what he wanted and he didn't ask permission. He wasn't big on consensus building. Garth seemed to be in actual pain when he realized he wouldn't be able to include Joseph in their "strategy session" for how to work with Bobby McGee.

"Let it go, Garth," Solita said. "Joey bought us ninety days. Now you've gotta figure out how to get rid of that little shit."

Solita understood the situation. Callie was right—Garth was in over his head. If Joseph owned a cell phone, he would probably be sitting in his truck right now listening to Garth's convoluted plan for how to work things out with a man who didn't respect him.

Respect. That was Red Cross's number one objective.

Don't care what any con or CO thinks of me. Not looking for friends. But if a man don't respect me, we're going to have a problem.

It was hard to live by Red Cross's rules in prison, but it was even tougher on the outside. At Florence, every day was a life or death situation, and following those rules had kept Joseph alive. But out in the real world the stakes weren't as clear. More and more, Joseph found himself breaking the rules and he was about to violate another one. *Never make a move without having a plan. In the joint and even more when you get out, you need to think three moves ahead.*

The Dixie Café was just a block away. Joseph wanted to check it out. He wasn't ready to see Mallory yet, but he could handle seeing something she had created. But what if Mallory was there? What would he say to her? How would he act? Why was he doing this? He couldn't answer any of those questions. He just knew he had to do it.

The café was next to the entrance to the park, nestled among palms, pines, and cacti. The parking lot was on the street side and the entrance to the café was around back. There was a patio on the front of the café and a mini-playground so parents could enjoy a drink while their kids played. It was a nice setup. There was a young woman at the entrance taking names. There were several parties enjoying their lunch on the patio.

The bubbly greeter offered a welcoming smile for everyone. Joseph walked up to her, still not thinking about what he was doing. She looked up from her seating chart and her smile froze. Joseph, in his dirty jeans and T-shirt and his long, frazzled hair clearly didn't belong here.

"Can I help you, sir?" she asked. Worry lines appeared around her mouth.

"Is Mallory here?" Joseph asked. He was making a mistake, but he couldn't stop himself.

"I'm sorry. Who are you looking for?" She stole a glance over her shoulder to see if there was someone who could help her. Joseph frightened her.

"Mallory Stewart. Isn't she the owner?"

"Oh." She relaxed slightly, deciding he was more of a flake than a terrorist. "No. She's not here."

Like a hiker who knew he was on the wrong trail but just kept plowing ahead, Joseph asked, "When will she be back?"

"I don't know. Do you wish to be seated?" She all but cringed when she asked him.

"No. Thank you." Of course she wasn't here. Joseph didn't know whether he was relieved or disappointed. He walked back through the playground, headed for the parking lot. There was a park bench just outside the fence. Joseph had screwed up. Now he was uncharacteristically tired. That was what happened when he got off his program. He sat down on the bench. A few minutes of rest would help him clear his mind.

On the playground, a young girl about twelve sat on one of the swings, her long legs dangling, kicking up dust. It reminded Joseph of the day he met Mallory at Roadrunner Park and they drove out to Lake Pleasant to find TJ. That was the day he fell in love with her. Mallory was just a kid who idolized Joey Blade. She didn't love him. Joseph made himself accept that reality, but he couldn't stop himself from believing she might have fallen in love with him if things had worked out differently.

Stop thinking like that. There are no mulligans in life. No time machine where you can go back and fix things. You play the hand Joey dealt you. It's a shitty hand.

The girl on the swing was staring at him. He smiled at her and she quickly looked away, frightened. She jumped off the swing and ran to the table on the porch where her parents were eating. Joseph laughed remembering how Kristi suggested he try modeling. Most models didn't scare people.

Visiting Mallory's restaurant was foolish. He knew that. Nothing good would come of it. Thinking about Mallory weakened his defense system. He needed to rebuild. Tomorrow he'd install that solar panel and finish reading *The Sound and the Fury*. On Saturday he'd go for a long run. Maybe all the way around Sutter Lake. Let the dry heat purge his mind of all his magical thinking.

On Sunday, he would drive over to Mrs. Landis's place and ask her if she could help him find a way to get rid of Bobby McGee. She had wealthy friends. She might know someone who could help. He would stay busy with his running and reading, and he would help his mother save the company. He would not allow himself any time to think about Mallory.

He pulled out his schedule and quickly wrote down those activities. He liked having a full list of things to do. It made him less anxious. More focused. He took a relaxing breath and was about to stand up when two police officers approached him, their hands on their holstered weapons.

"Sir! Sit down. Keep your hands where we can see them."

Joseph raised his hands. He was back in the truck bed of Lawrence Darville's Toyota Tacoma, hands raised, confused. Why was that DPS trooper so nervous about All-American good guy Joey Blade?

The officer stood in front of him while his partner slipped behind the bench out of Joseph's field of vision. Both men were trim and fair with military haircuts. Neither could have been much over twenty-five. Scottsdale PD was stitched on the pocket of their khaki uniforms.

"What's your business here, sir?"

"No business," Joseph said. He stared hard at the cop. *Give the man nothing,* Red Cross warned him. *Don't respect him, don't disrespect him. Give the man nothing.*

"Can I see some ID?"

Joseph pulled his driver's license from the front pocket of his jeans.

"You don't have a wallet?"

"No."

The officer squinted at the license and looked Joseph up and down. He handed it to his partner. "Check it out."

The partner trotted packed to their squad car. The questioning officer put his foot up on the bench and leaned over. "This is private property. You are trespassing, sir."

Joseph stared back at him. Silent.

"Hey, Cory!" The officer checking the ID waved from the car. "He's got a record." He quick-stepped back to the bench and handed the license to his partner. "Nine years in Florence. Rape and racketeering."

The officer named Cory took the license back and studied it again. "Well, Mr. Blade, it sounds like you were one badass. You want to explain to me why you're hanging around a kiddie playground?"

Explaining that the rape charge had been dropped wouldn't do any good. For most people, cops especially, getting charged was all the evidence they needed. "I wasn't hanging around. I was just resting."

"Stand up, Mr. Blade."

Joseph stood up. He stared at the officer, drilling him with his eyes, even though he knew that was the wrong thing to do.

"Cuff him, Charlie. I don't like your attitude, Mr. Blade. You need to come down to the station. Folks around here don't like ex-cons hanging around their kids' playground."

"Are you arresting me?" Joseph asked. He put his hands behind his back as the other cop slipped the nylon restraints around his wrists.

"Do you want me to?"

"I haven't broken any law."

"Not so sure about that. Sex offenders can't hang around playgrounds."

It was pointless to argue with them. He wasn't changing their mind.

"This way, Mr. Blade." The officer who cuffed him gripped Joseph's arm and started to escort him to the squad car.

"Hold it, Cory. Wait till this group passes."

An attractive blonde was strolling down the path flanked by two men dressed like lawyers or bankers and a younger woman trailing behind with a large briefcase. The blonde woman was dressed in a businesswoman's skirt suit. She pointed to the patio and then to the playground, and then she saw Joseph, standing there, his hands cuffed, accompanied by two officers of the Scottsdale Police Department. She stopped talking in mid-sentence.

She was poised, confident, clearly in charge. But there was no mistaking those soulful, compassionate eyes. Joseph always believed that one day he and Mallory would meet again. But not like this. He hoped she didn't recognize him. He wanted her to keep walking and ignore the poor loser being rousted by the cops.

"Joey? Joey!" She ran to him and then saw he was handcuffed. "What's going on here?"

"Do you know this man, ma'am?" Officer Cory asked. His confident swagger was gone.

"He's my friend. Why is he in cuffs?"

"Trespassing. Someone complained. And uh . . . he didn't say why he was here. With the playground, and everything . . ."

"Mallory? Everything all right?" asked the young woman assistant. The two suits were staring at her, trying to figure out what her connection was to this homeless guy.

"Go in and get a table. I'll be there in a minute."

She turned to the officer. "Please uncuff him immediately. This is my restaurant, and he is certainly not trespassing." She was polite but commanding. "Joey, I'm so sorry they've treated you like this."

"Sorry, ma'am. Misunderstanding. Let him go, Charlie."

Charlie released the restraint.

Joseph rubbed his wrists. Part of his life plan had been to never be cuffed again. The plan was in shambles.

Cory tipped his hat to Mallory and the two cops headed back to their squad car, walking as fast as they could without breaking into a trot.

Joseph stopped rubbing his wrists and tried to look at Mallory without revealing the turmoil he was feeling. "Hi, Mallory. Sorry to mess up your meeting. You have a nice place here."

Mallory glanced over her shoulder. Her group had gone inside. "Those are investors. I need to be nice to them, but can we talk later?" She pulled out her cell phone. "I'll call you. What's your number?"

Joseph wanted so much to talk to her, but now it was clear to him that he couldn't. His carefully constructed life worked as long as he didn't think about everything he had lost. Talking to

Mallory would break him. He would start thinking about what might have been and that would destroy him.

"I don't have a phone." He forced a weak smile. "One of these days I'm going to get one."

Mallory frowned and stared up at the sky. It was the same look she had whenever she was thinking something through. She opened her purse. "I'll be back here next Monday. Can you meet me here at noon?"

Joseph hated lying to her, but he had no choice. "I don't know my work schedule. Give me your card and I'll call you if I can make it." I still know how to use a phone."

Mallory handed him her card, but she didn't let go of it when he took it. "You will call me? Right, Joey?"

He nodded, as if that would be less of a lie than speaking. He slipped the card into his jeans pocket. "Thanks for the help with the cops." He turned around and stepped quickly toward his truck. He could feel Mallory staring at him, but he refused to turn around. When he got to his truck, she was gone.

CHAPTER 46

Thirteen years earlier...

SUNDAY - APRIL 11, 2004
FLORENCE CORRECTIONAL CENTER

Joey Blade had been sentenced to 4 to 10 years. He was eligible for parole on June 8, 2004 – his four-year incarceration anniversary. Red Cross sat on the edge of his bunk while Joseph sat on the bench across from him. For the last two weeks he had been prepping Joseph for his parole hearing, going over and over every detail.

"Okay, the guards escort you into the hearing and sit you down in this chair, just like you're sitting now. There are two men and a woman on the board. They'll be sitting at a table ten feet away from you. What do you do?"

"I look each of them in the eyes. My expression is serious, but not angry. I don't smile. At any time."

"How do you address them?"

"Yes sir. No sir. Yes ma'am. No ma'am."

"Now the tough part. They'll ask you why they should consider your application for parole."

It was the tough question because Joseph didn't want to say what Red Cross insisted he must say. Joseph sighed. "I made a—"

"No! Goddammit, Blade." Red smacked his fists together, making the bunk beds rattle. "You act like you're fucking constipated. Like it hurts you to tell the truth."

"But it's not the truth."

"We don't have truth in here, Joseph. That's for people out there in the real world. You tell those motherfuckers what they want to hear and win this fucking parole. I'm tired of sharing my goddamn cell with you."

Joseph held up his hand. "Alright, alright. Let me try again." He waved his hand in front of his face like he was erasing his expression. "Thank you for this opportunity. I made a foolish mistake. I got involved with the wrong people when I was younger. It was my fault and I am truly sorry. I have learned my lesson and I will never go down that path again."

Red Cross stared hard at him. "Okay. That's better. Try it again without that fucking smirk face."

Joseph grinned. "I gotta get to work. Dogs and kraut today."

Red Cross scoffed. "Jamal's right, you know. That shit will kill you." He tugged a cardboard box from under his bunk and handed Joseph four packages of Ramen. Red Cross got the Ramen cheap from one of the guards. Solita deposited a hundred dollars in Red Cross's account every month and he kept Joseph supplied with Ramen, which Joseph gave to Jamal. Jamal was Chico's man. When Chico got Joseph his position in the kitchen, the deal was that he would give Jamal four packages of Ramen a week.

"Are you done with Jamal's book?" Jamal loaned Joseph *Devil in the Blue Dress* by Walter Mosley. Joseph read it in one night and reluctantly shared it with Red Cross.

"Yeah. I liked that one. That dude, Easy Rawlins, he's one bad motherfucker." He handed the paperback to Joseph. It was twisted up like a roll of paper towels.

"What the fuck did you do to it?"

Red Cross scowled. "I'm an enthusiastic reader."

Joseph pressed the packets of Ramen down on the book

trying to flatten it out. "Jamal will have to learn to eat prison food if I make parole," Joseph said.

"Nah. Whoever replaces you will have the same deal," Red Cross said. "Wouldn't surprise me if Chico doesn't up the ante. He gave you a sweetheart deal."

Joseph stuffed the Ramen and the book in his shirt. "Time to roll. Don't want those dogs undercooked."

At meal time, the kitchen crew divided into cooks and servers. The teams rotated every day. Serving sucked. It was not so much a problem when the meals were crap, like the gray meat patties that were more soy meal than beef, but wieners and sauerkraut was a favorite. There were always a few cons who weren't satisfied with their portions and they would hassle the servers. COs weren't supposed to allow that, but they rarely did anything.

Tonight, Joseph was a cook, which meant he would steam the hot dogs and kraut and replenish the food trays for Jamal and Rabbit who were the servers. Jamal was in Vatos Locos, Chico's outfit. Rabbit belonged to the Aryan Brotherhood, but that was only so he could survive. He was a crooked white bookkeeper with skills the Brotherhood could use. The kitchen was neutral territory. It didn't matter what your gang affiliation was, kitchen was the primo gig, so no one would fuck around and risk losing that position. Détente ruled.

Jamal just shook his head when Joseph handed him the book. "Red Cross does that every time. He gets too wound up in the story. I ain't loaning you this one."

Joseph peered at the book cover. "The Blues Eye?"

"The Bluest Eye. Belinda gave it to me."

Belinda had cerebral palsy. She had just turned sixteen. She was six when Jamal went to prison and she'd be twenty-six when he got out. If he didn't screw up. And if he survived.

Jamal opened the book. He read to Joseph what his daughter had written to him. "When I grow up, I want to write books like Toni Morrison. She inspires me. Just like you, Daddy." Jamal's voice had become husky and he swallowed hard as he stared at the book. "Girl's stuck in a wheelchair her whole life and she's trying to cheer me up." He set the book down on the counter. "Damn," he whispered.

Inmates started filing in at 5:30. The cool thing about the kitchen was it kept you busy, which made the time fly. Meals ended at 6:45 and it was close to 6:30 when Joseph brought out the last batch of dogs. Both of the servers were too generous with extra dogs for their gang members and now they were running low.

"This is the last batch, guys," Joseph said. "No more freebies. Make it last."

"It's just newbies eating now. There won't be no problem," Jamal said. "As long as Rabbit don't get fucking carried away trying to make new friends." He winked at Joseph.

"N . . . n . . . n . . . no sir. I don't give away extra." Rabbit's face was florid, like it had been steamed.

Joseph patted him on the back. "Relax, Rabbit. Jamal's just busting your balls. But remember. Only two. Make those dogs last."

Joseph started draining the steam pot when Jamal was confronted by a newbie from the Brotherhood. "What the fuck? Two skinny dogs? Gimme another!" The inmate, a skinhead with tattoos covering his neck and arms, had seriously ugly teeth. Must be a meth-head. Meth-heads were to be avoided— the drug rotted their brains along with their teeth.

"Move on, fuck face," Jamal said.

The kid's chin was trembling and his eyes were wild. He

spotted Rabbit. "Hey, I know you. Bunnyman! Gimme another dog. Take care of your brother. This coon's fucking with me."

Rabbit froze. He looked down at the tray of dogs, hoping if he didn't look at the kid, he might disappear.

Jamal dropped his tongs. His fists were clenched.

"Come on, shithead. That one right there." The kid tapped on the glass.

Joseph put his hand on Jamal's shoulder. "Take it easy, J." He took the tongs from Rabbit, who willingly relinquished them. "Keep moving, kid. Two dog limit for everyone."

The inmate's jaw dropped and he stared at Joseph. "I don't believe it. Joey Fucking Blade!"

It was TJ Grimes. No hair, but the whiny voice was unmistakable. The two men stared at each other and then, with an inhuman scream, TJ launched himself over the food counter. His hands raked Joseph's face and neck and as Joseph flung him to the floor, blood spurted from Joseph's neck and cheek. He pressed his hand to his neck. With every beat of his heart, blood was spurting from the razorblade gash.

He fell to one knee as TJ picked himself up off the floor. "You killed my brother, motherfucker." He was about to slash Joseph again when Jamal grabbed him from behind. The last thing Joseph remembered was TJ howling like a wounded animal as Jamal violently twisted his arm and slammed his face into the counter.

o o o

Joseph awoke several hours later in the prison hospital. His face and neck were bandaged. The gash in his cheek was minor, but TJ had managed to slice the carotid artery in his neck. If Jamal hadn't been there, Joseph would have bled out in minutes.

TJ's right arm had been nearly ripped off, and his skull fractured. The arm would be next to useless and there was the likelihood of brain damage, but with TJ it would be hard to measure.

TJ was moved out of gen pop and Joseph and Jamal both got a month in the SHU. Joseph lost his shot at parole. He would have to wait two years for another hearing. If Chico hadn't intervened, they both would have lost their kitchen jobs.

Joey Blade was the All-American boy until TJ Grimes changed that. Joseph Blade was the model convict. TJ Grimes changed that too.

CHAPTER 47

Joseph's plan to keep busy and not think about Mallory was working. Over the next few days, he completed all of Lua's maintenance jobs, fixed the solar panel on the roof, chopped and split a cord of firewood, and filled the wood box so he'd be ready for the colder winter nights. He finished *The Sound and the Fury* and started on Joyce's *A Portrait of the Artist as a Young Man*. With all that activity, thoughts of Mallory were kept at bay.

But then, as he was driving home from Chandler on Friday afternoon, he switched on KNIX and the first song he heard was Clint Black's "Killin' Time" about a lovesick cowboy who can't kill the memory of his lost love. The opening line shattered his delusion that he wasn't thinking about Mallory all the time. Today, as he ran around Sutter Lake, Mallory was with him every step of the twenty-mile run. His dry heat therapy failed miserably.

He still had Mallory's business card. Even if he wasn't meeting her on Monday—and he wasn't—he should contact her. He would borrow Lua's phone on Monday morning when he came out with the work schedule. If he texted, he could avoid talking to her. He'd let her know he couldn't make it and that would be the end of it. This time he would stick with the plan.

As he ran the final section of trail that led to his driveway, his thoughts turned to those Scottsdale cops. Recalling that humiliation stoked his anger. He'd been out of prison almost seven years and thought his past was mostly forgotten. More foolish magical thinking. And to be rousted right in front of Mallory. Anita was wrong. He had not used up all his bad luck yet.

He was getting an anger-fueled adrenalin rush. He thought about running another loop, but as he reached his driveway, he noticed a car parked in front of the cabin. A black Acura MDX with tinted windows. He slowed to a walk and approached carefully. No one other than Lua ever visited him. There was a man sitting on his porch in the rocking chair. When he spotted Joseph, he stood up. He was trim and silver-haired with an unmistakable eye patch. Chico Torres still looked like he should be featured in *GQ*.

Chico stepped down off the porch, grinning broadly. "Joseph, you're looking good. Love that hair." He held out his hand.

Joseph hadn't seen Chico since the day of Dutch's funeral. "I like your hair too," he said. He waited to hear what Chico had to say. The man didn't make social calls.

Chico rubbed his head. "Yeah. Sucks getting old. But beats the alternative." His smile couldn't hide the meaning behind that observation. "How far you run?"

Joseph shrugged. "Around the lake. It's about twenty miles. You want a glass of water? Sorry I don't have any beer."

"Water would be great."

Joseph gestured toward the rocking chair. "Have a seat. I'll be right out." He poured two glasses of water from the chilled water in his fridge. Chico was standing on the edge of the porch looking out at the mountains.

"It's beautiful. I can see why you're hiding out up here."

Joseph handed him the glass. "I'm not hiding. I like the open space." He didn't have to say that after nine years in a prison cell, living here was the closest thing to heaven he could hope for. "What do you want, Chico?"

Chico took a long gulp of the ice water. "Ah, Joseph, you get right to the point. I always liked that about you. No bullshit. Just like your old man."

Lua told him Chico was no longer running the gang. He was supposed to be a legitimate businessman, but Joseph didn't believe that.

"I need your help with something, but first I've got some news I think you'll like."

Joseph knew that anything Chico had to offer would come with strings attached. "What's the news?"

"TJ Grimes is dead. CO made a mistake and left him in gen pop for an afternoon. He didn't last an hour."

"COs don't make mistakes like that," Joseph said.

Not without encouragement.

Chico frowned. "Everyone makes mistakes, Joseph."

Joseph had hoped that someday TJ would confess and clear his name. Magical thinking. Joseph knew better. With TJ gone, the case was closed for good. If Chico thought killing TJ would make Joseph grateful, he was mistaken. "You said you needed my help on something?"

Chico tilted his head, bemused. "Damn. You are just like your old man. Okay on to business. That banker your brother-in-law is tangled up with. McGee?"

Joseph snorted. "Yeah. I just met him."

"I know. He's a piece of work."

"Is this a collection call?" Joseph asked.

"I want you to put a cap in that motherfucker's prissy ass," Chico said. He was staring hard at Joseph and he wasn't smiling anymore.

Stare the man down. Don't let him know how scared you are. If he sees fear, you're dead. Joseph's mouth was dry. His eyes stayed wide. He willed himself not to blink or swallow or look away.

Chico must have read the same book. His eyes didn't waver. Then he grinned. "Joey, I'm busting your balls. I'm a businessman. I don't do that kind of shit, man."

Joseph took a deep breath. "Fucking asshole." He tried to smile, but he doubted his frozen face got the message. "You had me going."

Chico pulled a business card from his pocket. "I've got my own bank now." The card was premium stock paper. It had a sun rising over a desert landscape. "Desert Capital: Your Southwestern Loan Specialist in Phoenix, Albuquerque, and Tucson."

"Three locations?"

"Three phone numbers. I have a proposition for you."

"I'm not involved with the company. Garth and Callie are calling the shots."

"Hear me out."

Joseph took a breath.

Don't react. Don't give him anything. He's not your friend.

"McGee's screwing your company with that hard-ass approach. He's trying to squeeze you so he can buy the company cheap. But he's got his own problems."

"What kind of problems?"

"His investors aren't happy. McGee overpromised. Big mistake. These are not the kind of guys you want to make unhappy. I don't think he knows who he's dealing with."

Joseph nodded but didn't say anything. He didn't know what Chico was about to propose, but he was pretty sure he wouldn't like it.

"I got a little friend inside his company. I know Blade Engine is into him for almost three-and-a-half mil. You need to offer him two mil right now to go away."

"Why would he take that?"

"He won't. Not at first. But when his investors hear about it, they'll change his mind. I guarantee it. They want out."

"So where does the two million come from?" Joseph figured he might as well play dumb.

Chico winked and tapped Joseph on the knee. "Desert Capital, your Southwest loan specialist. We'll charge you three over prime—that's about eight points better than McGee."

"What's the catch?"

Chico stepped to the edge of the porch and stared up at the mountains. "It is beautiful here. I can understand why you'd like to hide out here forever. But you owe me. And I'm not talking about TJ. That one was a freebie. You have debts to pay, Joseph. Have you forgotten?"

Joseph closed his eyes. He hadn't forgotten, but some debts could never be repaid.

"You did your time like a man, Joseph. I knew you would. Now you need to get back to work. I ain't trusting my money with some golf pro wannabe."

"So that's the catch? I have to replace Garth?"

"You remember Jamal's kid, Belinda?"

Chico's words were like a slap in the face. How could he ever forget? "Yeah, I remember her."

"She needs full-time care. It's expensive." Chico stared hard at him. His eyes were cold. Killer eyes. "I need you on my team, Joseph." His expression softened. "Hey, I don't care about your brother-in-law. You can keep him on. I hear he's a good salesman."

This wasn't just another money-laundering scheme, like the one that tripped up Dutch. This would be a life sentence without parole.

But Chico was right. Joseph had debts to pay.

Chico glanced at his cell phone and frowned. "Dinner tomorrow. Six o'clock. I'll bring the paperwork. We need to get this deal done ASAP. Time to get back in the game, Joey."

PART 3

Joey

CHAPTER 48

Joey Blade had a plan. Red Cross would be proud. There was no magical thinking in it, but it was a chance to end the story on his terms. That was the best a man like Joey could hope for.

The sun was peeking through the mountains as he steered the Silverado up Anita's driveway. She would be doing sunrise yoga on her patio as always. He clicked her garage door opener and took a moment to admire its smooth operation. He enjoyed fixing things. It made him feel useful. Needed. It was great therapy after nine years in hell.

Anita was sitting at her kitchen counter, wrapped up in her robe, having a cup of coffee. She smiled as he stepped into the kitchen. "Didn't know you worked on Sunday. I thought this was truck wash day."

"I'm changing my plan. I need a favor, Anita."

Her eyes went wide, her coffee cup suspended halfway to her mouth like a stop-action photo. "Three years I've known you. You've never visited on Sunday, never deviated from any of your crazy plans, never asked me for anything. And you called me Anita when we weren't having sex! This must be serious." Her smile couldn't hide her concern.

"I want you to cut my hair."

She exploded with her donkey laugh. "Oh my God, Joseph.

You scared the shit out of me. I thought you were dying or something. Cut your hair? Wow."

"You can call me Joey. I've always liked that name better."

"Well, come here, Joey." She patted the chair at the counter. "Take off that shirt and let me find my shears."

It took her almost an hour to cut off his shoulder-length hair, but when she was finished, Joey Blade was back.

Anita held up her makeup mirror. "Do you like?" she asked.

Joey glanced at the mirror and quickly put it down. He recognized the face immediately. It was the grown-up version of the boy they sent away. "Looks good. Thanks."

"Good? You're a freaking Adonis. Thank God, Kristi's not here. I'd have to hose her down. Why don't you jump in the shower, get those loose hairs washed off? I'll help."

Tempting, but not part of his plan. "Garth told me you were on the committee to hire a new golf pro at his country club. He said you were an awesome golfer."

Anita beamed. "Coming from Garth Lynch, that is a serious compliment. He's the best golfer at Troon. Easily."

"Why don't you offer him the job?"

She stared at him, hands on hips. "You are full of requests today. Garth would be a fabulous club pro. I've watched him with his daughter. He's got a real knack." Her brow furrowed. "Is there something happening at the company?"

Joey rubbed the back of his neck. Without the blanket of hair, he felt exposed. Revealed. "We've got some problems, but nothing to do with Garth. He would jump at a chance to be the club pro. And you're right. He would be great at it. He loves the game."

Anita glanced toward the ceiling like she was actually considering the possibility. "If he's available, why not? It would save me countless hours of boring committee meetings."

"You can make it happen?"

She fluttered her eyelashes like a Southern belle. "I've always been pretty good at getting my way." She wrapped her arms around him and squeezed his butt. "So, how about that shower?"

Joey pulled her close and whispered in her ear, "I have to go, Anita. I have one more favor. It's important."

She stared at him, her eyes wary.

"I need your gun." Anita kept a SIG Sauer P220 in her nightstand. It was a parting gift from her ex when she married Ted Landis.

"Joseph! Joey! No! What are you thinking? No. You don't need a gun."

"I wouldn't ask if I didn't need it. The less you know, the better. This is something I have to do, but if you can't help me, I'll get it someplace else."

"Oh, Joey." She buried her head in his chest. "Goddammit." She sobbed. "Will I ever see you again?"

He wanted to say yes, or at least maybe. But that would be wrong. More magical thinking. "No, Anita."

It was a shitty thing to ask her, but he knew she would come through. Anita was standup. And she was his friend.

His eyes were welled with tears, and his chest was tight as he drove away from her home. Red Cross's words echoed in his head: *There ain't many problems you can solve without somebody getting hurt. And that somebody might be you.*

CHAPTER 49

Joey was on his porch, ready to roll in his going-out Wranglers and his Frye harness boots. He'd shaved and showered and checked out his new haircut in the mirror. He was getting used to it. He felt less exposed now. It made him feel free.

Not hopeful, but free.

The sun was warm on his face as he admired the peace and beauty of the mountains that had been his home for the last seven years. Chico was right; he had been hiding out.

You can't hide from yourself forever. That chapter is over.

Lua's truck was kicking up dust as he climbed the last hill to the cabin. Joey smiled, anticipating Lua's reaction to his haircut. When Lua stepped out of his truck, he was reading something in the newspaper, and he didn't look up until he was ten feet from the cabin.

"Holy shit!" Lua dropped the paper. "Joey!" He bounded up the stairs and wrapped him in an embrace that lifted him off his feet, just like he used to do when they were in high school. He set him back down and held him at arm's length. His eyes were shiny. "You're back. Goddammit. Joey Blade is back!"

Lua was happier than he had been the day Joey was released from Florence. "I am back. But I'm going away."

Lua's smile disappeared. "Why?"

"There's too much history here. It's everywhere. I'm—"

Lua picked up the newspaper and handed it to him. "I know, Joey. I get it." He scowled. "Where you goin'?"

"Haven't worked it all out yet. I need to get my coins. Can you come with me to the bank?" The safe deposit box was in Lua's name.

Lua studied him, his lips pressed tight. "Okay. Want to ride with me?"

No questions asked. That was Lua. Always there for Joey. "I'll follow you. I have a few more stops to make." He picked up his bag and his empty toolbox and carried them to his truck.

o o o

The Thunderbird branch was on Thirty-Second Street two blocks north of Shadow Mountain High School. It had been seventeen years since the high school bonfire that changed the arc of Joey Blade's life. The bank officer ushered Lua and Joey into a windowless vault-like room and left them. Lua grunted as he carried the safe deposit box to the table.

"Damn. How many coins you got now?"

Joey checked his register. "Should be three hundred and eight-one. That's only twenty-five pounds. Thought you were a muscleman, Lua."

"Fuck you, Blade. I want to watch you try and carry that toolbox out of here."

Lua opened the safe deposit box. The coins were in clear plastic tubes. Twenty to a package. "You know you could get a cashier's check. Might be a little easier to handle."

"I like gold," Joey said, picking up one of the tubes. "Each one of these is worth about twenty-four grand today."

Lua whistled. "You must have three hundred thousand here."

Joey looked at his register again. "Should be approximately

$462,000." There were twenty tubes of coins. They fit easily into his toolbox. "Follow me out to the parking lot," he said, grinning. "You still look tough enough to scare off any muggers."

"Fuck you, Blade."

Joey placed the box on the floor of the cab. Anita's gun was in the console. No one would be taking these coins from him. He grabbed two sleeves of coins from the toolbox. "I'm heading over to Callie's now," he said. He handed Lua the coins. "This enough to buy the truck?"

Lua frowned. "That truck's worth four thousand, tops. And I'm not selling it to you. It's yours. Always has been."

Joey expected that reaction. "I need you to look out for my cabin. Pay the taxes. You can give the books away. I won't be back. I want you to have that money. It's important to me."

Lua bit down on his lower lip. "Fuck, man. You gotta go?"

"Yeah. I'll miss you," Joey said, his voice barely a whisper.

Lua wrapped him in another embrace. But gentle this time, like he was afraid he would crush him. "You take care, Joey Blade. Call me any time." Then he shook his head, remembering. "Get a fucking cell phone. This is the twenty-first century, shithead."

CHAPTER 50

C allie was sweeping the walk when Joey pulled into her driveway. She had the same reaction as Lua when she saw him. It was as if Joey Blade had been missing for years and finally returned. He didn't have to say a word.

"It's so good to see you, Joey." She leaned into the truck window and brushed the side of his head. "Very professional job."

"Can I park in the garage?"

She opened the garage door. "Do you want some coffee?"

"Still have that stash of beer in the back of the fridge?"

She grinned. "I think I might have a couple of cold ones. Meet me on the patio."

It had been years since Joey enjoyed a beer. Callie did her total mom bit, putting a slice of lime in the beer and bringing out guacamole and chips. "This is nice, Mom. Thanks." Joey smiled, savoring the moment.

"The way you're dressed I'm guessing you're planning to do something with that son of a bitch McGee."

"Can I borrow your cell phone?"

"Sure. You don't want to use our regular line?"

"I mean borrow it like Solita would borrow a blouse. As in never return it. You don't use it, do you?"

Callie dismissed that notion with a wave of her hand.

"Solita insisted I have one in case I broke down someplace. Haven't used it in months. But it's all charged, just waiting for that emergency." She jumped up from the table and returned a minute later with the phone and the charger. "Be my guest."

"Thanks." Joey slipped the phone into his pocket.

The front door opened. Joey knew Solita came over most every day for lunch. His plan was on target.

"Hey, Mom, it's me," Solita called.

"Grab a beer and join your brother on the patio," Callie yelled.

Solita walked out from the kitchen clutching her cell phone in one hand and a beer in the other. "Holy shit, Joey! You look great." She rushed over to the table in her high heels. "And you're drinking! My baby brother is back!"

"Joey has a plan for the banker," Callie said.

Solita rubbed her hands together. "Please tell me it involves kicking his ass."

"I'm hoping that's not necessary," Joey said. "But it's complicated."

Solita settled down at the table across from Joey, staring at him like she hadn't seen him in years. "Let's hear it."

Joey took a deep breath. Anita and Lua were the easy pieces. The part of his plan that involved Callie and Solita was a lot more complicated. "First off, I want to talk about Garth. Troon is going to offer him the position of Club Pro. He needs to take it."

Solita's brow furrowed and her mouth opened like she was trying to say something but no words came out.

"That's where he belongs," Callie said.

"But how?" Solita had regained her voice. "What's going on, Joey?" Her face darkened like it always did just before she exploded at Dutch.

Joey held up his hands and lowered them slowly to the

table, signaling for Solita to calm down. He spoke softly. "Anita Landis will see to it that the committee recommends him for the job. I will work something out with that asshole banker, but Garth can't be part of what I work out."

"Well, who will run the company?" Solita asked, her voice rising.

Joey leaned across the table and took hold of his sister's hands. "You will."

Solita's jaw dropped. "Are you crazy? I can't . . . what are you talking about?"

"You're smart and you're tough and you're fair. And you know the business. Mom will be around to help you. So will Garth. But you won't need much help."

"What about you?" Solita asked.

"I think Joey's leaving us," Callie said. Her eyes were red. "It's a good plan, Solita. You can do this. You are your father's daughter."

"When does Garth get home?" Joey asked.

"He plays in that Nine-hole league. He'll be home around seven."

That messed up his timetable. Joey wanted to give Garth the news himself, but maybe this was better. Red Cross always said a good plan has to be flexible.

"Hey, Mom. I need the keys to the office," he said.

Callie walked over to the pegboard next to the phone and grabbed the keys with the yellow key ring keychain. "These are the spares," she said and handed them to Joey.

"What are you going to do," Solita asked.

"I'm meeting McGee at the plant. Meanwhile, your first job as CEO is to tell Garth the good news about the golf pro job."

Solita smirked. "Do I do that before or after I tell him he's being fired?"

"You will be a great boss," Joey said. He kissed her forehead and pulled out the cell phone his mother gave him.

Solita frowned, pretending to be angry. "So, what's your plan for Mr. Dipshit Banker?"

Joey leaned forward and whispered, "I'm making him an offer he can't refuse."

CHAPTER 51

The Blade Engine office was a small, framed structure tacked onto the front of the plant. Accounting and personnel functions were on the first floor. In the eighties, Dutch built an executive office and conference room in what had been the attic. He put in a large picture window with a great view of the employee parking lot. It was impossible to keep the room cool so Dutch added dark, louvered blinds that he kept closed most of the time.

Joey hadn't been in Dutch's office in nearly twenty years. Back then it was a classic eighties-era man-cave, with fake mahogany paneling, black leather sofas, and framed posters of NASCAR action. When Joey became a football star, Dutch replaced the posters of Richard Petty and Dale Earnhardt with a collage of Joey Blade in action. Garth, or maybe it was Solita, had redecorated. Now the walls were crème-colored, and there were framed prints of Tiger Woods, Jack Nicklaus, and Arnold Palmer. Joey was surprised and pleased that Garth kept the Joey Blade football collage.

The couch had been removed and in its place was an artificial putting green. Dutch's massive desk was gone. There was a small antique student desk and a glass-topped table with four chairs. The biggest change, which Joey didn't notice at first, was that

Garth's office had no discernible odor. Dutch's office always smelled like a mélange of Aqua Velva, cigar smoke, and sweat.

Dutch had refused to air-condition the offices. The plant was swamp-cooled and he didn't want to treat the office different from the shop. But after he died, Callie installed air-conditioning for the office and the shop and she removed the blinds. Garth's meeting table was in front of the window. Joey took a seat at the head of the table and arranged his bags next to his chair. From this position, he could keep an eye on the parking lot and the door to his office.

At 5:55, right on schedule, Bobby McGee called Callie's cell phone. "I'm here, Mr. Blade. The door is locked." He sounded annoyed. That was good.

"I'll buzz you in. Come on up." Joey hit the door buzzer and waited by the entrance to the office.

When McGee spotted Joey, he did a double take. "My goodness. You've certainly cleaned up your act, Mr. Blade." McGee was gray-suited like before, but had replaced his yellow power tie with a blood-red one.

"You can call me Joey." He stepped back and let McGee into the office. "Do you want a soda or bottle of water?"

McGee waved his hand. "Nothing, thanks." He stopped and studied the collage. "You were a football star."

"Yeah. I don't know why Garth kept that. It was a long time ago."

"What inspired you to cut your hair, if I may ask?"

"It was time." Joey walked over to the table. "Have a seat, Bobby."

McGee frowned and tugged on the sleeve of his shirt. "I told you I have a dinner engagement at seven. You said you had a proposal."

"I have an offer. Just waiting for someone else." Joey checked the parking lot. A black Acura rolled up. A few seconds later the cell phone rang. "I'll buzz you up," Joey said.

"You told me Garth was out of the picture. Who's joining us?"

Joey held up his hand. "Hang tight, Bobby. This won't take long." He walked back to the office entrance. "Hello, Chico. Thanks for joining us."

Chico Torres, as stylish as ever in khakis and a black sports jacket with a black silk shirt, had a what-the-fuck-is-going-on look as he studied Joey. "Finally outgrew the hippie look, huh?" His eyes darted past Joey as he scanned the room he was about to enter.

"Chico, this is Bobby McGee, head of RM Capital. Bobby, this is Chico Torres. Chico runs Desert Capital. I thought it would be a good idea for you two to meet." He led Chico over to Bobby, and the two men shook hands. Chico was cool. McGee was wary. Both men were trying to figure out what Joey's game was.

"Water, soft drink, Chico?"

Chico scowled. "What the fuck are you doing, Blade?"

"That's a good question, Mr. Torres. I concur," McGee said. He folded his arms and his mouth curved into a serious frown.

Joey rubbed his hands together. "Gentlemen, I'm going to solve our problem. But first I need to tell you a story. It won't take long. Bobby, you won't have heard this story, so it's especially important that you pay attention because you need to know who you are dealing with." He stared hard at McGee.

"I'm listening."

"And Chico, you think you know this story, but you have a lot of the facts wrong. So follow me close."

Chico smirked. "Lay it on me, dude."

"I was in prison for nine years. Chico knows that, and I'm

pretty sure that you are aware of that too, Bobby. The prison system wants to help the incarcerated prepare for life on the outside. I know that because it was on a bulletin board in the kitchen where I worked. They offered courses. I took one on public speaking." He shook his head. "It wasn't all that good. The instructor was a fast-talking con artist. But he did have a few good tips. He said even if you aren't a smooth-talking motherfucker like him, you could make your point with effective use of props. You know, the old adage, 'a picture's worth a thousand words?' Well, obviously I'm not a smooth talker so I brought some props."

Joey reached into the bag at his feet and grabbed a cylinder of Krugerrands. He set it on the table. "That's twenty gold coins. South African. That one cylinder is worth twenty-four thousand dollars. I got a bunch of them here."

McGee leaned forward. Worry lines creased his forehead. Chico arched his eyebrows and tried to act disinterested, but he was definitely paying attention.

"That's the carrot." Then Joey reached into his other bag and grabbed the gun. "And this is the stick." He set it on the table next to his right hand.

McGee jumped up from the table so quickly his chair fell over. "I think I better leave. I don't want any—"

"Sit down!" Chico grabbed McGee by the elbow with one hand and reset his chair with the other. "Let's hear what he has to say." He pushed McGee back into his chair like he was a life-sized doll.

Joey leaned across the desk and patted McGee's hand. "Take it easy Bobby. A gun is a tool, just like a personal guarantee. It's used to encourage the appropriate behavior. You say you don't want to use those guarantees to destroy my family and I believe you. But you will if you don't get what you want. And you can believe me when I tell you, I don't want to shoot you. But you need to listen to my story."

He paused. McGee was pressed back in his chair, his face pale. Chico was alert, still trying to figure out what the play was.

"So I'm sent to prison. I will add, for Bobby's benefit, that I was innocent. Most everyone who goes to prison makes that claim. Most of them are lying. But I wasn't. Chico knows that. He tried to help me find the kid who was guilty of the crime I was charged with. The man we were looking for was named TJ Grimes. Chico didn't find him, but he did find his brother. And soon after that, TJ's brother was killed."

Chico glared at Joey, not enjoying the story anymore.

"Okay, that was way back in 2000. Fast forward to 2004. I'm doing my time, working in the kitchen and hoping to be paroled, when who should I encounter, but TJ Grimes. And guess what, Bobby?"

McGee shrugged.

"TJ blamed me for his brother's death. Gave me this beauty mark." Joey stroked the scar on his cheek. "That one wasn't so bad. But this one"—he pulled the collar of his polo away from his neck so they could see the scar—"hit home. Slashed my carotid artery. I would have died right there if my friend Jamal hadn't stepped in and disarmed TJ."

Joey sat back in his chair and opened the bottle of water he borrowed from Garth's refrigerator. "Not used to talking this much." He set the bottle back down and turned to McGee. "Now Jamal was one of Chico's men. Chico, even though he was never in prison, had some . . . uh, let's call it influence, on how the prison was run. He was a good guy to have on your side.

And after that incident with TJ, he was able to keep me and Jamal from losing any privileges. Thank you, Chico. Keeping that job was important."

Chico frowned. He was getting impatient. McGee was still too scared to have any attitude.

"I should have mentioned that Jamal did serious damage to TJ. Almost ripped his arm off and cracked his skull. He wasn't the brightest bulb in the lamp before that happened, and after, he was stupid-crazy. Spent most of his time separated from gen pop so we didn't have any more contact with him. Fast forward again. It's 2009, two months from my parole hearing. I'm pretty much a sure thing. Clean record and I've served eighty percent of my sentence. So, of course, that's when they decide to let TJ out of the SHU. That's what they call solitary, Bobby.

"One night we're cleaning up in the kitchen, just me and Jamal, and I hear him scream. I rush into the pantry, and Jamal is face down on the floor, and TJ is sitting on his back, stabbing him. Blood everywhere. I grabbed TJ and ripped him off Jamal. He dropped the knife and started crying like a little bitch. I wrapped my hands around his throat and I'm choking the life out of that useless motherfucker. Then Jamal groaned and said, 'Don't do it, Joseph. Freedom, man.'"

Joey swallowed hard. His throat was tight. "Jamal didn't want me to blow my shot at getting out. That was the kind of guy he was. So, I didn't kill the son of a bitch. The guards dragged his sorry ass away and Jamal died.

"Chico and everyone else figured I let Jamal die because I wanted to be free. But they were all wrong. I would have done it, but Jamal said no. He wanted me to have a life. And I realize now that I've let him down. Hiding away for the last seven years. Running from something I can't run away from."

Joey picked up the gun in his right hand and held up the

sleeve of Krugerrands in his left hand. He stared at McGee. "Carrot or stick. What it's going to be, Bobby?"

McGee couldn't take his eyes off the gun.

"You look confused, Bobby. I guess you need a little more information. My sister will run the company. Garth's out, like I said. Solita's smarter than all of us and she's tough. And fair. She will be a great CEO."

Joey reached into the bag and pulled out three more sleeves of coins. He pushed them in front of McGee. "That's a hundred grand. Give or take. It's my going-away present. I'm leaving and you're going to reduce your interest rate to three over prime and give my sister a chance to run the company my father built. It will be up to her to decide if she wants to keep you as a banker or find someone else." Joey looked at Chico. "It will be her call."

"B-b-but I can't . . ." McGee knew he was supposed to say he couldn't accept Joey's gift, but he was trying figure out how he might be able to.

Joey held up his hands. "Sure you can. Share it with your investors if you want. As a good faith gesture on your part. It's totally off the books. But you have to cut that rate and give Solita some slack." Joey took the gun and pushed the sleeves closer to McGee. "Now or never. Take them and get out of here, or I'll turn this mess over to Chico. I'm pretty sure he knows how to use a gun."

McGee swallowed hard and slowly picked up one of the sleeves.

"Just stuff them in your pocket, Bobby, and get the fuck out of here. Now!" Joey raised the gun and pointed it at the knot in McGee's tie.

The banker picked up the other sleeves, stuffing them into his coat pockets as he ran out of the office.

Chico watched him go, his expression grim. "You sort of fucked me, man."

Joey shrugged. He didn't really care. "Do you think McGee will go to the cops?"

Chico shook his head. "Not a chance. If he's smart, he'll give that money to his partner. It'll keep him alive." He laughed. "For a little longer anyway. But that doesn't help me."

Joey knew he shouldn't like Chico. The guy was a stone-cold killer. But he couldn't help himself. "Like I told you, Chico, I'm moving on. I want to leave things right with you." He reached into his bag and pulled out ten sleeves of coins. "That's almost a quarter million. I'm hoping that will help with Belinda's care. And buy me peace of mind."

"Peace of mind?"

"Yeah, I don't want to be worried every time I start my car."

Chico scoffed. "You been watching too many movies. I told you I don't do that kind of shit. You got a bag for these coins? I don't have pockets like that douchebag banker."

o o o

Joey stood at the window and watched Chico drive off. He ejected the magazine from Anita's gun and put the gun into the top desk drawer of Garth's desk and the magazine in the side drawer. His plan had worked to perfection. But there was one more thing he had to do.

He took out Callie's cell phone. With a shaky hand, he keyed in a message. He looked at what he had written. He deleted it. Four times he tried and four times he deleted the message. Finally, he wrote, "Roadrunner Park 7:30," and left the phone on the desk.

CHAPTER 52

The Arizona sky was bright with stars. Joey sat on the swing, his feet dragging in the dirt. The air was crisp and chilled. It reminded him of the day so long ago when he sat with Mallory watching the millennium bonfire. He remembered the warmth of her body as she told him she was pregnant.

This was the last piece of his plan. The long shot. The magical thinking part. He had texted Mallory and left the phone in the office so if she texted him back that she wasn't coming he wouldn't know. He didn't want it to end that way. He didn't need to hear why. That wouldn't help. This was the best way.

His watch read 7:45. A sweet, wistful sadness held him. It was almost satisfying. Like a good novel where the ending wasn't happy but was true.

Mallory wasn't coming.

He understood. It was time to head out. He shivered. The chilled night air had been refreshing when he arrived. The adrenalin of pulling off the deal had him stoked, but now he was getting cold.

He needed to leave. But where should he go?

"You're too big for that swing."

He turned around. Mallory. He closed his eyes and when he opened them, she was still there. It wasn't a dream.

"Hey," he said.

"Oh my God. You cut that long beautiful hair? What happened?"

Mallory was wearing jeans and an ASU hoodie, just like she wore in high school. "You changed out of your corporate hottie outfit," Joey said.

"Well, it is a playground," she said, grinning. "Aren't you cold?"

"A little. Walk with me. That'll get me warm. There's something I want to tell you."

"Oh my, a Joey Blade speech."

As they walked across the soccer field, Joey told her about the years at Florence. How the two- to four-year sentence ended up being nine. He told her about the years he spent living in the mountains working for Lua. Those were the easy parts. As they crossed over to the softball diamond, he paused.

"Are you okay, Joey?"

Mallory wrapped her arm through his. The warmth of her body was achingly familiar.

He took a deep breath and exhaled slowly. "We were together a long, long time ago. You were just a star-struck kid, the girl next door, and I was a big football hero." He stopped walking and looked up at the stars. "When I read about how you built your restaurant in Seattle, I was so impressed. You escaped from your past and built a great life. I'm proud of you."

She smiled. It was that genuine Mallory smile that had made him fall in love with her. "Thank you. That means a lot to me." She snuggled closer.

"I need a fresh start. I thought I might get a job working for one of those places that counsel ex-cons. Or maybe kids who are in trouble. I've learned some things. I could help."

"You would be great at that, Joey."

He stopped walking. "We were so young. I loved you back

then. I still do. I know you cared for me, but you didn't really love me."

Mallory made murmurs of protest.

"It's okay," he said. "Hear me out. Everything was so messed up back then—your father, the pregnancy, goddamn Wendy and TJ—that nothing could happen in a normal way. Look, I made some bad choices. I know that. But I've been working on improving myself. I know I didn't go to college. But I read . . . a lot. And I work hard. I fix things and I like that. My friend in prison told me to avoid magical thinking. He said if you don't ever believe things will get better, then you won't ever be disappointed. But I don't want to live that way. I want something better.

"I don't want this to sound creepy, like I'm some kind of a stalker, but I was thinking I could move to Seattle. I have some money saved. I could get a nice place. Get a job doing something I like and then maybe I could call you. We could go on a date. I know it's a long shot, but sometimes long shots win. There's even a chance you might fall in love with me. I think—"

"Joey!" Mallory yanked on his arm. She faced him. Her expression stern, determined.

Joey's heart felt like it was being crushed. He slowly closed his eyes. He had given it his best shot. There was a tug on his shirt.

Mallory cupped his cheeks in her hands.

"Joey Blade. Sometimes you talk too much."

She kissed him hard. Joey wrapped his arms around her and melted into her.

It was a very good kiss.

THE END

ABOUT THE AUTHOR

Len Joy has published three previous novels: *Everyone Dies Famous* (2020), *Better Days* (2018) and *American Past Time* (2014).

He is an All-American triathlete and competes internationally representing the United States as part of Team USA.

He lives in Evanston, Illinois with his wife Suzanne Sawada.

OTHER BOOKS BY LEN JOY

PUBLISHED BY BQB PUBLISHING

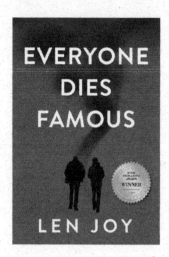

As a tornado threatens their town, a stubborn old man who has lost his son teams up with a troubled young soldier to deliver a jukebox to the wealthy developer having an affair with the soldier's wife.

It's July 2003 and the small town of Maple Springs, Missouri is suffering through a month-long drought. Dancer Stonemason, a long-forgotten hometown hero still grieving over the death of his oldest son, is moving into town to live with his more dependable younger son. He hires Wayne Mesirow, an Iraq war veteran, to help him liquidate his late son's business. The heat wave breaks and the skies darken. Dancer tries to settle an old score while Wayne discovers the true cost of his wife's indifference and turns his thoughts to revenge. When the tornado hits Maple Springs, only one of the men will make it out alive.